Praise for Jenny Hale

One of "19 Dreamy Summer Romances to Whisk you Away"—***Oprah Magazine*** on *The Summer House*

One of "30 Christmas Novels to Start Reading Now"—***Southern Living Magazine*** on *We'll Always Have Christmas*

Included in "Beach Reads Perfect for Summer 2020"—***Southern Living Magazine*** on *Summer at Firefly Beach*

"Touching, fun-filled, and redolent with salt air and the fragrance of summer, this seaside tale is a perfect volume for most romance collections."—***Library Journal*** on *The Summer House*

"Hale's impeccably executed contemporary romance is the perfect gift for readers who love sweetly romantic love stories imbued with all the warmth and joy of the holiday season."—***Booklist*** on *Christmas Wishes and Mistletoe Kisses*

"Authentic characters and a riveting story make it a keeper worth savoring."—***Publisher's Weekly*** on *The Summer House*

"This sweet small-town romance will leave readers feeling warm all the way through."—***Publisher's Weekly*** on *It Started with Christmas*

"Adorable contemporary romance... a tender treat that can be savored in any season."—***Publisher's Weekly*** on *Christmas Wishes and Mistletoe Kisses*

the
memory
keeper

USA TODAY **BESTSELLING AUTHOR**

JENNY HALE

HARPETH ROAD
PRESS®
Nashville

HARPETH ROAD

Published by Harpeth Road Press (USA)
P.O. Box 158184
Nashville, TN 37215

Paperback: 978-1-7358458-0-7
eBook: 978-1-7358458-1-4

LCCN – 2020921910

THE MEMORY KEEPER: a heartwarming, feel-good romance

This is a work of fiction. Names, characters, places, and incidents are the product of the author's imagination or were used fictitiously, and any resemblance to actual persons, living or dead, business establishments, events, or locales is entirely coincidental.
First printing: January 2021

To the greats in this industry who nurtured and inspired me—and put up with me—you know who you are.

Chapter One

She'd made it.

"That'll be thirty-eight bucks," the taxi driver said, his breath puffing out into the winter air as he lumped the bags that Hannah Townsend had packed for herself and her boyfriend Miles onto a mound of sludge piled next to the sidewalk at LaGuardia airport.

"Thank you," she said, preparing to make a run for it through the falling snow. She maneuvered around the clumps of winter road debris to hand the driver his fare with shivering fingers. It was icy cold outside, but Hannah barely noticed. Her pulse raced, eagerness zinging around inside her, all the while mentally counting down the seconds she was wasting standing there.

Hannah had to get to the baggage claim by the time Miles's flight came in. Miles Monahan was owner and CEO of Monahan Enterprises, the leading developer of application programming interface technologies in New York City. *ME*, as he termed the company, was his spoiled child, he'd said. Miles spent all of his time building the company, nurturing it, and giving it everything it wanted, spending an obscene amount of time away from Hannah to focus on work. But it would all pay off in the end, he'd told her.

He was flying in to New York from Chicago, winding up one final business meeting just before he took some much-needed time off, which worked out perfectly because—he had no idea—Hannah was planning to reveal that they had two hours until their *next* flight.

As the newly appointed art director for *Farmhouse Living* magazine, Hannah had been working incredibly long hours as well. She'd taken time off of work, bought herself and Miles tickets to Barbados, and booked a glorious week at a luxury beachfront hotel. With temperatures in Barbados reaching a balmy eighty-four degrees in February, she couldn't wait. She'd even reserved a couples massage the first day.

Hannah was turning the big thirty-five tomorrow, and she planned to tell Miles on this trip that she was ready to start a family. It wouldn't be a complete surprise—they'd both mentioned it before, and he'd even stopped into Tiffany's with her once while they were running errands to see what she'd like as an engagement ring—but he'd always put it off because of his work.

Hannah fiddled with the stargazer lily she'd tucked into her hair just above her ear. Tomorrow they'd be reclined side by side in lounge chairs, her arm stretched across the sand to hold his hand while they sipped on piña coladas and talked about the future. They were but a flight away from feeling the warmth of the sun and the only sounds around them being the quiet lapping of the waves—she couldn't get there fast enough.

While she hopped up and down in little wiggles to keep warm, waiting for the traffic guard to signal that she could cross, her phone rang. She fumbled to get it out of her coat pocket, unsuccessful in her attempt to wipe the droplets of precipitation off the screen.

Mom.

Hannah would have to call her back. As soon as she reached Miles at baggage claim and told him the plan, she'd return the call.

The traffic guard waved Hannah across, so she dropped her phone back into her pocket and readjusted her bags, jogging as quickly as her wedge heels could take her on the slippery surface.

The airport terminal's sliding doors hissed open and Hannah ran through, her head swiveling right and then left, looking past the red and pink Valentine's displays for signs directing her to baggage claim. Once she spotted where to go, she dashed over to the elevator.

"Please wait!" she said to no one in particular, throwing her hand between the closing doors as they slid back open.

Hannah stepped through and pulled her bags into the crowded elevator to exhales and throat clearing, as everyone rearranged themselves to adjust to less personal space. Her phone rang once more and she slipped her hand into her pocket to silence it. She peeked at the call: her mother again.

Her mom always got excited about Hannah's birthday, and since this one was a milestone, she was probably antsy to have a long, sweet chat like she loved to do. Hannah couldn't wait to talk to her, but she wanted to take the call when she had enough time to give her mother the attention she deserved.

The doors opened, and Hannah ran to the baggage claim turnstile that flashed Miles's flight number from Chicago. Her shoulders relaxed when she arrived with a few minutes to spare. The conveyor belt hummed to life, the anticipation of the surprise making her buzzy.

Hannah had packed Miles's bag for him, making sure to bring all his favorite summer attire. She'd even remembered the tennis visor he liked to wear on the beach to shield his eyes from the sun. Of course, Hannah had all her sundresses, the new upscale strappy sandals she'd bought for the summer season, and a super cute swimsuit she'd gotten

As she looked for him again, a wave of fear simmered slowly in her gut and then burst through her veins. So many thoughts were racing around her mind. The two very different parts of her life—the southern roots of her childhood and this new version of herself she'd created in adulthood—were suddenly converging, and she was struggling to handle all the emotions she was feeling. Hannah felt as if she were on autopilot, silently scolding herself for going so long without seeing Gran.

The most important people in Gran's life were her family, and with Hannah in New York, and Hannah's parents now in Florida, Gran had been all alone. Hannah couldn't imagine Gran's bungalow filled with silence, or the quiet that must have saturated the place after everyone had left her. And with the shop literally falling apart around her... Hannah felt the prick of tears. *Okay, focus*, she told herself. *Find Miles and tell him what's going on.* She needed him now more than ever.

Frantically, she scanned the crowd of passengers, but Miles hadn't reached the baggage claim yet. She would need his support to deal with this, and while the circumstances were less than ideal, it would be good for them to be together without the demands of their jobs. She hadn't even introduced him to her parents yet. It was time to do that.

A group of people walked towards her, but still no Miles. She took a few steps to get out of their way.

"Excuse me," a guy about her age said when he accidentally bumped into her, as she started to make her way to the outskirts of the growing crowd.

They locked eyes for a second, familiarity swimming around at the edges of her distraught brain. Cloudy flashes came into her consciousness of a bare-chested boy, showing off and jumping into the river while she and her childhood friend Morgan Pete giggled bashfully. The man in front of her was polished, somber, but there was definitely something about him she couldn't put her finger on that made it seem as if she knew him. *Wait, Liam McGuire?*

As if he could read her thoughts, his gaze lingered on her while he worked to unwind the bag that had gotten tangled with hers when she'd rolled her suitcase over it. "Sorry," he added.

Hannah attempted to pull her things out of his way. Liam tugged quickly, obviously in a rush to get out of there, the seriousness on his face doing nothing to diminish the incredible good looks he'd held on to since they were kids.

"It's no problem," she said, trying to help. By the way he was rushing, she wondered if he didn't want to be recognized. She didn't really have time to catch up right now, anyway.

Her fingers found his bag and pulled, but she only succeeded in jerking it in the wrong direction, having been distracted by a new group of passengers arriving at the baggage claim. She turned toward the escalator to see if Miles was heading down yet.

"I've got it," Liam told her, but she barely heard him. When she finally responded, he'd walked off, taking a call on his cell phone, and fishing his laptop out of his bag. She turned back toward the escalator full of passengers.

Suddenly time stopped still.

Hannah squinted toward the escalator to make sure her mind wasn't playing tricks on her. She could clearly see Miles making his way down, but he had his arm around another woman. To Hannah's horror, he then leaned in and kissed the other woman's lips, his hand moving up her back and to her neck the way it always had when he'd kissed Hannah. An icy cold shock slithered down her spine, and her throat began closing up with emotion. Hannah stood silently aghast, her heart hammering, as Miles and the woman moved down toward her level.

A shudder ran through Hannah just as Miles noticed her standing there at the bottom. His eyes widened and he jolted to attention before jogging down the last few steps, leaving the woman behind.

"Hi," he said with shifty movements, guilt written all over his face. "What are you doing here?"

Hannah wanted to scream at him, but her mouth was locked shut, tears spilling from her angry eyes.

"Hannah…" he said in a weak attempt to try to smooth things over, but both of them knew there wasn't anything he could say to undo what she'd seen. Clearly knowing he was caught, he relented, shame sliding down his face. "I'd been wanting to tell you," he said. "But I needed to find the right time…" He didn't even seem upset, just embarrassed.

Hannah looked away, her stare landing by accident on Liam. He was watching the scene curiously and had swayed as if he were going to move toward her to intervene, but perhaps she'd just imagined it because then he broke eye contact, facing the baggage claim turnstile as if to give her privacy, if that were possible. The last thing she needed was Liam jumping into all this anyway. She could handle it.

The striking woman with whom Miles had descended the escalator came swishing over to them in her fashionable heels and long coat. "Hello," she said with a smile, before her expression dropped to concern at the sight of Hannah's obvious anguish. "I'm Becky," she said cautiously. "And you are?"

"Miles's *ex*-girlfriend," Hannah said, her attention sliding over to Miles, piercing his complacent face like razors. Her entire body trembling, she kicked the duffel bag of toiletries she'd packed for him to his feet and pushed forward his suitcase. "These are yours," she said. "How fitting, they're already packed. When I get home, the rest of your things had better be gone as well." She put the other duffel bag's strap

over her shoulder and lifted the handle on her suitcase, steeling herself
so as not to break down completely and make a scene.

As she started to walk away, Miles caught her arm. "Hannah, wait,"
he said halfheartedly.

"I'm done waiting." In that moment, she understood the reason she'd
worked such long hours was because she needed to keep herself from
the realization she'd really been waiting for Miles to come around when
he probably never would. She needed more than this, and it was clear
that she'd been wasting her time thinking Miles would give it to her.

Hannah walked off at a clip, pulling her suitcase behind her until
she rounded the corner, out of his sight. Then she stopped and leaned
against the wall to keep her balance, trying to push down the sobs
rising in her throat with an avalanche of emotion that felt as if it were
crushing her. Her entire future, everything she'd worked for, had been
ripped away from her in the span of a single moment. She tore the
lily from her hair, tossed it in a nearby trash can, and slid down to
the floor. Completely overcome, she hung her head and began to cry.

Chapter Two

Hannah knew she had to get herself together enough to stand up and figure out how to change her flight, but she needed another minute, her body feeling as though it were submerged in quicksand. The boarding passes she'd printed and tied with a ribbon, so that she could hand them to Miles to add a special gesture to the surprise, had fallen out of the front pocket of her bag and lay next to her on the floor. She picked them up and slid off the ribbon, peering down at them, all her plans crushed—her entire world changed.

Dropping the papers back onto the floor, she hugged her knees, and hid her face in them to try to get herself together so she could concentrate on the issue at hand: she needed to figure out a way to get to Gran. But how could she be her grandmother's support in this state? Hannah's chest ached with a kind of pain she'd never felt before, the realization of what she didn't have in her life settling in. She was hollow, empty.

"Tough, innit?" a woman said from above her.

Hannah recognized her southern accent right away, and it felt like home. She lifted her head up to find a woman who looked to be in her mid-forties, with a giant smile and dark eyes staring down at her. She was naturally beautiful without even trying, her wavy amber-colored hair twisted into a messy bun, and it didn't look like she had a stitch of makeup on.

She held a carrier with something whining inside it, a portfolio of some sort was jammed under her arm, and a camera bag dangled from her neck in front of her, as she stood next to a suitcase that was larger than she was. The woman smiled down at Hannah, revealing the wad of chewing gum between her back teeth. Despite her smile, however, there was an undeniable sadness etched deeply behind her eyes that even her beauty couldn't mask.

The woman turned her head sideways to view Hannah's boarding passes, her trendy oversized gold earrings jingling with the movement. When she stepped closer to get a better look, her long sweater-like coat swished around her thin denim-clad legs. "Especially when you were going to Barbados. That's *really* tough," she said casually as she played with a lone tendril of hair that had escaped from her bun, addressing Hannah as if they'd just met at a coffee shop.

Her mind still in a fog with everything that had happened, Hannah stared at the woman blankly, unsure of what in the world she was even talking about. How did she know that Hannah wasn't still catching her flight to Barbados? Had she seen her confrontation with Miles?

Then the woman pointed to the flight departures screen and everything became crystal clear. Hannah's mouth fell open. A sea of red filled the right side of the monitor, nearly every single flight now saying, "Cancelled."

"The storm's a bad one," the woman said, shifting the tattered bag on her shoulder. "If you manage to get a hotel room, I'd be happy to split it with ya. You look nice enough... My name's Georgia Graves."

"A hotel room?" Hannah asked, her voice croaky from her emotions.

deep breath and tried to collect herself. Okay, she'd call the car rental companies first to see if they had any cars. She could put a reservation on the books by phone—yes, that was the smartest idea.

Hannah sat down on a nearby bench, pulling her suitcase toward her and lumping her other bag on top. She took a second to catch her breath and then swiped her phone to life. *What?* Her office knew she'd be out of contact but she had two missed calls and five emails from work. She'd have to look at them later. She searched for the number of the first rental company and hit call.

Busy.

She checked another one.

Busy.

A television monitor was reporting the weather, and all major roads and thoroughfares were bright red, jammed with traffic from crashes and people trying to move about the city in the snowstorm, the afternoon rush hour beginning early as commuters attempted to make it home before the worst of it.

Hannah continued to dial the rental companies anyway, over and over, unable to get a single person on the phone. Slowly, she put her cell down in her lap and let the tears come. How could everything have gone so wrong? *Think*, she told herself. But as she looked around at the pandemonium, she just felt bewildered.

Unsure of what she was even doing, Hannah got up and began walking, hoping a new idea would come to her. Some people had spread coats and blankets on the floor, making beds for the night. A woman nursed her fussing baby, rocking her while looking around dazed. Two toddlers ran in circles, playing and chasing each other while their parents were lost in conversation, alarm on their faces. Others were chirping madly into their phones and tapping on laptops. Airlines passed out snacks and offered sodas and bottles of water. Travelers barked at service desk employees, frustrated, while the desk clerks attempted to calm them down. The more Hannah paced, the more she understood that everyone was stuck; no one was getting out of there. It was total chaos.

As she resigned herself to the fact that she wasn't going anywhere, Hannah leaned against a large window, trying not to totally break down. She noticed some people had made signs with their destinations, in an attempt to find other passengers going to the same place. In surrender, with no other options that she could think of, she found an open spot on the floor where she could put her bags against the wall behind her and take a seat. She decided it couldn't hurt to make a sign—she could at least try like the others. She pulled out a pad of paper from her carry-on and wrote "Franklin, Tennessee" in big letters on it, setting it beside her on the floor. It occurred to her that Liam might be going to the same place, and for a while she watched the passers-by to see if she could locate him, but it was like trying to find a needle in a haystack.

Hannah's feet were tired and her head pounded from stress. She closed her eyes and tried to drum up happy thoughts. She imagined walking in through the glass-paned front door of Gran's little blue bungalow with her grandmother's signature red seasonal flowers flanking the entryway, passing the porch swing full of pillows, the buttery glow of evening lamplight illuminating the front hallway, the quiet shifting sound as the old woman moved around the kitchen while she danced to vintage music she had playing, and the sugary vanilla scent of her snickerdoodle cookies when she carried them to the back porch overlooking the lush green yard. She conjured up Gran's soft movements as she settled with Hannah on one of her white rocking chairs, draping a blanket over her legs... Hannah squeezed her eyes tightly to keep in the tears, but they spilled down her cheeks anyway.

Then suddenly, tearing her away from her thoughts, she was aware of someone standing beside her, and she quickly wiped her face. When she tipped her head up, she pulled back, surprised and relieved to see Liam. He had the same green eyes with flecks of gold in them that she remembered from when they were young.

"Hannah?" he asked, looking even wearier than she did.

She nodded as she blinked at him through her wet eyelashes. Every time she attempted to clear the tears, more came.

He stood quietly next to her. Even though it was awkward with her crying, it felt comforting to have him there; it made her feel as though she wasn't so alone. When her tears slowed, he squatted down next to her, obviously unsure of how to approach her. He cleared his throat, and then out of nowhere he asked, "Do you remember when we were young, and your friend Morgan refused to swing on that vine over the river because she was too scared to climb up to the rock to grab it?"

"Yeah," she managed.

"Remember what you told her?"

She shook her head.

"I still remember it. You said, 'Sometimes, you have to push yourself through the hard stuff to be able to enjoy the fun stuff.'" When he said this, there was a power behind his look that made her wonder if he'd learned that advice firsthand somewhere along the way.

She grinned through her emotions. "My gran used to tell me that. It's funny, she's always so positive about everything that I have to wonder if she ever faced 'hard stuff.' I know she must have, but it's difficult to imagine." Her lip started to wobble at the mention of her grandmother.

She turned toward him, his face returning to a melancholy expression. He seemed so different now from the boy she'd known back home.

That boy had been fearless, laughing all the time, quick-witted, and confident. Now, he seemed serious, grounded, focused.

"Your gran gave wise advice," he said.

Her mind went to a memory of Gran twirling around her flower shop, nestled out of the way and down a side street, popping chocolates into her mouth as she pulled flowers from their buckets for an arrangement she was making, music from the old record player filling the air. A woman had come in through the double glass-paned antique doors, the bells jingling to alert Gran to a visitor—her old friend. "Oh, hello, Darlene!" she said, setting down her flowers to pull out a pitcher of iced tea so she could offer Darlene some. She handed Darlene the beverage, and the two of them boogied like a couple of schoolgirls before Darlene finally put in her order for a basket of wildflowers to take to her book club.

When Darlene left, Gran had said, "Darlene's been feeling lonely since she lost her job and had to take on one she doesn't really love. She joined the book club to find a little joy. And I made her smile today. There's nothing dancing can't solve." She laughed as she grabbed Hannah's teenage hands and gave her a spin. "Most of our problems are of this world—they're created by us—when really our souls just long to sing and dance. When we do that, we become ourselves again, and we rise above whatever worries us. But we have to get through the hard stuff first. That's how we see good—when we can compare it to the bad." Despite how wise she was, Gran always seemed so young for her age, her skin glowing, her eyes vibrant and happy. She could melt all Hannah's fears in an instant.

"My gran's not well right now," Hannah told Liam, as she grabbed her handbag and started rooting around inside it. "I don't have any

The gravity in his face right then was burned into her memory. "Why not?" he'd asked. And she didn't have an answer for him. He'd rolled his eyes, frustrated. "Suit yourself. If we ain't good enough for you, then maybe you *should* go."

The memory still on her mind, she texted Ethan back: *I'm coming home to see Gran. Have you heard?*

He replied: *Do you know me at all? I've already been to see her three times.*

Hannah wondered if the question about knowing him was that frustration from years ago coming through. That final summer night before she'd left for college in New York, they'd been sitting on the massive exposed root of the old oak tree in his yard, the sun going down on the horizon over the horse fields. "You're gonna forget me," he'd worried, his thin lips set in a straight line. "You're gonna forget all about this place…"

He'd been right. Guilt settled in the pit of her stomach. She returned: *I know you plenty well. I just wasn't sure you'd heard about Gran, that's all.*

Ethan texted back. *You don't know me as well as you think you do anymore. Lots has happened since you left your boots behind and hightailed it outta here. I'll fill ya in when you get home. Can't wait for you to get here!*

She let out a little exhale of relief when she read the last line. A part of her expected him to still hate her for leaving, and there probably was a side of him that did, but he was being kind to her anyway, which was just how he was.

Another text floated onto her phone: *And hey, happy birthday!*

He'd remembered. Suddenly, like a tidal wave, she missed the time they'd spent together growing up so much that she could hardly bear it. Ethan was the kindest person she knew—why had she left him without a word like she had? Tears pricked her eyes as she typed, *Thanks. See you soon!*

Hannah focused on the endless expanse of snow-covered concrete and city life out her window to try to clear her mind, before she turned her attention to her work emails.

"I've got more snacks if anyone wants some," Georgia said as she removed Liam's bag and shoved a fistful of assorted packs of crackers through the gap between the two front seats, sending Jerry wriggling again.

"No, thank you," Hannah said, reaching back and petting Jerry. Her stomach was in knots and her appetite was nonexistent from everything she'd dealt with today, as well as the idea of a fourteen-hour car ride that propelled her toward all the people she'd basically abandoned.

"That's all right, thank you," Liam replied. "We can probably stop for dinner once we get out of the traffic." He pulled off on the exit, merging onto the highway and coming to a halt in another mass of cars that stretched as far as Hannah could see.

"Maybe I *will* have a chocolate," Hannah said, reconsidering. The sweetness of it might help her mood.

Valentine's Day was two weeks ago, but the chocolates at the airport had still sounded deliciously festive. She and Miles had been so consumed with their respective projects that they'd both missed the holiday completely. She had woken up that morning and briefly wondered if he'd surprise her with anything, but then she'd arrived at work and been so frenzied with her tasks that she'd forgotten about it—until her coworker Amanda had received a big bouquet of roses and two Mylar heart balloons. On her way home from work, Hannah had bought Miles a card, but it just didn't seem right to give it to him since he'd forgotten hers, so she'd stuffed it into her laptop bag until she could toss it in a public trash bin. She'd put on a brave face at work when everyone was sharing what their significant others had given them the next day at lunch, but inwardly she'd felt lonely and sad.

Georgia passed the heart-shaped box back up to the front, and as Hannah surveyed its contents Georgia pointed to a round one with coconut flakes on top. "That one's really good," the woman offered. "I got one of these hearts at the airport too, but I already finished mine."

"Was that what you were eating when you asked me to help you get your suitcase off the conveyor belt at baggage claim?" Liam asked with a chuckle, his eyes on the road.

"Yes!" Georgia said. "My mouth was full, and I couldn't talk," she explained to Hannah, "but my heavy bag was going around the thing faster than I could grab it. It had already circled the loop twice by the time I asked Liam. I was scrambling to get it while I searched for my boarding pass. At that point, I still thought I was gonna have to sprint to my next plane." Georgia put Jerry on a cushion in his carrying case and set it beside her on the seat.

Georgia's mention of catching her plane brought back the image of Miles and Becky on the escalator. "I was on my way to Barbados," Hannah told them. "I've always wanted to go there, and finally I decided to make it happen." He looked over at her as she pinched the coconut-covered chocolate between her fingers. "I was surprising Miles…" She hesitated. "My ex—with a trip for two. But it seems like he'd already had a romantic getaway with someone else."

Liam's face clouded with thought. "I'm sorry."

They fell into a heavy silence. The only sound was the shushing of the tires against the snow on the highway and the radio in the background. Hannah looked out the window again, but the view wasn't registering. Instead, flashes of the last two years swarmed her mind. All the nights Miles had come home late, tiptoeing in after she was asleep, the times he'd said he had to run out instead of staying at the apartment, the wine a "coworker" had spilled on his shirt, the gift she'd found in his dresser when she was putting away his laundry that he'd said he was shipping to his mother... It was becoming clear that he'd been deceiving her for a while. She popped the chocolate into her mouth, her focus on savoring the rich flavor of it to avoid the alternative, which was crumpling into tears in front of Liam and Georgia.

"Guys can be such jerks," Georgia said. "No offense." She leaned forward and patted Liam's shoulder, causing his attention to waver from driving for a second before his gaze returned to the road.

"None taken," he said quietly.

That moment of confrontation at the baggage claim returned to Hannah, and she wondered again if Liam had been about to intervene between her and Miles. She looked over at him now, just as his head swiveled toward her, and they locked eyes for a second. He offered a knowing smile, as if he could read her thoughts, and it gave her an unexpected flutter. The surprise of it made her turn around to talk to Georgia and refocus, but Georgia had put her headphones on, and she'd begun doodling on a pad of paper in her lap. Liam's eyes were back on the road, and Hannah sank into her thoughts once more.

She stifled a yawn and Liam looked over at her again. All the emotion today had taken a toll on her.

"Assuming we take turns driving," she said to him, "I'll never make it if we try to drive the entire journey tonight." Hannah yawned again. "Are either of you two night owls who can drive tonight?" she asked loudly, twisting around to get Georgia's attention.

Georgia pulled one of her earphones from her ear. "I have night blindness so there's no way y'all want me to drive," she said while she opened a pack of peanut butter crackers, causing a stir from the crate beside her. She slipped her doodling into the large leather portfolio she'd been carrying when Hannah had first met her. "But I'll pay for gas." Georgia popped a cracker into her mouth and brushed the crumbs off her thighs. "Jerry'll need a potty break at some point, too."

"Just let me know when you all want to stop. And then let's see how far we can get through the trip today before everyone gets too tired," Liam said, as he surveyed the traffic in front of them. "If we have to break it into two days, we'll need to get far enough out of town to even find a hotel with vacancies. They'll be full for miles. And we'll need to get a hotel that's pet friendly."

"Aw, that's nice of you to think of Jerry," Georgia said, "but you don't have to worry about a pet-friendly hotel. I just hide him in my bag, and he sleeps until I get him to the room. No one will even know he's there."

Liam nodded, clearly unsure. "Hopefully we'll get moving soon."

Hannah pulled out her phone and opened her emails from Amanda, her assistant director on the design staff, who was filling in for her this week to keep things moving. Amanda had always been a great friend at the office, and Hannah knew she'd be fair and kind, so she'd given her a large number of duties on the spread Hannah was working on. The magazine was in very capable hands while Hannah was on vacation.

The first message was just telling Hannah they needed the signed permissions form from one of the photographers they'd freelanced in LA. She attached the file to her reply, the attachment struggling to upload with a patchy signal. Then she sifted through her other messages: budget approval needed for cropping and adjustment work on two of the images, deadline change request for the October shoot, suggested layout amendment on the lifestyles page... She fired off emails, one after another.

"How long since you've been back home?" Liam asked.

She clicked her phone off and set it in her lap.

"A few years," she replied, "but it's been much longer than that since I've actually seen anyone we knew. Most of my visits were quick—I flew home and saw Gran or my parents, and then left right away. I always had work demands…" Her excuse sounded flimsy now, coming off her lips. All the stress and rushing around seemed insignificant compared to not spending time with the people she cared about. "How about you?"

"I visit quite a bit," he said. "I live in Charleston now…"

"Charleston? I expected you to be cutting records in Nashville."

He offered a nostalgic chuckle. "No, I ended up going in a totally different direction. I went into business instead. And started a family… I have a son—his name is Noah."

Hannah regarded him with interest.

"My mother gets antsy if we stay away too long." The lines creasing at the corners of Liam's eyes revealed his fondness for his mother.

"You have a son," Hannah said, the word feeling strange in her mouth. A tiny piece of her remained grounded in their youth when she spoke to him, and it felt odd that they'd both gone through so much life between then and now.

"Yep. Noah's four." He looked over at her pleasantly, but there was another emotion lurking in his eyes that she couldn't pinpoint. Hesitation of some sort. "Do you have any kids?" he asked.

"No," she replied, shaking her head. She huffed out a soft laugh to keep from crying again.

"I don't know why, but I imagined you'd have lots of kids," he said.

"Really?"

"Yeah. You always had a very nurturing way about you."

"Thanks," she said, breathing in the happiness his comment had given her.

They fell into silence again when the traffic got heavy, and Hannah texted her mother to ask whether Gran could receive calls or texts. Her mother responded, telling her that Gran did, in fact, have her phone, and she'd probably love to hear from Hannah. So, with nothing but gridlocked traffic to keep her busy, Hannah texted Gran.

I'm on my way to see you, she typed. *I'd call, but I'm in a car full of people from the airport. It was the only way I could get home in this storm.*

Right away, Gran responded: *I can't wait to see you. Are you safe with those people in that car?*

I think they're fine, she typed. *One is someone I grew up with in Franklin, and there's a Chihuahua named Jerry in the backseat that's wearing a light-blue sweater with "Angel" written on the back.*

Gran came back with, *I needed your humor. I miss you terribly. How are you? How's Miles?*

Hannah didn't want to bring Gran's spirits down in her state. She had to think about how to answer her honestly. *I'm not sure*, she typed back. *I'll fill you in when I get there.*

Tell me now, Gran returned.

The very last thing Hannah wanted was to break down in the car with nowhere to go, but at the same time, it felt comforting to know Gran was there to listen. She'd been there through all of Hannah's breakups growing up, and Gran had always had the best advice. *I thought he was The One*, she typed, *but it turns out he isn't. He's a jerk. We broke up.*

What happened? Gran asked.

She replied: *I found him kissing another woman today.* Just texting the words sent a flash of heat through her skin.

Today? My gracious. I'm so terribly sorry to hear that, dear, Gran texted. *Remember this whenever it hurts, because it will for a while: It may not feel like it right now, but it's just a step in the path to make you who you're meant to be.*

Gran was always saying things like that, but Hannah wasn't sure she believed any of it anymore. Was there some sort of golden path they were all meant to take, or was her life just a collection of chance encounters, millions of variations, and possibilities? As a girl, she'd believed Gran when she'd said those kinds of things, but now it had become more difficult. Hannah considered her choices. Would she have been happier spending her mornings like she used to: reading in one of Gran's porch rocking chairs, with a blanket over her bare legs to keep the morning chill off her skin before the sun filled the sky? Would she have been a different person if she'd stayed? Would she have been happier?

Thanks Gran. I'll call you whenever we stop next, okay?

Gran came back: *All right, my sweet girl. I'll count the minutes until I see you.*

Just texting with Gran filled Hannah with a kind of warmth she hadn't felt in years. Gran could make everything seem okay.

The snow fluttered down around them. Visibility was extremely low, and the only distinction between the road and the ground was the string of brake lights on the barely moving cars in front of them stretching as far as Hannah could see. Liam had both hands tightly on the wheel at ten and two, the windshield wipers going like crazy but only succeeding in smearing two large semicircles of precipitation across the windshield.

"Does anyone know a five-letter word for a kitchen item that starts with a P?" Georgia said, still wearing her headphones, her voice too loud for the confined space. She leaned forward and tapped the row of squares in the puzzle book she was working on.

"Plate," Liam said, his eyes still on the road.

Georgia huffed. "How did I not get that?"

They all fell quiet again, and Liam turned up the radio to fill the void—some call-in radio station. "We're asking people to tell us their answers to this question. Are you ready?" the radio announcer said. "What's the craziest thing you've ever done? We'll be back to hear from our callers after these messages."

Liam checked his rearview mirror to change lanes. "Besides going on a fourteen-hour road trip with two people from the airport after spending all morning in flight? I'm not sure," he said with a laugh, answering the radio announcer's question.

"Oh, come on," Hannah teased. "I knew you as a teenager. You've done crazier things than that, I'm nearly certain."

He looked over at her, amused, and she caught a glimpse of the boy she'd known. "I climbed the old Franklin water tower once, when I was sixteen," he said.

"Rebel," Georgia teased from the backseat.

"It's higher than it looks," he said with a laugh, turning the radio back down so they could hear each other. "I was actually dared to paint something on it, but I chickened out," he added.

"What were you going to paint on it?" Hannah asked.

"I have no idea. My friend ended up painting something instead. It was Billy Robertson. He went to my high school—do you remember him?"

Hannah shook her head. "Wait, was that the time someone painted 'Party's Here' with an arrow pointing into town? I remember my gran was on the town board and they debated on whether or not to keep it—some people actually liked it."

"Yes, that was it! Billy painted it. The arrow was actually pointing toward Leiper's Fork, where I lived. My parents were going out of town that weekend, and he kept threatening to have a party at our house."

"Did you?" Georgia asked.

"No. I went out to a bonfire instead." He grinned at Hannah, and she instantly made the connection.

"So that's the craziest thing you've done?" Georgia asked, rolling her eyes playfully. "*Almost* painting a water tower? Or going to the bonfire?"

"I suppose I have one more. In college, I made one of those full-court basketball shots they offer one fan at halftime, and I won a huge prize."

"What did you win?" Hannah asked.

"Twenty thousand dollars for charity. I gave it to a local boys' and girls' club."

Georgia leaned forward. "Are you a real person or some sort of storybook character?"

Liam laughed. "So what's the craziest thing you've done then?" he asked.

"At eighteen, I left home to be a photographer," Georgia told him. "I lived in the woods for three years, photographing landscapes and doing odd jobs to pay for my food. I mailed my parents letters every week to let them know I was okay, and I lived my life my way."

"Wow," Hannah said, nearly speechless, she and Liam looking back and forth at one another in complete surprise.

"I sold one of the photographs I'd enlarged and framed for five hundred dollars, and followed the guy who bought it to Chicago. That's how I ended up there. We didn't last long, but I just never left." She shrugged as if the whole thing had been no big deal.

"I think you win for the craziest thing ever done by any of us," Liam said. "Unless Hannah can top you... Done anything crazy?"

After a couple of rings, Gran picked up.

"Hello?" Her fragile voice came through Hannah's phone, and Hannah's heart sank. It didn't sound like her grandmother's usual bubbly self.

"Hi, it's Hannah," she said, trying to sound happy despite the alarm she felt at the idea that Gran was truly not well. She hadn't been able to tell at all when texting, but Gran's voice certainly revealed it.

"Oh, my dear Hannah." Gran perked up. "It's wonderful to hear your voice. I've been so bored sitting in this bed all day."

The sound of her grandmother's voice was reassuring, despite the raspiness to it.

"I heard Ethan's been to see you," Hannah said.

"Lord have mercy, that child."

Hannah laughed. Ethan and Gran had an unusual friendship. Growing up, Ethan would do anything for Gran, but he loved to tease her. His favorite was when she'd come into the room and he'd be stretched out on her sofa with his big man-feet in her slippers.

"Get those things off your feet," she'd snap.

"I'm cold," he'd whine. "You don't want an innocent child to catch a cold, do you?"

Gran would roll her eyes and snatch them off him, the whole time pouting to keep her amusement from showing.

"I hadn't seen that boy in years," Gran said. "It was kind of him to drop by."

Hannah nodded, even though she knew there was no one to see it, emotion swelling in her gut.

"How are you managing after the breakup with Miles? Are you all right?" Gran asked. "You're quiet."

"I'm fine!" she lied, wanting to keep the focus on her grandmother, although it was already taking everything she had not to allow herself to get even more emotional about the frailty of Gran's voice. She needed to stay strong for her.

A pleased exhale sailed through the phone. "I'm so glad to hear that, Hannah, my lovely girl."

"Let's talk about you," Hannah said. "How are you feeling?"

"I'm all right, I suppose. But, Hannah, I need your help." Her words suddenly sounded quietly desperate.

"Anything. What is it?"

"I'll bet the shop hasn't been opened in at least a week and no one is taking orders. Don't let it flounder."

Hannah hated to think of The Memory Keeper failing. If the shop closed up, so would Gran. But the shop was deteriorating despite her grandmother's best efforts, and Hannah knew Gran was entirely too old to run it. No amount of love could save it at this point.

"Your mother's there now," Gran said, "but she said she isn't staying because she's coming to see me here at the hospital. What if someone stops by and the shop is dark?"

"I'll get there as quickly as I can," Hannah assured her. "It's taking me a little longer to get home because of the snow. Flights are grounded, which is why I'm driving. But as soon as I get there, I'll go straight to the shop."

"Thank you," Gran said with obvious relief.

"Gran, how are *you*?" Hannah asked.

"I've been better," Gran said. But then, to Hannah's dismay, she turned the conversation back to the shop. "Steven, my accountant, needs to get my profit and loss from last year so he has it for taxes. He likes to have it by the end of February. It's saved in the system under P&L. Do you remember how to get into the system?"

"No, but Dad can get into it for me," she said as Liam opened his car door.

He leaned in and passed her a cup of cocoa before shutting his door again and walking around to fill up the gas tank. Hannah offered a smile of thanks through the window. She kept her eyes on him for a minute, her hands wrapped around the cup to keep warm, as Gran started talking again.

"And I'll bet no one's been taking in the geraniums at night," Gran continued, "so they're probably dead and a total eyesore. See if you can find anything at Nell's nursery to replace them. Also, Speckles probably hasn't had milk or food in days. I'm terribly worried about her."

Speckles was the jet-black feral cat that Gran had befriended. In the mornings, Gran always put out a bowl of fresh water for the dogs who came by with their owners, and milk for Speckles. Sometimes, Speckles would follow Gran home from the shop too.

Georgia shuffled over to the car and got in with Jerry, giving Hannah a wave before she settled the dog back into his carrier and put her headphones on.

"What about that guy you hired?" Hannah asked. "Doesn't he still work for you? Can he come in for a few extra hours?" She popped the lid off her cup to inspect its contents, the rich aroma dancing into the air. Floating on the top was a solid mass of marshmallows, making her smile.

"He left for college," Gran said. "I'm the only one on the books right now, which is why I only open the shop a couple of days a week… I'm expecting inventory tomorrow. It usually comes by ten o'clock. When will you get into town? If no one's there, the distributor will leave the boxes on the stoop, and the flowers will freeze in the cold."

"With this storm, I'm not sure when I can get home, Gran," Hannah replied, knowing that she was only placating her grandmother. "We'll get everything done for you. I'll text Mom to be there for the delivery. You just rest."

"I don't want to rest," Gran snapped. "And my leasing agent is giving me fits again," she said, sounding frustrated. "They're threatening to close the shop and take on a new tenant if I don't agree to the latest hike in rent, but it's astronomical." Her voice broke. "There's no way I'm letting it go. I need to have a phone meeting with the company's owner about it, and I'm stuck in this hospital. I keep calling, but no one's answering," Gran carried on. "I've left quite a few messages."

Gran didn't talk much about her problems. She preferred to deal with them head on rather than having a lengthy conversation about them, she'd told Hannah once. But she had let Hannah know a bit about her disagreements with the leasing agent. The company was called Mercer Properties and they'd bought the building a few years ago from the original agents, and had kept hiking the rent up on Gran, making it nearly impossible for her to turn a profit.

"Gran, we've got it. If you don't rest, you won't get better," Hannah told her gently. That comment seemed to quiet Gran for the time being.

Liam finished filling up the car and started the engine, sending a plume of heat through the vents; welcome warmth in the icy cold.

"Hey, Gran, I'll call you back in a bit, okay? We're about to hit the road again."

"Okay," Gran said. "But one more thing. Your mama and daddy are already staying at my house. When you get there, if they're out, the spare key's still under the mat where I usually keep it."

"Thanks, Gran," she said with a smile. Gran lived her whole life taking care of people. It had to be difficult for her to be in the position she was in, but it was time she focused on herself. Hannah just hoped she could convince her. She couldn't wait to see her. It was certainly going to be quite a visit when Hannah got home.

Chapter Four

They were a few hours into the trip now and making good time. Both the heavy traffic and the snow had tapered off, although the storm had left a thick gray cloud cover in its wake that seemed to want to explode with another downpour of frozen precipitation at any moment. The roads weren't much better either.

Hannah had been quiet, sipping her hot chocolate, lost in thought while Georgia made small talk from the backseat occasionally.

"So, did I hear you say you were from Charleston, Liam?" Georgia asked, piping up again.

"I grew up just outside Franklin—in the same area as Hannah," he replied, his gaze fluttering over to her, "but I've lived in Charleston for the last five years."

Hannah and her friend Morgan had both had a crush on Liam when they'd been younger. But he'd asked Morgan out instead of Hannah, and her friend had fallen head over heels for him. Hannah had consoled her friend when he'd broken her heart.

"How about you, Hannah?" Georgia asked, leaning forward.

"I live in New York City."

"Mm." Georgia sat back, tipping her head against the seat in thought. "Funny," she said. "You look very New York with your fancy clothes and your super shiny manicure."

Hannah smiled in response, but the comment made her self-conscious. Growing up, Ethan had always made her feel like there was something wrong with being glamorous, but once she'd gotten to New York, she'd fit right in.

Georgia shook her head. "Isn't it crazy that we'd probably never have met up were it not for this snowstorm?" She folded her arms with a content smile.

"Are you traveling to Franklin for vacation, Georgia?" Hannah asked, still not fully committed to the conversation at hand, but needing to refocus to keep her mind from returning to that kiss at the airport.

"Not really. I'm meeting my parents for the first time in my life."

Georgia's answer caused Hannah to turn around to make sure she'd heard right. Georgia was beaming.

"My birth parents," she clarified. "I was adopted."

Liam gave her a quick glance in the rearview mirror, obviously interested. But Hannah couldn't get her head around the enormity of the statement and the way Georgia was so nonchalant about it, as if it were something people did every day.

Unable to hide her astonishment, Hannah asked Georgia, "So this is the first time you'll have ever laid eyes on the two people who gave you life?"

"Yep," she replied. "The adoption agency couldn't tell me much, but they did remember that my parents were incredibly young when they had me, and they felt like they couldn't offer me the life I deserved."

"That was a very selfless and honorable act," Hannah said. "I can't imagine being faced with that decision. It would be so incredibly hard."

"I'm excited to see them," Georgia said. "I have no hard feelings at all. I just want to know who they are, you know?"

"Of course," Hannah said.

They fell into a lull after that, and Georgia sat back in the seat, stroking the dog, who'd closed his eyes and stretched out on Georgia's lap so she could rub his belly.

"How about you, Liam?" Hannah asked. "How long will you be in Franklin?"

"I'm doing business in the area, and I'm helping my mother with some insurance details. My father passed away six months ago and we're managing his assets…" Then, quietly, he added, "I'm picking up my inheritance."

Caught off guard by the sad news, Hannah looked over at Liam, but he seemed quietly composed, as if he'd practiced saying this. "I'm so sorry," she said.

Liam nodded in thanks, but he didn't elaborate. He kept his focus on the traffic in front of them, leaving Hannah to dive into her thoughts once more. She had a lot of very uncertain days to navigate ahead of her. She tipped her head back against the headrest and closed her eyes.

"Hannah?" A masculine voice sailed into her consciousness, but it wasn't Miles's. She wasn't quite aware of where she was at first.

"Hannah?" A warm hand rested on her forearm, giving her a sense of security, like everything would be okay.

She took in her first fully cognizant inhale, opening her eyes and registering that they'd parked somewhere. Liam was facing her from her open car door. A gust blew, and she was suddenly aware of the frigid temperature around her.

"We've stopped for dinner," he said.

Hannah cleared her vision enough to focus on his face in the darkness. She couldn't see what was behind him. The sun had disappeared completely.

"Georgia was starving, and this exit had a restaurant that was still open." He stepped to the side, revealing a tiny structure that looked like some sort of hodgepodge between a saloon and a thrift shop. The hesitant look on his face suggested he shared Hannah's skepticism that this was the best option. "Georgia's inside with Jerry in her handbag, getting us a table."

With a punch of amusement over the dog, Hannah slipped her arms into her coat, which had slid down behind her on the journey, and then grabbed her purse.

"How long did I sleep?" she asked, walking beside Liam on their way to the restaurant.

"About three hours."

"Really?"

It was only now that she realized how exhausted today had made her. She felt as if she'd been hit by a bag of bricks. Her eyes ached for more sleep, and the hollow sadness of her breakup and worry over Gran had settled upon her like a weighted blanket. She really just wanted to curl up somewhere and sleep until everything got better, but she knew she had to push through for Gran.

Liam opened the door to the restaurant, allowing Hannah to enter.

The aroma of fried food hit her right away, along with a surge of heat from the old wood-burning fireplace at one end of the narrow establishment. An empty stage with a single guitar and stool stood at the other. As they made their way further inside, the scent of burning oak took Hannah back to the winter nights she used to spend at Gran's.

Georgia waved from a minuscule table midway down the room, across from the bar, her handbag in her lap revealing an unusually large, moving lump. She placed her hands on top of Jerry to settle him, and his shiny nose peeked out. When they reached Georgia and Jerry, Hannah scooted the faded silk-flower table arrangement to the edge next to the salt and pepper shakers to give them all more room.

Liam pulled out a chair for Hannah.

"Thanks," she said, sitting down next to him.

"All right, y'all. It's getting late and we need to have a game plan," Georgia said, slipping a rubber band off her wrist and onto her newly piled ponytail in one fluid motion, copper-brown tendrils falling around her face. "Are we driving all the way through, or are we gonna stop for the night?"

A waitress clunked three plastic cups of tap water and a pile of menus onto the table beside them, as she eyed and then dismissed the bag of dog treats next to Georgia. Liam had been busy catching up with missed messages on his phone when he finally turned his attention to the waitress, only then becoming aware of what Hannah was already taking in: the waitress, a tall woman with a generally bored expression and wiry ringlets that fell in frizzy bundles to each shoulder, was wearing a sweater with the words *Yep, this is my life!* embroidered on the front.

Liam and Hannah shot a quick glance at one another, and Hannah hid behind her menu so as not to burst into laughter at the sight of his face when he'd seen the woman's sweater. They both must have been loopy from exhaustion because the two of them were biting back their amusement. Hannah looked away so as not to make a scene, but when she turned back to Liam, she caught him gazing at her curiously.

"Back in a sec for your orders," the woman said. "I'm Rose. Just call over if you need me. I'll be behind the bar."

Hannah scanned the appetizer options: loaded onion rings, chili-cheese fries, two-alarm jalapeño nachos… None of the choices hitting the mark, she looked up from her menu. "How far into the trip have we gotten?" she asked. Despite the lighter atmosphere, her head was still aching from stress, and she had a pinch in her shoulder that was making it difficult to sit. She maneuvered around awkwardly to have space at the small table.

"We're not even halfway yet," Liam replied, scooting his chair into the aisle a bit to give Hannah more room between him and the wall. "We've got about nine more hours to go, so I can't imagine pushing through. Are we all on board with staying the night somewhere?"

"I'm definitely up for finding a hotel," Georgia said, unzipping the bag of dog biscuits and discreetly dropping one into her handbag.

Although Hannah wanted to get to Gran as quickly as humanly possible, she needed to climb into a warm shower, lather herself up, stand in the stream of water until the heat of it soaked through to her bones, and then crawl into bed. She nodded. "Me too."

"While we eat, I'll see if I can book something a few hours from here." He tapped on his phone screen. "That'll get us to the midpoint."

Hannah texted her mom to let her know where she was, and to tell her about Gran's delivery tomorrow at ten o'clock. When her mom didn't respond, the niggling worry that things wouldn't get done at The Memory Keeper bothered her. The last thing Gran needed right now was to pay for inventory she couldn't sell because it had all frozen outside the door. Hannah put her phone down and looked at her menu again while Liam scrolled through hotels on his cell.

The waitress materialized. "Are you all ready to order?" she asked, her fountain pen poised above a pad of paper.

Hannah tried to scan the options quickly, none of them sounding at all appealing. Everything was fried, and given the events of the day, it would all settle like a cinder block in her stomach if she tried to eat any of it. "I'll just have your side salad," she said, unable to find a suitable meal option.

The waitress observed her inquisitively for a second before she offered an indifferent shrug and scratched the note down on her pad of paper. The lights of the stage at the end of the restaurant came on, and a man set up a microphone. "What dressing?" the woman asked. "We've got ranch, blue cheese, and Italian."

Hannah deliberated. "I'll take ranch, please. Is he going to sing?" she asked, waggling her finger at the man.

"No, that's the manager. Our singer is late. He'd better hurry or he'll let down all the fans," she said dryly, while waving her arm around the near-empty restaurant.

Amusement floated its way back into Liam's face, and he tipped his head down to make his dinner selection. "I'll have the same," he said, offering Hannah a grin of solidarity from behind his menu.

"Ranch dressing okay?" the waitress asked, unaffected.

"Ranch is fine," Liam answered.

Georgia tapped her finger on the menu under one of the entrees. "I'll have the double cheeseburger with the works, an order of fries, the cheese stick and marinara appetizer, and the loaded potato skins." She closed the menu and handed it to the waitress.

Liam and Hannah peered over at Georgia in unison. How could Georgia even fit that much food into her waif-like body?

"What?" Georgia said, as the woman collected the menus. "I'm starving. I'll share my appetizer with y'all if you want."

"That's okay," Hannah said, smiling at her, laughing inside again as Liam caught her eye. She liked how they kept doing that, and she realized this was the first time she could remember all day when she was actually enjoying herself.

A loud squeal from the microphone pierced Hannah's ears, sending her gaze over to the stage. "Sorry, folks," the manager said, his voice echoing through the amplifiers. "Our singer tonight is… late. We're trying to find a replacement."

An older woman sitting with a small group at a table behind them groaned. "Marty, find me some music," she shouted to the manager. When Hannah twisted around in her chair to view the woman, she told Hannah, "It's my birthday."

The manager acknowledged her with a friendly nod, before turning around nervously, his cell phone pressed against his ear.

"Happy birthday," Hannah told the woman.

"Thank you," the woman said, taking in a heavy gulp of air. "It's the second year since my husband passed—he used to play here," she explained, scooting her chair closer to Hannah, her gaze floating back up to the stage. "I know it's nothing fancy, but it's the only place to hear live music around here, and it helps me forget that he's gone for a while." The woman's eyes glistened. She grabbed a napkin then excused herself.

Hannah turned to Liam and realized that the woman heading to the bathroom had his attention. The manager on stage dialed a number on his phone with a sigh. "I feel terrible for her," Hannah said. "I wish we could do something."

Liam nodded, looking pensive, a slight crease forming between his eyes.

"Why don't you get up there and play like you used to at the bonfires when we were young?" she suggested in a whisper. "You're amazing."

"Oh… no." He shook his head. "I don't play anymore. I haven't performed in years."

His reply shocked her. "How come? You're so talented."

"I was a kid, Hannah," he said gently. "I grew up." He turned his attention to the empty stage, a distant look in his eyes.

The woman at the table behind them returned and took her seat, a few others filtering in.

"Oh, come on, Liam," Georgia chimed in. "Now I'm curious. I cannot for the life of me picture you singin' anything."

"Why not?" he asked, the surprise at her comment causing a glimmer of humor in his eyes to take over.

"Because—with all due respect—you look like a banker."

Liam threw his head back and laughed. "I do not."

"Your hair could not be more perfectly combed if you tried. It rivals Clark Kent," Georgia said. "And that is *not* the outfit of a rock star."

Liam looked down at his jeans.

"His hairstyle is fine," Hannah said, sticking up for him. "Although it was a little longer and messier when you were young."

Liam ran his fingers through his hair.

"I'm sorry," the manager said into the microphone on the stage. "Looks like we won't have any music tonight, folks."

The woman behind them sniffled.

"Try, Liam," Hannah pleaded. "Who cares if you're rusty? That woman should have music for her birthday."

He eyed the lone guitar on stage.

"Just a song or two," she urged.

He shook his head in disbelief. "I can't believe I'm letting you talk me into this," he said with a chuckle as he shrugged off his coat, pushed his chair back, and stood up.

Hannah broke out in an enormous smile and clapped her hands.

"Clark Kent saves the day," Georgia teased.

"You haven't heard him play. Maybe he'll surprise us and turn into Superman," Hannah added.

Liam didn't respond to Hannah's comment and made his way over to the manager. After a brief conversation, he grabbed the guitar and climbed onto the stool on stage, tilting the microphone down to his mouth and leaning into it.

"Uh," his voice boomed around them. He cleared his throat. "I hear that the performer wasn't able to be here tonight, so I'm filling in. I hope that's okay."

The room was silent.

Liam strummed the guitar uncomfortably, tuning it, and it was clear that he was reacquainting himself with the feel of it in his hands. He looked so different from the boy who'd played for her all those years ago. Hannah remembered sitting in the back of Ethan's truck in the field where they used to gather as kids, her bare feet swinging above the wild tumbleweeds. At dusk, the boys would all drive their trucks there and drop the tailgates so the girls could have a place to sit. And when Liam showed up, all the girls' heads would turn. He'd had an electric charge that had surrounded him wherever he went, a current that made people pay attention to him. She could still remember that particular night when he was sitting in the back of his truck, playing guitar. He'd looked her directly in the eyes when he sang, and she'd looked away, but she'd gotten a flutter like no other. She'd hoped he'd come and talk to her, but he never did.

"It's someone's birthday tonight," Liam said from the stage as Rose set their salads onto the table. "So we can't let her go home without a song or two." He offered a friendly wink to the woman.

Hannah got up and moved her chair closer to the stage. The woman moved up too and set her chair beside Hannah's. "I'm Daphne," she said, holding out her hand. Hannah shook it and introduced herself. Daphne tipped her head toward Liam. "Is he any good?" she asked.

"Yeah," she replied. "I think he'll surprise you... and maybe himself."

Liam began to strum the guitar, the notes taking shape, forming a melody. He hummed into the microphone, getting his bearings. "This is one I wrote myself," he said.

Then he began an old song that he used to sing all the time. It was about how chances could slip away if you didn't grab them. Hannah remembered it well. Her senior year, she'd gotten lost in the lyrics, dying to get out of that town and promising herself she'd never let an opportunity pass her by.

"He's good!" Daphne said.

"Yes, he is," Hannah replied. He still had it.

Once he'd gotten into his stride, Liam's fingers played effortlessly, just like they had when they were kids. His voice was more reserved than it had been, and he was quieter, but that kid was definitely still inside somewhere. As he played, Hannah closed her eyes for a second and could almost smell the summer wind back home. When she opened them, Liam's gaze was on her the same way it had been so many years ago, but this time, she didn't look away. Instead she smiled, this shared moment giving her relief from everything she was going to face when she got home.

Chapter Five

"I still can't believe you can sing like that," Georgia said as she slung her bag with Jerry over her shoulder, leaving the carrier in the car and peering up at the towering hotel. They'd gotten back on the road after dinner, and a few hours later, they'd stopped for the night in Northern Virginia.

"It's been a while," Liam said.

To Daphne's delight, Liam had ended up playing about five songs. She'd told him it had been the best birthday she'd had in years.

"When did you stop playing?" Hannah asked.

"You know, I can't remember the exact day when I didn't pick up my guitar," he replied, shutting off the engine. "I played a little in college, but after graduation, I got busy with finding a job and then marriage, and having a child… Before I knew it, it had been years since I'd played, and it didn't really feel like it fit me anymore."

Hannah nodded, considering his reply. She knew what it was like for a part of her not to fit anymore. They got out of the car, and as he pulled their bags from the trunk, she wondered about his wife and the life he'd built for himself. The whole idea of Liam as a family man had changed the dynamic between them.

The first hotel they could find close by was a gorgeous, shiny structure with a rooftop bar and a lobby that rivaled the Taj Mahal.

Since it was housing wedding guests who seemed to take up most of the building, there were only two rooms left, so Hannah and Georgia agreed to share while Liam took the other room.

Hannah could tell by the look on Georgia's face that she wasn't used to this sort of lavish accommodation, but luckily, Hannah had accrued some frequent-visitor points for this particular chain from traveling with Miles a few times on his various business trips. She'd always put the rooms in her name because he couldn't care less about the points, so tonight one room was free of charge, and the three of them agreed to split the cost of the other.

"Did they say they have bathrobes and slippers in all the rooms?" Georgia asked Hannah wide-eyed, as she slid her room key across the illuminated sensor for the elevator while shifting Jerry in her handbag. The doors swished open and Georgia loped inside. "I'm gonna take a long, hot bath and curl up in that robe, and watch TV with Jerry in my lap until I pass out. The burger I had earlier made me so sleepy," she said with a yawn.

Hannah felt the total opposite. She was starving from only having the meager salad back at the restaurant, and she'd disrupted her normal sleep rhythms so long ago that now she was wired. "It looks like the downstairs bar is still open. I think I might see if I can grab a bite to eat, and then I'll come up." She felt grimy and needed to get in the shower and scrub the day's awful events off her, but her hunger had won out. Their bags had been delivered to the room already, so as soon as she finished eating she'd shower, change into her clean pajamas, and sink into bed, drifting off to dreamland.

"I could do with some food, too," Liam said.

Hannah liked the idea of having someone there to distract her from all her thoughts. Then she wouldn't be tempted to think about everything that had happened at the airport. "Oh, good. We can grab a table together."

Contemplation washed over him, and heat spread through her face. Only then did it occur to her that perhaps he hadn't meant his comment as an invitation. A married man might not be up for late dinners with another woman, no matter what the situation was. Hannah inwardly scolded herself for not thinking it through. It was really late, and he probably just wanted to grab some food and take it to his room. She hadn't meant anything by her suggestion but now it was awkward.

Oblivious to their moment of uneasiness, Georgia obstructed the elevator doors with her foot as they pinged to alert her that she'd held them open longer than acceptable. "We should exchange numbers in case we need to talk to each other," Georgia suggested, already tapping on her phone screen, ignoring the pinging.

They all got out their phones and put in their contact numbers.

"I'll probably be asleep when you get up to the room, so I'll see y'all in the mornin'! When you come in, just say, "Hi, Jerry," so he won't bark. Bye!" Georgia said as the doors closed, leaving Liam and Hannah in the lobby.

With the tension of eating a meal with Liam when he might not have meant to spend it with Hannah settling in, they walked over to the hostess at the restaurant.

"We're closing in ten minutes," the woman said with an apologetic look. "But the rooftop bar is open until eleven. They have a kitchen too. And room service is open until 2 a.m."

"We could do room service," Hannah suggested, glad to be able to correct her blunder.

"No, it's fine," Liam said, to her surprise. Now he was probably trying to smooth things over, when really he just wanted to retreat into a dark room, eat, and pass out for the night. "We'll go to the upstairs bar."

She glanced over at the promotional sign in the lobby for the bar's special Valentine's month-long soirée. Hannah wasn't at all dressed for the rooftop bar. The image on the sign dripped with glamor, and Hannah was still in the jeans, sweater, and wedge heels she'd chosen for the plane. She hadn't combed her hair all day, and she was nearly certain she didn't have any makeup remaining on her face.

Liam also seemed to be considering the trendy sign. "I'm up for skyline views and confused looks if you are," he said. "I'm famished."

With no other real options, Hannah shrugged. "If you say so," she said, grinning.

That was twice now that, in the oddest of circumstances, he'd made her smile in the midst of her awful day. He was so quiet and mysterious—nothing like the boy she'd once known. She wondered who Liam McGuire really was in his regular life. Perhaps he'd share a bit about himself and his family over dinner. As she considered this, the question occurred to her: Who was *she* in her regular life? With so much of herself wrapped up in her work and in Miles, she wasn't really sure of the answer anymore. Her milestone birthday was tomorrow, so she needed to figure it out sooner rather than later.

Chapter Six

"I have to say," Hannah said, from across the candlelit table that stood against a wall of glass overlooking the Northern Virginia skyline, "I can't believe I ended up driving home with someone I know. What are the odds?" She eyed the candle with its ring of beaded hearts and the sushi appetizer they'd decided on clumsily, when they realized it was part of the Valentine's light menu package, the only offering at this late hour. It was all a bit awkward to share with someone else's husband, sitting in that atmosphere.

Liam pinched a piece of sushi with his chopsticks from the plate for two. "It *was* odd running into each other, after all these years."

"I know. We haven't seen each other since you dated Morgan Pete, right?"

Liam nodded, contemplative.

"Morgan was devastated when you two broke up, you know," Hannah told him with a wink, remembering the long talks she'd had with Morgan, trying to help her friend through the breakup with Liam while Morgan sobbed and swore she'd never find anyone as great as him again.

"I felt terrible," he said. "It was a misunderstanding that got out of hand."

"What misunderstanding?"

"Nothing. It's not important now."

"You can still tell me," she urged, her curiosity piqued.

His lips were set in a pout as he clearly decided what to say. "I had my eye on someone else, and I just didn't have the heart to tell Morgan…"

"Oh," Hannah said. "Why didn't you stop it earlier? You dated for about six months, if I remember correctly."

He cleared his throat, his chopsticks hovering in his hand. "I kept hoping to see her friend again."

"Her friend?" Realization dawned. "Nooo. Me?"

"Yep."

They both shared a little laugh. She felt embarrassed to have pressed him on the issue, but there were so many years between them, and he'd said himself that it wasn't important now. However, a tiny piece of her wondered what might have come of it had he said something.

Hannah remembered how kind he'd been at the bonfire where she and Morgan had met him that night, offering her a beach towel to put around her shoulders once the sun had gone down. While Morgan and Liam had chatted the night away, he would smile when he caught Hannah's eye…

"You didn't talk to me. You talked to Morgan instead."

"You made me nervous," he told her.

Hannah took a sip of her drink, thinking back to those carefree days.

"So the guy at the airport…" Liam said, switching gears. "Was he your boyfriend for… very long?" His words were careful, coming off his lips softly as if he didn't want to hurt her with his question, their common ground settling between them.

"'Was' is definitely the key word there," Hannah said, shaking her head and taking a long swig from the rim of her cocktail glass, ignoring the swarming fear which felt like she'd just realized she'd left her handbag in a taxi. "Miles and I dated for two years. We were supposed to do something together for my birthday. That's why I booked the trip…"

Liam's head tilted in response. "When's your birthday?"

"Tomorrow."

"*Tomorrow?*"

She nodded.

Liam looked around, helpless, for a second. "I wish I'd have known. I would've grabbed another Valentine's heart of chocolate at the airport at the very least… Last piece of sushi?" He scooted the appetizer plate toward her. "That's the best I've got."

Hannah laughed. "You know, as a kid, my mother would always bake heart-shaped cookies with pink roses made of icing that we could eat the entire week leading up to my birthday. And when I was really young, I believed that all the Valentine's candy I saw in the stores this month was really an early gesture to celebrate my upcoming birthday. Mom never told me otherwise."

"Is your mother staying in Franklin with you?" He motioned again for her to have the last piece of sushi.

Hannah nodded, picking it up and popping it into her mouth. She swallowed. "She and my dad are. They retired in Florida, but they just flew back to help with my gran. My mom called to give me the news when I was on my way to surprise Miles." She took another drink of her cocktail—some sort of pink concoction with rum and triple sec that the waitress had convinced her to buy, since it was part of the light menu package and the hotel only made them in February every year. The alcohol had relaxed her, causing her to open up a little more than she had in the car. "I'm really worried about Gran," she admitted. "Mama sounded panicked when I spoke to her, and she's never like that. She's always as cool as a cucumber."

"I'm sorry to hear about your grandmother," he said.

"I can't lose her," she said, working to keep the line that formed between her eyes when she cried from creasing.

Liam seemed visibly affected by her comment, as though something she'd said had bothered him. But the look was gone before she could make sense of it. Whatever it was, he obviously didn't want to share it with her.

"I keep trying to tell myself there's no sense in getting upset until I know the facts," she continued, trying to talk herself into the idea that everything would be okay. "But Gran sounded so frail when I spoke to her."

They fell into a moment of quiet; both of them sipping their drinks, Hannah's mind still going a hundred miles an hour.

"It's interesting that Miles was on your flight," she said, her thoughts coming out again. "It's like all the events lined up, and the universe knew where I really needed to go."

Liam watched her thoughtfully. "So maybe the universe made sure that Georgia and I were on that flight to get you back home."

She liked the idea that the universe would send people to keep her safe. "It's strange how things that seem so random end up being just what we need, isn't it?"

It appeared as though her comment sparked something within him. "Yes," he said, tipping up his bottle of beer and taking a drink. He leaned back in his chair, his shoulders more relaxed than they'd been previously, the beer bottle dangling from his fingers.

His phone rang, disturbing the moment. He grabbed it from his pocket and looked down at the screen. "I'm so sorry to do this," he said, getting up and setting his beer on the table, "but do you mind if I grab this call quickly?"

"What is that?" she asked.

He opened it, revealing a large piece of triple-layer vanilla cake with creamy icing and dark chocolate curls lying on its side. Liam opened his fist to divulge a single candle and a pack of matches. "Just a few minutes till midnight," he said. "Your birthday."

Hannah stared at the box of dessert, speechless. She looked into his green eyes. "Thank you," she said, her words heartfelt.

"It was the least I could do. Will you make a wish?" he asked, putting the candle in the cake, and lighting it.

She inwardly searched for the right words to construct her wish, and she knew instantly that, even though she had lots of things she could wish for herself, the wish should be for Gran to be well. But when she worded her wish in her mind, she wished for more than that—she wished for the memories yet to be made and for a life that would give her more time with her grandmother, Hannah's years in New York closing in on her.

She blew out the flame. "What an unexpected and wonderful surprise," she said.

Liam gave her a long look. "I couldn't agree more."

Chapter Seven

Hannah sat in the near darkness of her hotel room at the dinette table beside the box of birthday cake, anticipating her dinner, her tummy rumbling while Georgia and Jerry slept. Liam had texted her that he'd called in the order, so now there was nothing to do but wait.

Finally, there was a quiet knock, sending Jerry's head above the covers. Georgia turned over in bed but resumed the deep breathing of sleep. Hannah stepped out into the hallway so as not to disturb her roommate, and handed the room service guy a couple of bills.

"Thank you so much," Hannah whispered.

The man nodded and hopped back into the elevator across the hall.

Hannah pulled off the silver dome covering her plate to take a peek, her stomach in knots from hunger. A double burger and tater tots? That wasn't what she'd ordered. *Oh no.* Could this be Liam's order? If it was, that meant Liam might have her chicken, veggies, and potato wedges. She turned around to the door to open it, but it had locked behind her. Before she could start to panic, Liam stuck his head out his door down the hall.

"I've got your plate if you've got mine," he called quietly.

"Oh, good," she said. "But I've just locked myself out of the room. Could you hold my dinner while I run down to reception and get a key?" she asked, evaluating the patterned burgundy carpet under her bare feet, and wondering if she could squat down and eat right there. She was starving.

"You're welcome to eat at the table in my room."

"You sure?" she asked, not wanting to intrude.

"Of course… We could leave the door open if it would make you feel more comfortable."

"It's fine," she said. "I trust you."

She took the plate of food the few doors down the hallway to Liam's room. He propped the door open with the doorstop as promised, even though she didn't require that. She sat down at the table.

"Here you go," Liam said, swapping out the plate for the one in front of her.

They'd been in the car together the entire journey to Virginia and they'd just spent the evening at the restaurant upstairs, but here in his room, it felt more intimate, which immediately made her less talkative. Someone in the hallway walked by the room and looked in.

"You can close the door," she said. "I'm pretty confident that you won't… steal my potato wedges or anything."

He allowed a little grin. "You're putting a lot of faith in me," he said.

"Well, I eyed your tater tots when they were delivered to my room. I might have even stolen one…"

"You didn't," he said, chuckling, and it gave her an unexpected fizzle of happiness.

"I'd never tell," she teased, enjoying their banter. She got up and closed the door, plunging them into silence and solitude. "I feel like I've been up for forty-eight hours," she admitted, stabbing a piece of broccoli. "It's been a very long day."

"Yes, considering we're eating dinner after midnight. I'm usually out for the count by ten these days."

"Me too."

"Happy birthday," he told her, his face alight.

"Thank you."

Her gratitude was deeper than surface level. Liam was like a quiet light in the darkness, the one right thing in everything else that had been going wrong.

"Your cake is back in your room," he noted.

"Yeah, I'll have to eat it after I wake up."

"At least you got to make your wish. I hope it comes true for you," Liam said.

"Thanks."

They fell into another buzzy silence, only making a bit of small talk for the rest of the meal. She wanted to talk more, but she was so tired she couldn't think straight.

"Thank you for letting me eat with you," she said when they'd finished. "I'll just go wake up Georgia now."

"Of course," he said, standing up to walk her to the door. "Have a good night. See you in the morning." He stood in the open door to watch her go down the hallway.

Hannah went to her room and knocked, but no one answered. She knocked again and waited, her eyes aching for sleep and feeling terrible that Liam was standing there waiting for her to get into her room. He had to be as drained as she was. She didn't even want to shower at this point. She just wanted to fall into bed and close her eyes. She knocked again, this time as loud as she could. Jerry barked once but no one came to the door. She didn't want to make Jerry bark any more or they'd all get thrown out for having a pet in the room…

"No answer?" Liam called down to her.

She walked back over to him. "No," she said, exhaustion causing her voice to quiver. "I might be able to go down to the front desk and get a key."

"It's already almost one o'clock in the morning. I've got two beds in my room. You can bunk with me if you want. It's totally fine."

This was certainly awkward.

"We're going to be sleeping," he said, evidently reading her doubt. "Neither of us will even know where we are in about two minutes."

"True," she said.

He opened the door to let her in, and she came back into the room.

"You can wash up in the bathroom, and I have an extra T-shirt and shorts in my toiletries bag if you need to borrow them. I always roll up a few garments in my carry-on in case my luggage doesn't make it. Looks like it paid off this time." Before she could say anything, he went over to his bag and pulled out a gray T-shirt and a pair of navy-blue running shorts, handing them to her. "They're clean."

"Thank you," she said from the doorway of the bathroom. As she headed in to change, he walked over to the bed and pulled the covers back for her. The crisp white sheets were calling her name.

When Hannah came back into the room, Liam was on his side, facing away from her. She climbed into her bed, clicking off the lamp he'd left on by her bedside, plunging her into darkness until her eyes adjusted to the low light. Hannah lay in bed with the covers pulled up, her arms on top of the blanket, suddenly wide awake. She sharpened her hearing to home in on Liam's breathing, straining to hear over the hum of the heating, but she couldn't make out any deep breathing.

She'd enjoyed being with Liam tonight. She conjured up the look in his eyes when he'd listened to her. It was unique to him, and she doubted he even knew he was doing it, as if he were studying something that he really appreciated.

Hannah took in a deep breath and tried to unwind. Beginning with her toes, she focused on relaxing her muscles, moving to her legs, and then—

She squealed, throwing off the covers and jumping out of bed.

"What is it?" Liam said, clicking on the bedside lamp and climbing out of his covers, while squinting at her as his eyes adjusted to the light. His gaze slid down her bare legs in his shorts and up to the T-shirt, a hint of interest surfacing on the pout of his lips.

"I'm so sorry. I think I felt a spider," she said with a shiver. "I swear. It crawled across my shin." She lifted the sheet and shook it to see if she could find it.

Liam moved over to her and as he leaned around her, she felt it crawling on her. "It's on my arm!" she shrieked, sending her backwards and knocking into him, making him laugh out loud.

"That was my hand," he said. "I was just trying to get around you." He went over to the side of the bed and lifted the sheets, shaking each blanket. "I don't see it. Hopefully, you scared it away." He double-checked, letting her see.

Hannah took in a steadying breath. She hated spiders. But it looked like whatever it was had vanished. Perhaps it was a loose thread or something. "Thank you," she said. "Sorry again."

"It's no problem."

He switched off the light, and they both climbed back into their respective beds.

All riled up now, Hannah had to try again to bring herself back down and relax. She looked at the digital clock on the dresser: 1:45. *Ugh.* She turned her thoughts back to her muscles, attempting to clear her mind. Then, unexpectedly, she felt it once more. This time it was on her shoulder. In a panic, she jumped out of bed. Liam laughed again from his side of the room.

"I can't help it," she said into the darkness. "There's something crawling in my bed. I'm not joking." She put her hands over her eyes. "It's getting so late. I just want to sleep, and I know you do too. I feel awful."

"If you don't mind sharing, you're welcome to have the other side of my bed. I haven't felt a single critter in here," he said. "I'll just turn toward the window. And then let's be sure to mention it to the front desk in the morning, so they can let housekeeping know."

Hannah didn't make a habit of crawling into bed with people, but this was an emergency. She was not sleeping with a spider. And she was locked out of her room. So there was only one thing she could do, and that was to take Liam up on his offer. She slid under the covers, feeling his warmth beside her, making her skin prickle, every nerve on high alert as he lay on his side, facing the window.

Before long he'd dozed off, rolling onto his back, their arms and legs nearly touching. Hannah felt his fingers resting next to hers, and all she could think about was the softness of his touch when he'd rubbed her arm to wake her up in the car. She tried to remember the last time Miles had even rolled over and given her a kiss, and she couldn't recall. The more she thought about it, the further back her emptiness spread until she realized that she'd been lonely for a very long time. Tears welled up in her eyes, making her already aching head pound. One teardrop slipped out of the corner of her eye and ran down her temple. She tried to clear her mind of it all, but she was struggling.

She spent the next half-hour working on relaxation, and finally she started to feel the weight of sleep fall upon her, her limbs becoming heavy. Her breathing had slowed to a steady rhythm and her consciousness was waning. Then, her eyes sprung open again when Liam turned over in his sleep, draping his arm across her body, his face snuggled into her neck. She turned her head to try to view his face in the dark, the slightly spicy scent of his soap delightfully welcoming. She lay there, barely able to calm the pounding of her heart, unsure of what to do. If she tried to untangle herself, she might wake him up.

She wiggled a tiny bit, but then he pulled her in closer and his head tilted toward her, his lips finding hers. His kiss was soft and gentle, and it felt strangely perfect. Her shoulders relaxed just as his eyes flew open and registered the situation. He sucked in a short gasp, and she could tell he was horrified she'd think he was taking advantage of her. She offered a smile through the dim light of the room to let him know that she knew he wasn't. They both stared into each other's eyes, for what seemed like forever and a brief moment at the same time, before he swallowed hard, his face closing up.

"I'm so sorry," he said, breathless.

"It's okay," she assured him. "It was… nice."

"Let's get some sleep," he said, rolling over. His tone let her know, kindly, that the kiss had been an obvious blunder, but now she couldn't get the feeling of it out of her mind.

Staring at the gray of the ceiling in the dark, she tried to conjure up something else she could think about, but it had been the best and most surprising thing that had happened all day.

There was something reassuring about Liam being there—she couldn't deny it. It felt oddly right to have him next to her.

Chapter Eight

Liam stirred ever so slightly, and Hannah was quickly aware of the light coming in through the window, and the proximity of his body. His arm was around her again, warming her like a cocoon, his face snuggled up next to hers. She hadn't noticed when he'd done it this time, but his snuggliness made her happy.

He slowly opened his eyes, and they both took in the situation through their bleary, sleep-deprived consciousness. She wanted to wait to see how Liam reacted in the light of morning. He kept his sleepy eyes on her for a moment with a vulnerability that took her breath away. Slowly, he unwound himself from her, every muscle in her body screaming for him to stay put, and sat up.

Running his fingers through his disheveled hair, he turned back to her. "Good morning," he said softly, his gaze sweeping over her as if he wanted to drink in the sight but was forcing himself not to.

"Morning." She struggled to take her eyes off this more authentic version of him. She definitely liked it.

Until now he'd been so measured and serious, so businesslike. There was an underlying weight behind his eyes, and she had a feeling that if he ever decided to write down what he was thinking, he'd have volumes before he'd finished. But this morning, he seemed different. All of that was stripped away, and it was just him, the guy who'd laughed at her ridiculous fear of spiders, the guy who'd pulled back the covers for her, the one who'd held her and kissed her last night…

Hannah threw the covers off her legs and fluffed her pillow before getting out of bed. She felt she needed to focus on anything but Liam to avoid divulging the flutter she got whenever she looked at him.

"Coffee?" he asked, grabbing a hotel mug in two fingers, and loading the compact in-room coffee maker.

She padded over to him and, as she did, she caught the tiny bit of interest from the corner of his eye before he turned his attention back to the coffee.

"Yes, thank you," she replied, browsing the selection of miniature creams and sugars.

"Sorry I didn't give you much room to sleep," he said, his words careful as he prepared her coffee. "But on the other hand, the spider probably slept like a king." He handed her a steaming mug.

She laughed at his joke, a comfortable ease settling over her now. "I didn't mind." She looked up at him through her lashes as she sipped her coffee.

"You're definitely not a fan of spiders. I'll have to remember that…"

As he said it, it was as if he'd caught himself. Both of them seemed to consider the implications of his statement. Would he want to see her after today? She certainly would like him to. She was enjoying their time together.

"Happy birthday!" Georgia said in the open doorway, as Hannah stood in the hallway outside their hotel room. She scanned Liam's oversized outfit that Hannah was still wearing, lingering on the wad of Hannah's clothes piled in her hands, before continuing all the way down to her bare feet. "Somebody's having a *very* good birthday, it looks like." Georgia sucked her lips in, her eyes round as saucers, as she stepped aside to let Hannah into their room. She scooped up Jerry and followed Hannah over to her bed, which was still freshly made.

"It's not what it seems," Hannah said, dumping her pile of clothes on the bed, turning away from Georgia, heat rising under her skin. "I got locked out after dinner, and it was so late…" She yawned, still lacking enough rest to feel energized even with the caffeine from her morning coffee. Her eyes burned with the need to close them, but every time she did, the feel of Liam's kiss rushed through her. "Liam offered for me to sleep in his room."

"Did he, now?" Georgia said, grinning like the Cheshire cat.

Hannah didn't make eye contact for fear her bright cheeks would now completely give her away. She pushed her lump of clothes over and set her suitcase down on the bed, unzipping it. "Nothing happened…" Then she stopped, changing course. "Oh no," she said, wondering, as she stared at all the sundresses and tank tops she'd packed for sunny Barbados, what in the world she could wear that would be warm enough in this February snowstorm.

"Well, that's not good," Georgia said, standing in the hotel bathrobe, looking over her shoulder.

"I know…" Hannah chewed on her lip while she assessed her choices. "I was packed for Barbados."

"Not the clothes, the sleepover." Georgia poked her head into Hannah's line of vision. "The way he's been looking at you the whole trip, I'd have thought he would've at least tried to make a move." Then she pulled back as if to get a better view of her. "Unless he *did* try, and you didn't take the bait."

Hannah laughed incredulously, but she wasn't convinced that Liam hadn't felt the bit of chemistry that she had, and if she were honest with herself, she wouldn't be terribly put off if Georgia's assumptions were right. "He was asleep in seconds. And what are you talking about? He hasn't been looking at me like anything."

"When you're talking, he studies you as if you were some interesting new subject in college."

"He does not," Hannah returned, shaking her head. But as she went into the bathroom and started the shower, she couldn't deny the flurry of happiness she'd felt at what Georgia had said. She came back out to grab her shampoo and conditioner, and walked past a grinning Georgia on her way into the bathroom.

After Hannah's shower she'd checked her email, only to find a full inbox. When she'd responded to everyone at work, she and Georgia split up. Georgia ran out to walk Jerry and get a coffee, while Hannah went to see if she could find warmer attire in the gift shop downstairs.

"Hey," Liam said, waving fondly as he entered the shop. He was clean-shaven and wearing his clothes from yesterday.

"Hi," Hannah returned, holding a sweatshirt that said, "Virginia is Home."

"You need clothes too?" he asked.

"Yeah. Unless I want to wear my swimsuit and sarong. I was packed for a beach vacation."

He chuckled and reached around her, grabbing another sweatshirt. "At least you have something," he teased. "I should charge the airline for this." He held up the sweatshirt so Hannah could see what was on the front: "Sweet Lovin' Right Here." Hannah laughed out loud, sending the store clerk's gaze their way. "What? Not my color?"

"Orange isn't really anyone's color," she said, still laughing. She liked this humorous side of him. It reminded her more of the boy she'd known so many years ago. Perhaps their time together last night had loosened him up a touch.

Liam considered his choice once more. "But we could match." He grabbed another orange sweatshirt in a smaller size, this one reading: "Butter my biscuits."

"Never," she said, squeezing her eyes shut in amusement. She grabbed a green-and-yellow scarf, wrapping it around her neck.

"Stunning," he said. Then he plopped the matching beanie on her head. "Perfect. And it would go with *this*. He held out a white sweatshirt with the state motto—"Virginia is for Lovers"—in black block font, the state below it in green, with a zipper running through it. His gaze lingered on her long enough that she felt the need to slide the silly hat off her head and be serious. But then his phone rang, tearing through the moment. "It's my mother," he said, apologizing with a quick glance before hanging the sweatshirt back up and stepping out of the shop.

After paying for and putting on the warmer zip-up hoodie she'd purchased, Hannah sat beside her suitcases on a bench in the hotel lobby, waiting for Liam and Georgia. Liam was still on the call down the hall, and he hadn't noticed she'd come out. Georgia wasn't back yet, so Hannah sent a text to her mom to check in on Gran.

I haven't gone to see her yet today, her mother texted back, a long string of words filling Hannah's screen. *I've been at Gran's shop. I spent all evening going through the books to send off the P&L, and she's hemor-*

rhaging money. It's worse than your dad and I thought. I tried again to get in touch with the leasing agent, but haven't gotten an answer.

No one seemed to be getting answers from this leasing agent. She texted back, *Gran is such a levelheaded woman. She has to see it's time to retire.*

Her mother returned: *I fear with her health, she's going to *have* to retire. Not to mention that, if she doesn't, your dad and I won't have a penny to our names.*

Hannah replied, *I should be home this evening and we'll talk about all of it then.*

Her mother came back: *Okay, honey. Be safe and see you this evening.*

Hannah dropped her phone into her bag, and when she looked up, Liam had moved to another bench just down from her, his phone in his hand on speaker as he typed frantically on his laptop. He was so absorbed in what he was doing that he hadn't seemed to notice she was sitting there. Hannah picked her phone back up and scrolled through social media, waiting for him to finish the call, trying not to eavesdrop, but it was difficult with the way the sound carried down the empty, airy lobby.

"Have you considered going to see someone?" a woman's voice came from Liam's phone.

"That's not necessary, Mom," Liam replied, his eyes on the screen of his laptop as he typed feverishly. "I'm fine."

"You think you are, but I'm telling you right now, Noah definitely isn't, and neither are you. You can't just abandon your son."

Abandon his son? Hannah shifted her eyes discreetly toward Liam, his fingers now stilled on the keys. He was still staring at his screen, but it was clear that his mind wasn't on whatever was in front of him.

When he didn't respond, his mother's voice came through again. "He barely knows you, Liam."

Liam set his laptop on the bench and took his mother off speaker, putting the phone to his ear, standing up, and speaking quietly enough that Hannah couldn't hear what he was saying. She dove back into her social media, her mind not really into it as she considered how much had changed between the time she'd known Liam and now.

The man she'd spent the entire day with yesterday, the person she'd woken up to this morning—that person didn't seem like the kind of man who would abandon a child…

"Happy birthday," Liam said, suddenly joining her. "I should've said that earlier."

Hannah stood up to greet him. She had so many questions, but she knew she couldn't ask any of them. "Thank you," she said.

The corners of his mouth twitched upward as if he were trying to deny the grin that wanted to surface. His gaze slid down Hannah's new "Virginia is for Lovers" sweatshirt, and a glimmer of humor drifted into his eyes. "You took my suggestion," he said.

"Yes. Thank you," she replied, pulling her coat over the sweatshirt.

He finally smiled at her, a broad, honest smile.

Georgia came shuffling toward Hannah excitedly, bundled up and holding a paper to-go coffee cup in one hand while dragging her suitcase with the other. Jerry was peeking out of his bag. "How's everyone?" she asked.

"Great," Liam said.

After the conversation she'd just overheard, Hannah knew his answer was false.

"How's the birthday girl?" Georgia asked. "We should do something fun for breakfast to celebrate."

"It's fine, really." Hannah didn't want to take up everyone's time, but Georgia had already jumped in again.

"We could go to a nice restaurant and eat instead of grabbing something on the go," she suggested. "What do you think, Hannah?"

"You really don't need to make a big fuss…"

Liam tipped his head to the side and studied her. By the look on his face, he seemed interested in her newfound caution. "It's your *birthday*. It's the big thirty-five, right? You only turn thirty-five once," he said.

"Okay," she replied, hoping that by conceding, he wouldn't question her change in demeanor. She hadn't meant it to show.

Hannah really didn't want to delay the trip any longer than she had to. She wanted to get to Gran's as soon as possible. But it looked like she was outnumbered.

The closest place open for brunch was Dos Pablitos, a Mexican restaurant about a block away from the hotel. Hannah meandered through the crowd between Liam and Georgia as they followed the hostess to their table.

"Hang on a second," Liam said, sliding back out of the booth as soon as he'd sat down. "I'll be right back."

While he was gone, a waiter arrived and served them chips and salsa, handing them the menus. Hannah looked up and spotted Liam across the restaurant, eyeing an enormous sombrero that hung underneath a sign saying "Feliz cumpleaños," which Hannah remembered from her ninth-grade Spanish class meant "Happy birthday." He waved, grabbing the attention of the hostess. She nodded and Liam lifted the large hat off the wall, bringing it over. He slipped into the booth beside Hannah and set it on her head.

"That's better," he said, picking up his menu.

"It's a good look for you," Georgia said with a giggle.

Hannah grabbed hold of the enormous brim and adjusted it on her head.

"Yes, it's becoming," Liam agreed, the corners of his mouth twitching upward again with amusement.

"Ah! It is your birthday?" the waiter asked as he approached their table, smiling from ear to ear, showing off his bright white teeth.

"Yes," Hannah replied, feeling self-conscious as a few people turned to look.

"And how many years have you?" he asked, in broken English.

She tipped the front of the sombrero up to see him better. "Thirty-five."

"Thirty-five!" he called out, entirely too loudly.

Suddenly two guys with maracas came dancing toward her, all the wait staff falling in line behind them singing,

> *"Feliz cumpleaños a ti*
> *We know what we see*
> *A beautiful lady*
> *Not a day over twenty!*
> *Cha-cha-cha!"*

They all cheered, the two men shaking the maracas, as others in the restaurant clapped.

When they all left, Hannah realized Liam was looking at her warmly. "Your cheeks are the color of a fire engine," he said.

"That was the best thing I've ever seen," Georgia said. She grabbed a chip and scooped up some salsa. Then she subtly eyed Liam as if to say, "See how he looks at you?"

Liam's phone buzzed suddenly.

"Oh," he said, a wave of something crossing his face. "Do you mind if I take this video call? It's my son, Noah."

Before Hannah could process anything more, he'd answered it, and the face of an adorable boy filled the phone screen. He had freckles and dark hair, the shape of his serious mouth just like his dad's, his innocent face hypnotizing her.

"Hi, Daddy," he said timidly. "Grandma said I should call you."

"Hi, Noah," he said. "I'm glad you did."

The quiet lightheartedness that Liam had just shown them with the sombrero had quickly left him with this call. His shoulders seemed tense, his face full of thought. This wasn't the reaction a father would usually have when he hadn't seen his son in days. Instead of being jovial and silly, he was guarded.

"I'm having fun with Grandma," Noah said, his high voice like an angel's. "We played on the beach."

"That sounds like fun," Liam said.

Noah nodded. There was an underlying sadness in his face that mirrored the one Hannah had seen in Liam's at times, and she wondered about it.

"Who is the lady in that big hat?" she heard Noah ask, as Liam moved his phone closer to her. She only just remembered she was still wearing the sombrero. "She's funny," Noah giggled.

"This is Hannah. She was nice enough to come along with me on the trip home since I can't take a plane. And this is Georgia." He twisted his wrist to turn the phone around so Noah could see Georgia. "They're my new friends."

"Will I get to meet them?" Noah asked.

"Maybe," he replied, diplomatically.

His answer caused Hannah to consider the fact that, after this, they would all go their separate ways.

"Can we?" the little boy pressed. "I want to meet Hannah so she can bring her hat."

"You like this hat?" Hannah said, leaning into view. She grabbed a tortilla chip and scooped up some salsa, popping it into her mouth. Seeing the little boy's face lightened her mood considerably.

"I want to wear it. Would you let me wear it?"

"I would, except I borrowed it from this restaurant. It's my birthday today and this is the birthday hat."

"Will you eat cake?" Noah asked.

"I did have some cake earlier," she replied.

Noah's eyes grew round, and he broke into a delighted expression. "What kind was it?"

"It was vanilla on the inside and chocolate on the outside," Hannah replied. "Your daddy bought it for me." The waiter came by and brought them waters. Georgia told him they'd need a minute more.

"Daddy, will you buy me cake one day?" Noah asked.

"Sure," Liam replied, tilting the phone back in his direction so Noah could see him.

"What kind of cake did you have for your last birthday—can you remember?" Hannah asked, making conversation. It was easy to talk to the little boy. He seemed just darling.

"It was a white bread kind with the white icing on top," he replied excitedly. "And it had special balloons with my name on them! I love balloons…"

"That sounds like a fun cake," she said. "Did you pick it out? Or did your dad?"

"Daddy doesn't buy me cake. Elise does."

"Who's Elise?" Hannah asked.

"My nanny."

"Oh," Hannah said. "So did she pick out your cake?"

"Yeah, she always gets good stuff."

"It definitely sounds like it," Hannah said.

"I ate two whole pieces at my birthday party!" he said.

Hannah laughed. "And how many did your daddy eat?" She grinned at Liam but he looked worried, withdrawn.

"He didn't have any cake," Noah said. "He works till after I'm in bed."

"Hey, buddy, I'm going to go, okay?" Liam said. "I'll be at Grandma's to pick you up when you get home from the beach."

"Okay," Noah said, but he seemed more hesitant about that than excited.

"See you soon," Liam told him.

"Bye, Daddy."

It occurred to Hannah that when they'd talked about renting the car earlier, his reason for going to Franklin was to secure the real estate funding and collect his inheritance. Wouldn't any parent have first said they were picking up their son? Certainly that would come above money, right?

Maybe it would be better to focus on her life instead of someone else's, she thought.

As they resumed the journey home, Hannah alternated between pretending to read the book she'd brought for the beach and closing her eyes to give them relief. The latter won out, and not long into the second leg of their journey, she drifted off. When she woke, she realized that they'd driven well over half the distance to Franklin.

"I'm so sorry," she said to Liam. "I was absolutely exhausted after yesterday and I zonked right out. I thought we were going to take turns driving." She tucked the book she'd placed on her lap but had never actually read back into her bag.

Liam pulled into a parking space at a rest stop along the highway. "You looked too deep in sleep to interrupt you." He cut off the engine and turned around. Georgia was also asleep in the backseat, with her headphones on and her crossword in her lap.

"Wild bunch you've got here," Hannah teased, in an attempt to lighten the mood.

Liam smiled. "Wanna lock her in and take Jerry for a quick walk to stretch our legs?" he asked.

"Sure."

She pulled on her coat and zipped it up to her chin before she reached back to grab the leash and scoop up Jerry. She clipped on his leash and set him on the grass. The clouds had parted, revealing a bright-blue sky, the sun beaming down in long, glorious rays through the trees, but the temperature was still quite cold. Hannah paced beside Liam as they led Jerry across the yard at the rest area.

"We're making good time," he said, obviously trying to fill the silence with conversation, but the look on his face made her wonder if he had more to say. "We only have about two more hours left to drive."

"When will your son get there?"

"Not sure. They're flying home sometime tomorrow," he replied. "My mother watches him for me a lot when I travel for more than a night or so. He keeps her busy, which is good. She's been alone a lot since my dad died."

"I'm sorry to hear that."

"It's been a dark time for my family," he said. Then he stopped walking. Jerry sniffed around by their feet. "Can I admit something to you?"

"Sure."

"My attention went right to you yesterday at the baggage claim. You floated in with that big smile, a flower in your hair, as if you'd brought the light in when you came... It sort of made me notice the cloud I've been walking under."

Both their lives seemed to be full of obstacles at the moment, and they'd probably be terrible for each other, but Hannah was beginning to feel something for him. She wanted to be careful with her next steps, but there was something pulling her toward him. She couldn't put her finger on it. The two of them walked the path around the yard.

"I couldn't help but see you," he added. "You make things seem better just being there."

"Wow," she said, shocked that he was voicing these kind things to her. "I've never had anyone in my life tell me something like that before."

He turned to her, his face serious. "You should." The affection in his eyes was intoxicating.

While she knew they both had a lot on their plates and should probably go their separate ways, she found herself saying, "You don't have to stay in a hotel when we get to town."

"What do you mean?"

"You could stay at my gran's house with my parents and me until your mom gets back." She wanted to return the kindness Liam had shown her by giving her a ride home. "She has a third bedroom that won't be used. You're more than welcome."

"I'd hate to impose on your family," he said, shaking his head.

"You wouldn't. I'm sure they'll be fine with it. And you'll have your own bathroom and everything. I usually sleep in that room, but I can sleep in Gran's room, so you can have it. It's really fine."

"What if your grandmother gets better suddenly and needs her room?"

"Well, by the sound of my mother's worry on the phone, I doubt it would happen that soon," she said. "But if by some miracle she does, I can always take the sofa."

"That's really nice of you to offer." He seemed to be deliberating.

Hannah knew that getting involved in Liam's life might not be a good move for her, yet a buzz vibrated between them that she couldn't ignore. "There will probably be a heart-shaped birthday cake… Just saying."

"All right," he said. "You twisted my arm."

And suddenly, Hannah could see exactly what Georgia had described in the hotel room earlier. She couldn't deny the happiness she felt when she saw it.

Liam's phone pulsed in the car's cup holder between them. "Do you mind answering that for me while I drive? It's Noah," he said with his eyes on the road, focused on the navigation as the weather shifted again and they moved through the traffic in the falling snow.

Without a lot of time to think it over, Hannah accepted the video call and Noah's adorable face popped up.

"Hi," he said, with a big grin that stretched to his dimples on each cheek. "Did you have to give back your hat?"

"Sadly, yes," she replied.

"Oh. I wanted to try it on."

Hannah laughed. "If I see another one, I'll be sure to tell your dad where to get it."

"Okay," he said. "Where's my daddy?"

"He's driving in the snow and he has to concentrate. What are *you* doing right now?"

"I'm on the deck of the beach."

Noah wobbled the phone to reveal the glistening, turquoise waters behind him, giving Hannah a pang of wistfulness, as the reality of where she was compared to where she originally thought she'd be at this moment pushed its way into the front of her mind.

"It's beautiful," she said, lost in thought for a second.

Hannah had barely traveled anywhere, spending every minute of her time working. She'd wanted to change that, starting with the trip to Barbados she'd planned for this week, but it had all gone so horribly wrong...

"Grandma is behind me in the chair," Noah said. The picture on the phone pixelated and then the image of a woman, waving at the screen, became clear.

"Hello," Hannah called.

Noah came back onto the screen. "I was bored, and Grandma needed a rest, so she said to call Daddy."

"You're bored?" Hannah asked. If she were there, she'd be able to come up with a million things to keep him busy. "You know, there's a spot by the river in Franklin with a tire swing, and you can swing way out. So far that you can see the river. Maybe, if it's still there, I can show your daddy where it is, and he can take you to it when the weather gets warmer."

Liam glanced over at her with interest.

"Could you take me?" Noah asked.

"Me?" she replied.

"Yes. I want to go with you."

"Maybe we could all go…"

Liam's eyes stayed on the road, but by the way his lips were ever so slightly pursed, it was clear that something bothered him.

"What else can we do?" Noah asked.

"Well, when the weather's nice, there's a lot to do. We could hit baseballs at the park, get ice cream downtown, kayak…"

"Yeah!" he said, running around with the phone, the turquoise water sliding in and out of focus with his movements.

"With that kind of reaction, we're going to have to take him," Hannah said to Liam with a grin, once she'd gotten off the phone. "He's such an adorable boy. I'd have a lot of fun with him. His smile is so cute that it makes me laugh."

Liam stayed quiet, but looked over at her for a second, attentive. Then he turned his focus back to the road. Hannah looked out her window, wondering what in the world was going on between Liam and his family.

Chapter Nine

"Just drop me off here," Georgia said from the backseat when they'd exited the traffic circle, directing them onto the main route of the southern town of Franklin, Tennessee.

The street brought back nostalgic memories for Hannah, and the shame of being gone so long returned with a vengeance. It had been nearly three years since she'd walked down this street, although even then she'd breezed down it quickly on her way out of town. It looked smaller now, compared to the towering city she called home. The warm glow of sunlight filtered in through the trees that had started to bud early, signifying warmer days that had been enjoyed before the recent cold snap. They passed the side street where The Memory Keeper was, and she craned her neck to try to see it, but construction and overgrowth blocked her view. Like an old film, her memories assaulted her.

"Slow down!" Gran had called to an eight-year-old Hannah as she ran ahead to get to the ice cream shop. She and Gran always walked there on summer days when the heat would slow a person down to a near crawl, making something as simple as sitting on the porch swing difficult to manage. Impatiently, Hannah would stop at the crosswalk and wait for Gran.

The vintage stores that lined the two-lane road had been exactly the same since childhood. They were all open for business, their windows filled with pink and red decorations and heart-shaped wares for the month of February. Despite the cold, the sidewalks were full of people. Families lined up for the day's show outside the old Franklin theater, while others dipped into the local chocolate shop to get their taste of gourmet treats. Music sailed into the car from a street performer strumming gritty southern tunes on his guitar, as passers-by dropped tips into his cowboy hat.

"Are you sure you don't want me to take you somewhere specific?" Liam asked. "It's freezing outside."

"I'll be fine," Georgia replied, as she opened the pet carrier and leashed up Jerry. "There are lots of restaurants and coffee shops I can duck into if I get too cold on the walk, and I have your number if I get into any trouble." She waved her cell phone in the air.

"Want me to help you take all your bags somewhere?"

"I'm fine. I've been on my own long enough to handle a few bags. Pull over there." Georgia pointed to an empty parallel spot near the stoplight.

Liam complied and put the car in park.

"Well, it's been fun knowin' you two." Georgia gathered her things in the backseat and put Jerry on the sidewalk, where he immediately found a nearby tree.

Liam popped the trunk and got out to help Georgia with the rest of her bags.

Hannah put down her window. "You sure you don't want to head over to my gran's house with us? I can almost promise there will be birthday treats and a home-cooked meal."

Georgia grinned. "That's okay, but thank you."

"Text me if you need anything at all," Hannah said.

"Sure thing." Georgia slung her bag over her shoulder and picked up the pet carrier as Liam set her suitcase next to her on the sidewalk. "Catch y'all later."

Liam got back into the car and Hannah put the window up. As they pulled away, she watched Georgia shrink in the side-view mirror as she made her way through the crowds. "I have to admit, I'm going to miss her."

"It's weird, isn't it—being with someone for two days straight and then not knowing if you'll ever see them again." He glanced over at her, and the look in his eyes made her wonder if that particular concern applied to her as well.

"Yeah," she said, her attention lingering on him longer than she'd meant to. He caught it, offering another glance in her direction.

"Which way?" he asked.

She refocused on the task at hand. "Take a right on the next street."

After a few more turns, they finally pulled up in the drive at Gran's blue clapboard bungalow. Ethan's fully restored, turquoise 1977 convertible Ford Bronco Sport sat out front. He'd been tinkering with that thing since they'd driven off Old Man Samson's used car lot when they were eighteen. Hannah got out and walked up to it, peering into the windows. New leather seats.

"Wait, wait, wait—I gotcha," Ethan had said to her the last time she'd ridden with him, running around to her side of the truck to let her in. He'd spread an old beach towel over the soiled, torn seats and held his hand out, palm side up. "For you, milady," he'd said with a dramatic bow. Then he'd made some joke about her being too much of a princess.

She turned away from the truck and reached into the rental car to grab her things. Liam got the suitcases out of the trunk while Hannah piled the other bags next to them.

The porch swing swayed in the cold breeze, the pillows a bit more disorganized than Gran would have had them; the rocking chairs had been pushed aside, and her geranium pots were empty, which gave Hannah an immediate punch in the gut. Good thing Gran couldn't see that right now. She'd have a fit.

The front door swung open, and Hannah's dad, Chuck, waved, leaning on his cane, and filling up the doorway with his broad stance and oversized belly—too many dinners at home and not enough golf. Her father was still recovering from a heart attack he'd had last year, which had forced him into retirement. After the heart attack, which had been touch-and-go, putting all of them on edge, Hannah's parents had settled on the coast of Florida for a slower pace of life.

"My eyesight might be failing me these days," he said, working his way down the two steps to the drive, using the cane his doctor had suggested he now use, "but this young man hasn't been on your social media feeds."

"I don't put all my business on social media," she said, making a silly face at him, ignoring the niggling feeling of shame that her father had to search her social media feeds to find out about her life these days.

Ethan came out behind her father. His hair was a bit shorter and more stylish than it had been when he was younger, and somewhere along the line he'd developed a muscular build, having shed his lanky teenage body. She wanted to run to her best friend and wrap her arms around him, but seeing how different he looked now—how grown up—made her realize how many years she'd lost.

"You pickin' up strays?" He regarded Liam curiously before giving Hannah a lengthy look. "Hey, man. Good to see you."

Liam shook Ethan's hand in greeting.

"Liam drove me home when all the flights were grounded. He's a hero, not a stray," she said, with a big smile in Liam's direction.

When her father reached her, he gave her a giant bear hug. His squeeze wasn't quite as tight as it had been over the years, given his health, but the familiarity of it was still there, making her want to bury her head in his chest to shield herself from everything that was swirling around in there right now.

"Who knew that being overly cautious and booking a rental car could make me a hero," Liam said to Ethan.

"He did a lot more than that," Hannah cut in, sticking up for him.

Liam shrugged it off before turning back to her father, holding out his hand. "Liam McGuire. Nice to meet you."

"Chuck Townshend." Hannah's father offered Liam a firm handshake. "Let me help y'all with your bags."

"We've got it, Dad," Hannah told him, grasping the handles before he could. She noted the frustration in the purse of his lips, and she knew that it went against his nature not to help his daughter, but he was supposed to be taking it easy these days.

Liam carried the suitcases inside with her father leading the way, while Ethan took the duffel bag from Hannah. "Don't those designer jeans get dirty on the back of your horse?" Ethan teased Hannah.

"I haven't ridden horses in years, Ethan," she told him, hearing the drawl inch back into her voice as she responded to him.

"You ain't done a lot in years." He tossed her bag over his shoulder.

He wasn't going to let her off easy, and she knew that. Family meant everything to Ethan, and he'd considered her family. She'd let him.

"Were you ever plannin' on comin' home?" He ran his hand through his hair, and her breath caught when she saw the wedding band on his left hand. She'd always said she'd be a bridesmaid in his wedding since he didn't have a sister.

"What's that?" She pointed to it.

"Life's moved on since you left," he replied.

"You didn't invite me to the wedding?" she asked, hurt that he hadn't even so much as called her to tell her.

"I didn't think you'd care," he said honestly.

His words cut her like a knife. How could he ever think she wouldn't care? She'd have stopped everything and come home to his wedding. But then it hit her: while she'd been working like crazy, meeting deadlines, and moving up the corporate ladder, on his end, all Ethan had heard was silence. And her silence had felt like indifference. Sadness plumed in her stomach. She'd never wanted him to think for one minute that she was uninterested in his life.

"Did Gran know you were getting married?"

He shook his head. "We kept it small. I told her when I went to see her at the hospital, so she knows now…"

Still in shock, Hannah reached down and grabbed the last of the bags, slinging it over her shoulder. Ethan gently slid it back off and carried it for her.

"Your mama's been at the shop all day, organizin' to get it into some kind of order," Ethan said, moving the conversation on. "I'm sure she'll want to kick her feet up when she gets home. Good thing, since it's your birthday." He waggled his eyebrows at her.

Her dad called from the doorway. "We've got a few surprises for you."

"Y'all didn't have to do that," she said, but she was glad they had. She hadn't been sure what she was going to find when she got home, and Ethan's news had hit her like a ton of bricks.

But despite everything, a sense of home had settled upon her the minute she'd arrived, and she missed being around her family. Ethan was right to give her a hard time. It had been too long. She hoped she could make him see that she hadn't meant to stay away. She wouldn't let it happen again.

"How's Gran?" she asked as she made it to the front porch.

"Mama was with her some yesterday," her father said. "She's doing okay, all things considered." He opened the door, sending a wave of flavorful smells from Mama's famous stew her way, taking her back instantly to the savory aromas she knew so well from her childhood. "She'd get out of bed and walk home if they'd let her. You know Gran."

Hannah laughed, despite the weight of the situation. "Will I get to see her tomorrow?"

"Absolutely. You can go with your mama. Maybe you can convince Gran to sign a few business documents. Your mom tried to get her to entertain the idea of closing the shop, but she's not having any of it. You and Gran have always seen eye-to-eye, so maybe you can talk some sense into her." Her dad closed the door behind Ethan. "But enough about that right now. Your mother's gonna be home in just a bit, and we need to celebrate our birthday girl."

While Chuck made small talk with Liam, Ethan grabbed Hannah's larger suitcase.

"What room you sleepin' in?" he asked.

"I'll help you," she said, grabbing her other bag. "I'm staying in Gran's room." She turned to Liam. "I'll be right back."

Chuck patted Liam on the back. "I'll get you a drink. After that drive, I'm sure you need one…"

"So," Hannah said as they went down the short hallway. "You got married."

"Yup."

"Do I know her?"

"No, she didn't go to school with us. She grew up in Chattanooga."

"Ah," Hannah said, the topic uncomfortable for her. She'd always known everything about Ethan, and now he had a whole life she didn't know *anything* about. "What's her name?"

"Christie."

Hannah nodded, feeling like she'd lost all her oxygen. She'd been so selfish, and she hadn't even realized it.

"I'd love to meet her."

"Maybe..." He dropped her bags next to Gran's bed. "Let's talk about it later, all right?"

"No, let's talk about it now," she pressed. "Why wouldn't you want me to meet your wife?"

He pressed his lips together the way she remembered whenever he was worried about something. The last time she could remember seeing him do it was the day she'd left.

"Tell me," she urged.

"She thinks you put crazy ideas in my head."

"What?" she said, dumbfounded. "How? I haven't even spoken to you in years. And even if I had, what crazy ideas would *I* put into *your* head?"

He sat down on the bed. "This is where I belong. I'm happy here," he said. "But sometimes I wonder out loud to Christie, what if you were right about getting out of here and following your dreams? I wonder what's so good out there that you didn't even bother to come back. It must be pretty damn great."

Hannah lowered herself down next to him. "It's not that great," she said. "Not at all. It's just different." She hung her head, feeling awful. "I should've come back."

Her father stuck his head into Gran's room. "Quit hogging her, Ethan," he teased. "Y'all can catch up out here."

"Yes, sir," he said, and Chuck disappeared down the hallway. Standing up and tipping his head toward the door, Ethan told Hannah, "Let's talk later. We've got birthday treats out there."

She needed to get back to Liam anyway. Her father had probably cornered him with his coaster collection—he'd bought a coaster on every trip they'd taken since she was a little girl. Hannah got up and followed Ethan to the kitchen.

Liam's bags were stacked in the corner, and he and her father were talking next to Gran's antique farmhouse table, which was hidden by a red tablecloth. In the center was a stack of dessert plates from the family china pattern and Gran's nineteenth-century white French cake stand. Under its glass dome was what Hannah would bet was a red velvet triple-layer cake, the icing a mass of perfect peaks and valleys in buttercream. Two gifts, wrapped in pink paper printed with cascading bright white bows, sat beside it. And, of course, Gran's largest white milk-glass vase was filled with red roses and a balloon that said, "Happy Birthday."

"How did Gran do all this?" she asked, the sight stirring the desire in Hannah to see her gran.

Growing up, every year after having cake at home, Hannah had gone to Gran's. And whenever she visited on her birthday, she got this exact set-up. The only difference was that this time, she hadn't gotten to choose the "surprise" in the middle of the cake. Hannah's favorite had been the time Gran had added a peanut butter fudge swirl that marbled the entire inside. Hannah could still remember the creamy decadence of it. Gran had told her she'd teach her how to do the fudge swirl, but that had never happened.

"She helped your mama bake it over the phone last night," her father said. "Gran told her it was time she learned how."

Fear flooded Hannah with that last statement. Had Gran wanted to teach her mother how to do it so that she could carry on the tradition in her absence? She shook the thoughts free, the idea of being without Gran unimaginable.

"The top gift is from your gran," her father said. "She told your mother where to get it and how she wanted it wrapped."

"Leave it to Gran to still deliver gifts and flowers from her hospital bed," she said, after collecting herself.

Her father smiled. "That's your gran," he said.

"I'm home!" Maura Townshend's comforting voice sailed in from the entryway. She came into the kitchen, unwinding her scarf and pulling her light brown hair from under her collar. "Oh, hello, all." She kissed Hannah on the cheek. "You made it!" She held her hands out to get a good look at her. "I'm so happy to have you home." She turned to Liam. "Hello," she said.

"Mama, do you remember Liam McGuire?" Hannah asked.

"I think so…" She smiled at him.

"He drove me all the way from New York so I could get here," Hannah explained.

Her mother seemed surprised, and Hannah was pretty sure she was wondering why she hadn't brought Miles with her. "You are a godsend, young man," Maura said with a warm smile as she patted his arm in a friendly greeting.

"Liam is going to be staying in the spare room with us for a few days. I hope that's okay."

"Of course." She walked around Hannah and gave Ethan a hug. "Someone says 'cake' and Ethan shows up," she teased him.

Exhaustion lingered under her gracious smile, but she maintained her usual good humor, the worry from her initial phone call replaced by fatigue. With a playful shake of the head, her gaze doting as if she were looking at her own child, she said, "Missed ya. What ya been up to?"

"I dunno," he said with a shrug. "Same ol' thing. Workin' with Dad."

"Well, I've got a big dinner that's been going on the stove all day. And I've made mulled cider," she said. Then her eyebrows bounced at her daughter. "Your favorite." She gave Hannah a wink. "I'll just put another bread bowl in the oven for Liam. Ethan, you staying?"

"Naw, thank you, ma'am," he said. "I'm heading home. Just wanted to stop by and welcome Hannah back to our little corner of the world." He said the words "little corner of the world" patronizingly, but then laughed as if to play it off.

"Suit yourself," Maura said, wrinkling her nose at him. "Liam, you hungry?"

"Please don't go to any trouble on my account," Liam said.

Mama shooed away his comment. "It's no problem at all. Y'all go unpack and get comfortable. Hannah, show him where to put his things."

"I'll catch y'all later," Ethan said.

As he passed Hannah, he leaned close to her. "See ya," he said, just the way he always had when he'd dropped her off from school, as if to say everything would be okay. The sound of it made her want to cry with relief right there.

"This is where you'll be staying," Hannah said, as Liam parked his suitcase against the wall of Hannah's old room, and scanned the walls inquisitively.

Hannah sat down on the quilted bedding of her four-poster bed, considering how long it had been since she'd slept here.

"I remember Ethan well," Liam said. "He's a good friend, right?"

"He was my *best* friend. I've known him all my life."

"He likes to give you a hard time," he said, the corner of his mouth turning upward.

"Always." She chuckled fondly at the thought of him. "He's mad at me for not coming home over the years, so he's going to make me aware of that fact every minute I'm in his presence, I'm sure."

Liam nodded, strolling over by the window and peering down at the plaque Gran had displayed on a side table. "You won a pie-baking contest?" he asked.

"Mm-hm. My grandmother and I made key lime pie for the Spring Festival right after I turned sixteen… You know, it's about that time of year right now."

"I did hear something about the Spring Festival coming up," he said, looking back at the award.

"I'd entered the contest that day instead of getting my driving permit. That's why Morgan always drove whenever we saw you that year."

"That must've been a good pie to forego your driver's permit."

"It's award-winning," she said, teasing him and making him smile.

She shifted her gaze to the wall opposite them to avoid the flutter of happiness that it caused her, catching sight of the old shadow box of pressed flowers hanging on the wall. She ran her fingers along the frame.

Hannah's first memory of it was when she was five. She'd felt so grown up when Gran had allowed her to use the pressing board for the first time. She still remembered placing the lone poppy in the center, her tiny hands shaking as she held it down with all her might to keep the press together.

Liam picked up a frame with a grainy photo of Gran and eight-year-old Hannah, outside Nell Winter's old barn where Gran used to get her geraniums and have coffee with Nell. "I can still see traces of this little girl in your face now," he said, looking between Hannah and the photo. He paced further into the room. "You were on the high school gymnastics team? I didn't know that." He leaned over the dresser to get a better view of the trophies Gran had placed there.

"I don't know why she displays those," Hannah said. "I was packing them up before I moved to New York, and she was visiting at the house. She'd said she wanted to take care of them for me."

He was thoughtful, that undecipherable look that seemed to come and go at random washing over him again as he set the photo back into its spot. "She asked because she was going to miss you, and she didn't want to let you go," he said. "Having your things around would make it feel more like you were here."

"You think so?" she asked, already knowing the answer.

"I *know* so," he replied.

"How do you know?" she asked him outright, hoping he'd open up.

"I just do," he said, turning away from her toward the window and folding his arms. His back heaved with an inhale and he slowly released it, something seemed to be eating at him.

She wasn't sure what came over her, but she put her hands on his back, moving slowly to his arms, making him turn around.

"What's the matter?" she asked seriously, looking up into his eyes.

"Nothing," he said, but something substantial had taken hold of him.

His gaze roamed her face, settling on her lips, his hands finding hers. He intertwined their fingers hesitantly, as if trying on his affection for her for the first time. Their electricity was so new to Hannah, and it occurred to her, in the moment, that she and Miles hadn't ever had this kind of spark. If she wanted to be brutally honest with herself, the Barbados trip had been covering up the fact things were pretty bleak between them.

"You know, I'm great at listening. If you want to tell me what's bothering you, I'll listen."

He moved in closer. He was so near that she could feel his breath gently brush her skin. He gave her hands an affectionate squeeze, their bodies pulling together like magnets. Everything around them melted away as she looked into his eyes. His lips parted as if he were going to say something, and she hung on his every minuscule movement, waiting for it, wanting to know what was clouding that gorgeous face of his.

The door squeaked and the two of them flew apart instinctively.

Her mother pushed it open an inch further. "Dinner'll be ready in an hour," she said, ripping through the moment. "Y'all come on out and have a drink with us. I've got that mulled cider. It's been brewing in the Crock-Pot all day."

"Thanks, Mama," Hannah said.

When her mother had shut the door and retreated back down the hall, he looked white as a ghost.

"Are you okay?" she asked.

He didn't answer.

"Whatever it is, I want to help."

"You definitely can't help," he said, his words kind but final.

"Okay, then I at least want to listen."

He moved back over to her, standing close again. And she could tell by the shallowness of his breathing that their proximity affected him. "Now's not the time to explain it," he said, his voice gentle. He cleared his throat, looking at the door. "It's your birthday. Your mom has mulled cider, and she's dying for us to have some—she's mentioned it twice now." He winked at her, his spirit seeming to lift, but something told her that the burden he was carrying would return.

Hannah grinned up at him, drinking in the look he was giving her, and knowing that despite everything, something was definitely happening between them. It was like a rocket, its engines firing with no way to stop it.

Liam opened the door. "Let's get that cider."

Hannah went with him to the kitchen, her outlook brightening. She remembered how Gran had always told her, "To get to the treasure, sometimes we have to go through the stormy seas." Hannah couldn't help but think she was in the storm right now, but being back at Gran's and weathering it with Liam could be the best thing that had happened to her in quite a while.

Chapter Ten

The cake and gifts had been set aside until after dinner, and replaced with plates of fresh homemade bread that her mama had warmed in the oven. She'd scooped out the centers and filled the rolls with her creamy potato-bacon stew, topped with grated cheese. The savory aroma of it tickled Hannah's nose.

Hannah sat down between her father and Liam, and scooted her chair closer to the table.

"It's so good to have you kids home," Maura said, taking a sip of her cider, her shoulders finally seeming to relax from the day. "Where do you live now, Liam?"

"Charleston," he replied.

"Another out-of-towner," Mama said with a teasing wink in Hannah's direction. "We tried to keep Hannah here, but she couldn't be contained. She was drawn to the bright city lights."

Liam took in her observation, looking on thoughtfully.

"Remember how you used to put on your mom's high heels and walk around with a notepad, pretending you were at work?" her father asked.

Hannah's mother put her hand on her heart fondly. "Seems like yesterday."

"I'm so glad I didn't follow *my* childhood musings," Liam said. "I wanted to be a circus clown."

Hannah laughed out loud, his comment totally taking her off guard. "Now that I think about it, you might be able to pull off one of those giant curly wigs," she said with another laugh.

"You think?"

"Yes, but only with a squeaky nose." She liked the way he looked at her whenever they shared an amusing moment.

"I wanted to be the first clown magician famous enough to have his own show. I spent hours learning magic tricks from books, and at my best, I could make a quarter disappear from the palm of my hand."

"Can you still do that trick?" she asked.

"I don't know," he said. "I haven't thought of those days in a long time."

Hannah wondered why he wouldn't have tried to show the trick to Noah.

"I'd love to see you attempt it, Liam," Maura said, getting up from her chair and digging around in her purse. She returned with a quarter and handed it to Liam.

He took the quarter between the pointer finger and thumb of his left hand, holding it up. "Okay, I might be a bit rusty," he said, wriggling it back and forth. "You see," he continued dramatically, while holding up his right palm as if he were about to high-five someone, "I only have this one quarter." He moved with a fluid motion, transferring the quarter into the palm of his right hand. "Then I close my hand around it like so." He held up his right fist. "But wait." He opened it up and his hand was empty.

Both Hannah and her mama gasped in surprise.

"How in the world…?" Hannah's father said.

"Where is it?" Hannah asked.

He opened his other hand. "Right here," he said with a grin.

"That's fantastic," Maura said. "Perhaps you really should've been a magician."

It occurred to Hannah, as she soaked in his smile, that there was definitely a glimmer of magic floating around Liam.

"Gran was insistent that I make the cake this way," Mama said after dinner, as she set the glass dome to the side, her knife sinking into the waves of buttercream while they all sat around the table with their dessert plates. "So I did everything exactly as she told me to. I baked the entire thing on video chat, hoping the project would cheer her up." Maura eased out a slice of the cake and set it down on Hannah's plate, then motioned for Liam's.

"Peanut butter fudge swirl," Hannah said, nostalgia filling her up. "I thought it was going to be red velvet."

"Gran has been meticulously involved in what's going on here ever since she found out you were coming home. And she's had a hand in all of this. She chose the roses. She picked the cake—Liam, here you go." Maura handed Liam his slice.

"Thank you," he said. He was relaxed, setting down the plate and draping his elbow on the back of his chair, his mug of cider in the other hand.

Mama cut a piece for Chuck. "And the smaller present on top there—Gran was unrelenting about me finding it and wrapping it up for you." Mama cut herself a slice of cake and sat down.

Her father held up his mug of mulled cider. "To thirty-five, a golden age where we step onto the path of life and begin the journey to who we really are. Happy birthday, my dear."

"Cheers," Maura said, holding up her mug and clinking it with Chuck's. Liam and Hannah raised their mugs too.

As they all nibbled their cake, Mama handed Hannah the bigger of the two gifts. "This one's from your dad and me," she said, wrinkling her nose with fondness for her daughter.

Hannah untied the bow and then pulled the tape loose at the end of the gift, ripping off the red heart-printed paper. "Oh, that's so wonderful," she said, turning the new sweater around for Liam to see. "It's gorgeous." She got up and hugged her parents. "Thank you."

"I saw it in the store window and it just screamed your name," her father said.

"You'll look absolutely beautiful in it. I just know it," Mama chimed in. "Now, unwrap Gran's gift." She reached over and got it, passing it to Hannah.

"Should we get Gran on a video call first?" Hannah suggested.

"That's a great idea." Mama got up and retrieved her phone, tapping on the screen.

The phone pulsed as Hannah held the book-shaped gift in her hands. Then she heard Gran's voice.

"Hello, Faye," Maura said. "I've got Hannah here, and she's about to unwrap your gift." She turned the phone around. Gran was on the screen in a hospital gown, her gray hair in disarray, which was a far cry from the fashionable crop she usually styled every day.

"I wanted you to be here when I unwrapped it," Hannah said, trying not to panic at the transparent hue of Gran's skin or the way her eyes looked as though half the life had been sucked out of them. Gran raised a weak hand and touched her lips to hide her smile, revealing the IV in her bruised skin. Hannah chewed on her lip, the shock of seeing Gran spiking her emotions despite her attempt to stay calm. She looked so much older…

"Go on then, my love," Gran said.

Mama propped the phone up on the table while Hannah unwrapped her present, revealing an old journal, the pages yellowed with age.

"What is this?" Hannah asked, opening the book, and reading the first entry's date: *February 14, 1943*.

"It's the journal I started when I was eighteen," Gran said. "A collection of all the memories from my youth in Kentucky. It's all that came before I was your gran. And a story I almost didn't have a chance to tell you. There's never been a more important time than now to do that."

Tears sprung up in Hannah's eyes. She felt as though Gran was slowly getting her affairs in order, which meant she was preparing for the end, and Hannah couldn't bear it. She peered down at this gift, like a lifeline to her beloved grandmother, a keepsake that would stay with Hannah forever. "Thank you," Hannah said, her words heartfelt as she ran her hand across the tattered leather cover. "I'm coming to visit tomorrow," she said.

Gran gave her a weak smile. "I can't wait to see you."

"I'll get there first thing in the morning, okay?"

"Well, at eight, one of my nurses comes in to take my vitals. She's a chatter, bless her heart, and you won't get a word in edgewise. Better come at nine."

Hannah grinned. "Okay, Gran."

"I hope you have a lovely birthday," Gran told her. The picture was starting to shake, betraying her trembling hand as she held the phone. Her weariness was showing. "I'm going to go now so I can rest, all right?"

"No problem. I just wanted you to see me unwrap the gift—*and* to say thank you for the fudge swirl cake." Hannah pushed away more tears.

"Ah, you're welcome. And Hannah?"

"Yes?"

"Your mama knows how to make it now, okay?"

Hannah swallowed the lump that had formed in her throat. All she could do was nod. But then she mustered the strength and forced the words out. "*You're* gonna teach me, though," she told Gran. A tear escaped down Hannah's cheek and she quickly swiped it away.

"I'm sorry, excuse me," Liam said with a catch in his voice. He left the room.

"Stop at the shop on your way to see me tomorrow, okay?" Gran said. "Make sure you fill any orders on the online system."

"I will," Hannah assured her, knowing there probably weren't any orders. It didn't matter now. She'd stop by if Gran wanted her to.

"All right, dear. I'll see you tomorrow."

Hannah said goodbye to Gran and handed her mother the phone, taking a minute to get herself together. She took in long breaths and let them out, trying to make the aching in her chest subside. When she'd collected herself, she asked her parents, "Mind if I check on Liam? I'm worried that we made him uncomfortable with the call."

"Not at all," Chuck said.

Hannah left the kitchen and roamed the bungalow, finally seeing him through the glass front door. He was sitting on the step outside, his back to her. She opened the door and ventured out into the cold, folding her arms in a feeble attempt to keep warm. He turned around.

"I'm sorry to have gotten so emotional just then," she said.

But he immediately shook his head. "It's totally fine. I just needed a minute." His face didn't say the same. It looked heavy with thoughts.

"Wanna tell me what you're thinking about?" she asked, feeling bold after sharing such an intimate moment with Gran in front of Liam.

"There's nothing to tell," he said matter-of-factly. "That's just it: nothing. There's nothing at all."

She sat down beside him, hugging her knees for warmth. "Okay, with all those 'nothings' you just said, you implied that there's definitely something."

His phone went off and he opened up an email. Whatever it was caused him to change course, standing up and zipping his coat. "Hey, I have something to do for work. Mind if I step out for a while?"

"No problem." She didn't want to press him anyway if he wasn't going to tell her whatever was going on. She had enough worries of her own.

"Thanks." He took his keys from his coat pocket and headed down the steps, leaving Hannah there in a flash.

As his car pulled out of the drive, Hannah went back inside, wondering what all that was about.

"Where's Liam?" Maura asked.

"He had to leave for something with work." His quick exit was reminiscent of the rush of the career she'd been swept up in back in New York. She wouldn't ever allow herself to get that caught up in work again. She went over to the table and picked up Gran's journal and her new sweater. "I'm going to go take these to my room and have a look at them," she said.

Maura smiled sympathetically at her daughter. "Sounds good," she said.

Once she was settled in her room, Hannah opened the journal, interested to learn what Gran had wanted her to know.

Chapter Eleven

Hannah lay on her belly and gripped the journal Gran had given her. With a deep breath, she inhaled Gran's unique scent of lilac and powder that saturated the room, and read the first lines of Gran's familiar swooping script.

February 14, 1943

I wish I could send something to Charles for Valentine's Day. I count the days until I can marry him...

Originally, she'd thought Gran was talking about her dad, whose name was Charles, but then she'd written that she'd wanted to marry him. *Marry him?* The only man Gran had ever married was Pop-pop, and his name had been Warren Langley Townshend. She looked back at the date of the entry: 1943. That was the year Gran had told them all she'd met Pop-pop, right?

So Gran had been in love with someone else right before meeting Pop-pop? And she'd named her child after him? Gran's comment from earlier tonight came back to Hannah. She'd said the journal was "a collection of all the memories that came before I was your gran." It was hard to imagine Gran being anyone other than the woman married to Warren, mother of Hannah's father. Who was she before that? Hannah read on.

Curry's drug store has chocolates in sampler boxes from twenty cents. It's more than I should be paying for chocolate right now, with Daddy out of work, but I would if Charles were here, just to show him how much I love him. And I'd also tell him that I stopped into Buxton Floral Co. when I saw their sign that said they would wire flowers. They even assured me of prompt and dependable delivery anywhere. But "anywhere" didn't include Tunisia. And while it seems silly to send a soldier flowers in the middle of the war, it certainly would brighten up that dirty tent he told me he was sleeping in. But it might also distract him and make him miss home... So instead, I'm spending my twenty cents on a Valentine's supper for one at the town hall. It'll be good to get out of the house for a while. Mama and Daddy aren't going, but they told me to have fun. Fun. That's not a word I use very much these days.

Hannah set the journal down, rolled onto her back, and hugged one of Gran's pillows to her chest. While she didn't like the idea of her eighteen-year-old grandmother not having any fun, Hannah could hear her cheerful disposition even in such a turbulent time. It was a delight to read how innocent she was back then. Just thinking of how Gran wanted to put flowers in a military tent in the middle of World War II made Hannah smile.

She considered what Gran had been going through back then. Hannah could relate to having rough times. She couldn't even remember the last time she'd done something that had made her laugh until she cried, like she had so many times when she was younger. She and Gran used to get to talking about something funny and end up doubled over, gasping for breath, the two of them giggling like schoolgirls. She promised herself right then that she'd do everything in her power to laugh with Gran like that again.

Liam still hadn't come back from wherever he'd gone, and it was getting late in the evening. Hannah almost texted him, but she figured he was a grown man; he didn't need her checking up on him. He had enough manners to come back at a decent hour, she was certain.

There was a knock on the doorframe. Hannah twisted around to greet her mother, who was standing in her bathrobe and slippers, holding her nightly glass of water that she'd always taken to bed.

"I was just checking on you," Maura said. "You've been in here since dinner, and I wanted to make sure you were okay." She came in and sat down on the bed. "I know how hard Gran's situation must be for you. There's no way to prepare for something like this."

"It's making me question everything." Hannah pushed the journal to the side and sat up next to her mom. "I need to tell you about yesterday," she said. She told her mother about what had happened with Miles.

"My goodness. That's a lot to handle," her mother said. "How are you holding up?"

"As good as I can be. I need to be strong for Gran," Hannah told her.

Her mother sat, thoughtful, her hands wrapped around her glass of water. "I never got to meet Miles," Maura said. She huffed out an expression of resentment.

Hannah ran her fingers through her hair. "I'm so sorry I didn't bring him home."

Maura frowned. "Doesn't matter now."

"It *does* matter that I never brought him to meet you. I'm sorry I stayed away so long. I should've been better."

Maura smiled affectionately at her daughter. "We spend our lives trying to be better people than the ones we are now. That's all we can do."

"I missed you," Hannah told her, basking in the wisdom only a mother could offer.

"Aw, honey, I missed you too." Maura leaned over and kissed the top of her head like she had when Hannah was young. "I wish I could shield you from all the pain that life can bring," her mother said, "and I know I can't. But your dad and I are here whenever you need us." She patted Hannah's hand. "How are you really? Are you doing okay?"

"I feel like I spent so long and wasted so much precious time trying to make things work between Miles and me, and it was all for nothing," she admitted. Tears welled up in her eyes unexpectedly.

Maura scooted closer to her. "It wasn't for nothing," she said gently. "All this is supposed to teach you something. Every step in life is a teaching moment—we just have to figure out what we were meant to learn from it."

"Maybe it was teaching me not to waste my time," Hannah said. She wiped her tear away.

Her mother nodded lovingly. "You could be right. You've had a setback, but now maybe it's time to dial in to that inner drive you have."

"Yeah…" Hannah said, considering what she even wanted. "I'm at a loss for what I'm supposed to be doing."

"Maybe it's because the future is wide open. God's giving you time to deal with what you've got on your plate right now before you start your next journey."

"Maybe," Hannah said, grateful for her mother's insight. She always knew just what to say.

Maura eyed the journal. "Anything interesting in there?" she asked with a wink.

"Definitely," Hannah replied, picking up the book and fanning the pages with her thumb.

Her mother wiggled her eyebrows. "Well, enjoy it. I'm heading to bed. I'll see you in the morning." She stood up and started toward the door.

"Good night," Hannah told her, feeling a little lighter after their talk. As her mom left, she opened up Gran's journal and began to read another entry, hoping to escape her thoughts for a while.

February 27, 1943

I can't stop staring at the letter sitting at the top of my trash bin. I know that I'm being selfish to even contemplate feeling sorry for myself, but the tears come anyway. Maybe my emotion is displaced. Perhaps my tears fall for my love. Charles has been on the front lines in Tunisia without word for weeks, and I have no idea if he's all right. This war is definitely hitting us all hard, but our armed forces are taking the worst of it for us, for which I should be grateful. All I have to be anxious about is the acceptance letter to Saint Joseph College for Women in my trash can that will never be answered, and my awful boss James Williams on the assembly line at the metal company. But I'm safe and well, and I'm able to help provide for my family.

Wow, Hannah thought. She knew Gran had never gone to college, but what Gran hadn't told her was that she'd given up a place to work on a factory assembly line during World War II to help her family.

Hannah couldn't imagine what it would've been like to have the kind of pressure that Gran was under.

Just then, Liam's headlights flashed through Hannah's window, so she got off the bed and headed to the front door. When he started up the walk, Hannah opened it, standing in the doorway.

"Sorry that took me so long," he said.

"No problem," she returned. "Well, I think I'm going to head to bed. It'll be so nice to sleep in a familiar bed tonight."

Liam grinned. "No spiders."

The memory of their kiss in the middle of the night floated into her mind. "Definitely no spiders."

They shared a moment, both of them looking at one another, and she felt as though he had words on his lips just like she did. But instead, he offered her an uneasy smile. Hannah turned away from him and locked the door. They walked quietly down the hallway, neither of them saying anything more.

"Good night," she finally said, as she left him at his bedroom and headed down to Gran's room.

"Good night," he returned from the hall.

Hannah closed the door to Gran's room and flopped onto the bed, her mind whirring again with Liam's presence. She squeezed her eyes shut to try to clear her mind. She'd just read one more entry to help her sleep…

March 3, 1943

I got a letter from Charles! I'm so excited I can hardly mind my manners! I went screaming through the house and scared Mama half to death. Here's what Charles wrote:

We're quite safe at the moment and I'm thinking of you, wondering if you've changed at all. Just wait until you see how different I am after being here, Faye. I'm skinnier now, and my hair is much shorter, but I love you just the same. I've told the other guys about you. With them around all the time, it's a wonder I have time to miss you so much, but I do and I'm glad they distract me when they can. It keeps me from thinking of everything I'm missing back home in Kentucky. How about that school you wanted to go to for art? I'll bet you're already packed by now. Let me know all about it. I'm excited to hear about you and what you're doing, and I can't wait to come home to you.

What had happened between Gran and Charles? She scanned the entry again, the last sentence blurring in front of her tired eyes: *I can't wait to come home to you…* She set the journal beside her and changed into her pajamas. Her thoughts still on Gran's story, she clicked off the bedside lamp, crawled into bed, and closed her eyes. She couldn't wait to visit Gran tomorrow so she could ask her about Charles.

Chapter Twelve

"Hey," Liam said tentatively, as he met Hannah in the hallway the next morning. He was already dressed, hair combed, clean-shaven. There was caution in his approach.

"Good morning," she said, crossing her arms over her pink heart-covered flannel pajama shirt. "Heading out so soon?" she asked. She took a step toward him, but he backed up, giving her pause.

"I'm all packed," he said, the look in his eyes warning her of something. "My bags are in the car. Thank you for your hospitality last night. It was truly appreciated."

"You're leaving now?" she asked, not even trying to hide her confusion. "But your mother isn't home yet, right?"

"Hannah…" He trailed off, clearly struggling to find the words for what he wanted to convey. "I can't be what you need right now, and we have to stop before things go any further."

"What?" Her mind was still clouded from sleep.

"I'm not… available," he blurted.

She stared at him. Moments from their time together flashed through her mind as she tried to understand his abrupt change in mood. Then his mother's voice—*have you considered going to see someone?*—rushed into her consciousness. As in counseling? Marriage counseling? Fear washed over her.

"Are you still married?" she asked before her mind could run too wild. Surely, he'd set her straight.

Not only did he not deny it, the hesitation and remorse on his face was enough to cause Hannah to stumble backwards. She leaned against the wall for support. After everything with Miles, Liam had moved in on her, letting her believe he cared, all the while knowing what she'd been through. How cruel could one person be?

Her face contorted with anger. She tried to keep her voice down so she wouldn't wake up her parents, but she wanted to scream at him. How dare he lie to her?

This was not the boy she'd known. She stared into his eyes, questioning everything. An ache scratched at her insides, making her feel as if a cosmic force had just jumbled the puzzle pieces of her life and left them scattered on the floor.

"Hannah, I shouldn't have... I'm so sorry." He reached out to her, but she jerked away. "I needed to stop this before it got out of hand," he said. "It already has..." He shook his head, wrestling with his thoughts.

"Yeah," she said deadpan, her complete disgust with the situation making her unable to emote. "Just go."

"I'm so sorry," he said gently, but she ignored the pain on his face because he'd brought it all on himself.

When he walked out the front door, she didn't even bother to watch him leave.

Hannah had put on clothes and brushed her teeth on autopilot, her mind in a fog. And now she sat at the kitchen table, crossing her arms over the new sweater she'd gotten for her birthday. While her mother made them a cup of coffee, she'd explained what had happened this morning with Liam, the disbelief of it still stinging.

A light knock at the back door in the kitchen stopped their conversation. Ethan stood on the other side of the glass, holding a box.

"Are those what I think they are?" Maura asked, getting up and opening the door. "Tell me you brought us freshly made cinnamon donuts," she said.

"You know I don't come over before noon empty handed," Ethan said, setting the box on the table and opening it up, the buttery, sugary scent of fried dough wafting through the cold air around them and making Hannah's tummy growl.

He plopped down in the chair next to Hannah. "What's goin' on?" he asked, reaching in, and pinching a tiny donut between his fingers. He had on the mechanic's uniform from his dad's body shop: a dark-gray button-up with the logo on a patch over the right side of his chest. His father, Ardy Wright, had worn that uniform for as long as she could remember. It was strange to see Ethan in it.

"You working with your dad today?" Hannah asked.

"Every day," he said.

Hannah nodded and reached for a donut. The only time she'd ever seen Ethan get heated was when he talked to his dad about the future. Ethan was artistic, his creative genes making him appear to be all over the place, his attention span jumping from one idea to another. He didn't sit still well, and he was always buzzing around, so tedious mechanic work wasn't his strong suit—but when he was painting, he was the stillest and most focused she'd ever seen him.

His dad would tell him, "You can't raise a family throwing paint on walls, son. You need to have an honest profession where you put in a full day's work, every day. Some kids would die to have a father who's willing to just hand over his business…"

"The shop is *your* life, Dad," Ethan would argue. "Not mine."

Ethan took another donut from the box then slid it toward the middle of the table. "You goin' to see your gran today?" he asked Hannah.

Hannah nodded. "So explain to me exactly what's wrong with Gran, Mama," Hannah said with a deep breath, to steady herself for what her mother was going to tell her.

"Her heart isn't working like it should," her mother said, the sadness in her words causing her face to slacken, showing her age. Maura's eyes filled with tears and she blinked them away, clearly trying to keep it together for Hannah's benefit. She picked at her donut.

"By the time I got here, she was coughing terribly and had swelling in her legs." Maura traced the rim of her coffee cup, faint lines forming around her lips as she pouted to keep in the emotion. "She was diagnosed with congestive heart failure. They're monitoring her and running tests to see if they can do anything for her."

Hannah covered her mouth as if that would keep the fear from escaping. "Oh my God," she said through her fingers. Ethan put his arm around her shoulders protectively.

"We don't know what the outcome of this will be, but she's ninety-five, Hannah. I think it's important to spend as much time with her as you can over the next few days. Read her journal if that's what she wants you to do. She'd asked me about fifteen times if I'd found it. Get all your family questions answered. And show her how much you love her."

Her mother had only taken that tone twice in Hannah's life: once, when Hannah was eight and a tornado had ripped through their neighborhood, her mother had gathered Hannah, her father, and her childhood dog, and they'd hunkered down in the closet under the stairs as the house shook. The second time was when her father had had his heart attack. That phone call at nearly midnight was still fresh in Hannah's mind.

"In the journal, she talks about someone named Charles. Not Dad, but some other Charles. Do you know who that is?" Hannah asked, her hands trembling.

Her mother shook her head. "I have no idea." She reached over to the kitchen counter and pulled a tissue from the box, blowing her nose, the tears still swimming in her eyes.

Hannah clasped her hands together, leaning on them, lost in contemplation about the time she'd never get back while Ethan rubbed her shoulders consolingly.

Maura got up and walked around behind her, putting her arms around her daughter in a motherly embrace. "Go see her," she whispered. "It'll do the both of you good to talk to one another. I've always admired the way you two can communicate."

"Okay," Hannah said, clearing her throat in a feeble attempt to push the emotion away as she stood up.

Ethan gave her a squeeze.

"Do you have time to go with me this morning, Ethan?" Hannah asked.

"Dad told me I could have as much time as I need." Ethan looked her straight in the eyes. "I know how you like to process things. Take a minute and breathe. I'll hang out with your mama until you're ready."

"Okay." Surprising herself, she threw her arms around Ethan. "Thank you," she said, her face buried in his chest, his familiar cotton and cedar scent calming her immediately.

"No problem," he said quietly.

Hannah headed down to Gran's room to freshen up for the hospital visit. She shut the door and fell against it, her chest heaving with the emotions that came as soon as she was alone. Her gaze roamed the room—Gran's dressing table, her soft-bristled hairbrush with the silver handle sitting unused, her pair of slippers lined up neatly under the chair, a string of pearls nestled in a porcelain dish on her nightstand. She let the tears come.

Her phone pinged with a notification, and she pulled it from the back pocket of her jeans. It was work. Something from the IT department. She couldn't look at it in the state she was in. She'd read it later.

She grabbed Gran's journal, hugging it to her chest. It was a comforting force; Gran's voice when it was still vibrant and untainted by time. She'd take just a quick minute and read a few entries to compose herself. She had to be unruffled when she walked into that hospital room. With a deep breath, Hannah opened the journal and settled in to find her calm.

March 25, 1943

James Williams is not to be trusted. He worked Sally Mae and me all day on the assembly line and then wouldn't let us go until a whole hour after our shift had ended. He said he'd pay us overtime, but I don't believe it. Last time he said that, there was nothing new in my paycheck. I hate working at the factory. I understand that we're helping America by making guns for the war, and it's good money for my family, but it's the same thing day in and day out, and my feet hurt so much after standing on them all day. I should be thankful to have a job when so many still don't make enough money to support their households, and I'm helping the family because Daddy can't find work that pays enough. But it doesn't make me like the job any more.

While she still wrestled with her own problems, after reading about Gran's strength in her time of uncertainty, Hannah was feeling stronger herself about seeing Gran. She sharpened her hearing to make out Ethan telling her mom a story, the two of them laughing. Despite the circumstances that had brought her here, she was glad she was home.

Chapter Thirteen

"Hey, Gran," Hannah said, as she and Ethan entered the hospital room from the brightly lit hallway.

Gran's empty stare at the wall across from her bed shifted, her head slowly turning toward them as a smile emerged on her pale, weathered lips. She raised her arms for an embrace, the IVs pulling taut, the sight causing Hannah to hurry to her bedside. She wrapped her arms around her frail grandmother.

"It's so good to see you," Hannah said, through the shock of witnessing Gran in that state.

Gran pulled back. "Don't you fuss over me. I'm just fine. I always look like this," she said, reading Hannah easily. "It's just that I usually cover it up with makeup and hairspray," she teased. "And I've never been so hydrated in all my life." Her grandmother tugged gently on the IVs going into her arm.

Hannah smiled to disguise her worry.

"I see you've brought your partner in crime," she said with a wink toward Ethan. Gran had always teased them that there was no other name for two people who were capable of getting into so much mischief together.

"Knock, knock." A nurse in yellow scrubs came into the room. "I need to check your vitals, Ms. Faye." The nurse wheeled in the portable medical unit and parked it next to the bed. Then she addressed Hannah and Ethan. "I'm Lanelle, the day nurse," she said with a wide, friendly smile, her teeth like a set of pearls against her dark skin. She walked around the bed and checked the IV bags, typing something in on one of the machines.

"I'm Hannah, Faye's granddaughter. And this is Ethan."

"Oh, so you're Hannah. Ms. Faye hasn't stopped talking about you since she found out you were comin'." Lanelle placed two fingers on Gran's wrist and looked at her watch. "And I already know Ethan. He's been up here causin' trouble for days," she kidded.

"You'll miss me when I'm gone," he said back to her with a big grin.

Lanelle rolled her eyes playfully but then relented. "You might be right about that," she said. "He was sweet one mornin' and brought all the nurses coffee."

"Suck-up," Hannah called him, making Ethan and Lanelle laugh.

Lanelle leaned over Gran's bed. "How you feelin', Ms. Faye?"

Gran pouted. "I feel the same as I always do—antsy. When can I go home?"

"I know you're lookin' to get out of here, but we've gotta get you well first."

"Have you been to the shop?" Gran asked Hannah, while Lanelle checked the IV ports in Gran's arms. "How's it looking?"

"I haven't been yet," Hannah replied honestly. When Gran's face contorted with concern, she added, "But Mama's been there the whole time. She's got everything under control."

"How are the geraniums on my front porch?" Gran asked, as Ethan pulled chairs for both of them to the side of the bed. He eyed Hannah, having obviously noticed when he was there that there were no geraniums on Gran's porch.

"They could use a little TLC," he said, covering for Hannah.

"See y'all later," Lanelle said as she left the room. "Bye, Ms. Faye."

"Bye, dear," Gran called. Then she turned back to Hannah. "Don't forget, you can go over to the nursery at Nell's and grab some more if you need to. Buy them through the account they have on file for the shop."

Hannah nodded. That account probably didn't have any money to fund the purchase, but rather than get into it, Hannah changed the subject. "The cake Mom made with your recipe was delicious."

"I'm so happy to hear that," Gran said with a smile. "Did your mama put any out at the shop for Speckles?"

"The cat eats cake?" Hannah asked with a laugh.

"With milk," Gran said, her chest bouncing lightly with her chuckle. "When the shop is closed, she finds her way to the house. Has she been hanging around?"

"I haven't seen her," Hannah replied. "But I just got here yesterday afternoon. Maybe Mama's seen her. I'm sure she's fed her."

"Make sure there's food and water," Gran said.

"Don't worry, Gran. I'll go to the shop straight after this, and then I'll be able to tell you more about what's going on there, okay?"

Gran reached for her and Hannah came close. With near desperation in her eyes, Gran said to her, "Whatever happens, save the shop."

"Hello-o," Maura's voice interrupted the moment. She walked in with a file folder and her handbag over her shoulder. "How is my favorite mother-in-law?" she asked, leaning in and kissing Gran's cheek.

"Decent," Gran said. "Now that Hannah's here. She fixes everything, doesn't she?" Gran winked at Hannah, a blanket of pleasantries sliding across her face.

"Yes, she does," Hannah's mother said with a doting look to Hannah, giving Ethan a friendly squeeze on the shoulders as she moved further into the room. "Hopefully Hannah can help with this," her mother said, opening the file folder.

Hannah jumped up. "Mama!" she said. "I've already taken care of that old paperwork."

"But—"

Hannah cut Maura off and took her arm. "Don't worry Gran with silly purchase orders. I'll fill them out for you. We can get it done in a second in the hallway. Ethan, chat with Gran while we get some work done really quickly."

The skin between Maura's eyes wrinkled with confusion, but she closed the file folder and followed Hannah into the hallway.

"Make sure you have enough baby's breath," Gran called. "I'm always running out."

"Back in just a second," Hannah told Gran and Ethan, before she slipped down the hallway with her mom.

"What's this all about?" Maura asked. "I don't have purchase orders."

"I just couldn't upset her. She seemed so desperate for me to save the shop. What exactly were you going to ask her to sign?"

"They're the documents to release her from her lease at the end of the year—you know that."

Hannah chewed on her lip.

Maura rubbed the top of Hannah's arm. "You can't keep all this from her forever. At some point she's going to need to sign it. I know you don't want to think about this, and God knows I don't either," she said, her voice breaking. "But if something happens to her, without her signature, it's an ongoing lease. If she doesn't sign it, and then she..." Her mother took in a deep breath and let it out slowly. "According to their death clause, the responsibility for payment that year will fall on the beneficiary of the shop that she's nominated on the rental agreement, which is your father. Your father and I will be responsible for a year of rent, and we can't afford it. She doesn't have anything left of her savings to cover it."

Hannah tipped her head up to the ceiling, closing her eyes, the fluorescent hospital lighting making white rectangles in the blackness of her thoughts. Her chest ached and her heart felt as though it would break in half. She turned back to her mother. "Can we just not tell her yet?"

Her mother's shoulders rose and she shook her head, unsure.

"I know it has to be done, but can we do it tomorrow?"

"Every day we wait is heightening our financial risk if something were to happen to her, and it's ridiculous to keep that old place open. At her age, she should be resting at home."

"Give her some time. Perhaps me being here will make her feel more like herself, and she'll eventually sign the papers."

"All right. I need to be at home with your dad anyway. He noticed Gran's gutters are full of leaves, and I've got to call someone before he tries to get on a ladder."

Hannah let out a huff of disbelieving laughter. "Yes, get home to Dad. I've got this."

"Okay, but Hannah. We have to get her to sign the papers."

Hannah kissed her mother goodbye and headed back into Gran's hospital room.

"There's my girl," Gran said, as she handed Ethan a cup of water with a straw. He set it on the counter at the other side of the room. "Always looking out for your gran," she said, and blew Hannah a kiss.

Hannah plopped down in the visitor's chair by Gran's bed, happy she had settled the issue for now. "Finally, we can chat," she said, taking

Gran's hand. "I've been reading your journal," she told her. "I'm dying to know about Charles."

"Ah," Gran said fondly, putting her hand on her heart. "Lovely, lovely Charles."

"In the journal, you mention him a lot."

"I was smitten with him. He planned to marry me after the war," she said, a distant look settling over her as she tapped into the memory.

"What happened?" she asked.

"It's all there, Hannah," Gran told her. "I've already lived it once. I'd rather focus on right now, but it's important that you read it. I'm hoping it will shed some light on life for you."

"Okay," Hannah said, not wanting to push her.

"Besides, I want to hear about how many arrangements you planned for on those purchase orders."

Hannah couldn't deceive Gran much longer, because eventually she would see through it. She had one day to figure out how to tell Gran the news. She needed to get over to the shop so she could see firsthand what she was dealing with. It would be a whole lot easier for Gran to take the news about closing The Memory Keeper if Hannah could be the one to tell her, and she needed to build her case right now.

It wasn't long before Gran had fallen asleep. Ethan took Hannah into town on his way to work, so she could check on The Memory Keeper. While she was near Main Street, she also planned to stop by the boutiques to buy a few winter outfits to wear, since all she had in her suitcase were beach clothes.

On their way, she checked her work email. IT was asking for one of her department's program passwords, which she didn't know. She'd written it in a notebook that she kept in her desk at work, so she'd asked Amanda to find it for them. She'd also had another suggested layout change from her design team for the major spread they were working on. The team was proposing to use only a few larger photos from old stock in the spot where she'd had a montage of images from her last cross-country photo shoot, which was odd because Hannah had gotten all of that nailed down before she'd left. She'd have to make a call to Amanda about that at some point.

"You're missin' it," Ethan said, drawing her eyes up from her phone.

"What?"

"The green space," he replied, waving one hand in the air. "I read an article once that said natural green like these here fields lowers your stress."

Hannah grinned. "I didn't know you could read," she said, picking up their usual banter of throwing out jabs until they both fell over in fits of laughter.

"Only when I have to," he shot back with a grin.

Hannah laughed and looked out the Bronco's window as the early afternoon sun sent its beams down through the clouds that were rolling in. It looked as though the heavens were combing the fields with their long golden fingers.

"Ain't it nice?" he asked. "Not much longer and we can start up the bonfires again. I think there were some kids messin' around in the old field last weekend already." He pointed toward the lane that led to the field where they'd all gathered in high school to park their trucks, dance on the tailgates to music, and socialize. "Damn hot shot kids, always jumpin' the gun. I don't know anyone in their right mind who would try to start bonfire season weeks early." He wrinkled his nose playfully at his joke.

In the early days, Ethan had dragged Hannah out to the fields every year in the freezing cold, trying to get the season going after the long winter. Sometimes it had just been the two of them out there, and she'd had to convince him to put out the fire and head home before they turned into ice cubes. Once the kids from the neighboring schools started to come, he'd gotten less excited about going, and Hannah wondered if he'd preferred the smaller crowd of locals.

Ethan turned onto the road that led into town.

When they'd finally reached Franklin, he pulled over at The Memory Keeper. "Well, here's your stop," he said, reaching over her and pulling the door handle to unlatch it for her—something he'd always done since they were young. "Call me if you need me, all right?"

"Okay," she said, getting out. Hannah leaned back into the Bronco and gave him a quick hug. "Thank you for the ride."

"No problem," he said, slipping a ball cap with the logo for his dad's shop onto his head, the brim tattered and torn. "See ya later."

Hannah shut the truck door. As Ethan drove away, she stood in front of Gran's flower shop and understood right away what her parents had been trying to explain to her. Walking up the overgrown sidewalk, the weeds tall enough to tickle her ankles, her gaze fell on the shriveled, brown remnants of the plants that flanked the door. She stepped closer, noticing the faded paint on the building, picking up the silver water bowl Gran always left out for pets, and shaking the rainwater and dead leaves out of it. She set it on its side against the building to dry.

The exterior wasn't too bad, apart from needing a fresh coat of paint and some landscaping, but the wild overgrowth next to the side of it that separated The Memory Keeper from a strip of vacant shops had taken over, completely obscuring the freestanding store from Main Street that ran perpendicular to it. It looked as though construction was going on in the strip of shops, the orange cones on the curb narrowing the street further and making it nearly impossible to access.

Hannah fiddled with her key ring, locating the key Gran had given her years ago. She slipped it into the old lock and twisted the knob, pushing open the large wooden and glass-paned door. The hinges creaked with age, as if they were protesting her intrusion.

Once she got inside, there was an eerie silence. Sadness falling upon her, she turned the "open" sign to "closed," realizing it had never been switched from the last time the shop had been open, and clicked on the lights. The old music Gran used to play on the antique record player at the back was absent, the bright streams of light now dulled with both the winter weather and cloudy windows that needed a good cleaning.

Hannah let her gaze wander over the wall of silver buckets. When Hannah was a girl, Gran used to keep bright bunches of flowers in the lower ones. Now, cobwebs stretched from one to the other. The old wooden counter in the center of the room—a large space that was both an arranging station and housed the register—was completely hidden with stacks of papers, the display case in the bottom holding a couple of drooping arrangements.

The grit on the floor crunched beneath her feet as she moved over to the open delivery boxes that lined the opposite wall and peered inside. They were filled with the latest delivery of stunning flowers—red and white roses, hydrangeas, gerberas, freesias, anemones, daffodils, and baby's breath—all wilting. She pulled them out and filled the containers with water to save them.

Every day that Hannah could remember, Gran walked to work from her bungalow at the edge of town, bundling up if it was cold and wearing a rain bonnet on rainy days, absolutely delighted to get to work. Hannah had loved the effortlessness of Gran's style, both at the shop and in her life. She played records and hummed along while she gathered bunches of flowers to make bouquets. The white interior had showed off the rainbow of flowers. But now it just looked tired, like Gran.

She went to the back door and looked through the glass. Her gaze swept across the yard for Speckles, but she didn't see the cat. She turned the knob and stepped onto a small, cement landing, where Gran used to keep large bins to save discarded stems and leaves of cut flowers for compost. They were gone, the manicured garden now covered in leaves. A slip of white plastic jutted out from under the fallen foliage, so Hannah went over to retrieve it, recognizing it as Speckles's food bowl.

Tears filled her eyes, her mind racing with the thought that the poor cat might have been forced to abandon Gran in search of food. She took the bowl back inside and checked the bar fridge at the back for milk, but it was empty. With a heavy heart, Hannah set the cat's bowl on the counter where Gran used to leave a platter of fresh muffins for her customers, and returned to the front.

She caught the view through the display window to the tiny yard, past the walk from the road now patchy with weeds. The old sign out front was faded, making The Memory Keeper look more like *Th emor eep r.*

Once, when Hannah was about ten years old, she'd asked Gran why she'd named the shop The Memory Keeper, and Gran had explained, "Every time I create a bouquet for someone, I'm creating a memory. Think about it," she said, taking Hannah's hands and filling them with a bundle of hydrangeas. "Someone might get this bouquet for her birthday, and it will sit on the kitchen table while her family gathers around a cake full of flickering candles, singing to the girl they love." She leaned in close enough for Hannah to see the twinkle in her eye, and whispered, "She'll remember it." Gran took the bunch from Hannah and twirled around, holding it into the air. "And we'll have been a tiny part of that." She placed the flowers into a vase of water and began hunting for other blooms to complement it. Gran was right about the flowers making memories for others, although they made a whole lot of memories for Hannah too.

No one would make any memories in a place like this. As she stood in the old space, she decided it was time to figure out what she was going to say to Gran.

Chapter Fourteen

The least Hannah could do was help Gran get her affairs in order. She pushed up her sleeves and went over to the mass of papers on the center counter. Each pile was labeled with sticky notes in her mother's handwriting. One heap was categorized "recycle"; another said, "file." Hannah zeroed in on the pile marked "bills" and picked up the stack, flipping through them, her heart sinking. Gran had racked up hundreds—maybe thousands—of dollars in unpaid bills. She set them back on the counter.

Hannah stared at the invoices, thinking. She was thirty-five years old. She'd saved money for a family that, given her recent situation with Miles, and her age, she may never have… She set her phone on the counter and opened the calculator app, adding up every invoice in the pile, and even as the number got bigger, she knew she could still cover it with her savings. She could wipe these bills completely clean for her parents and Gran. But if Gran kept the shop open, the bills would keep mounting.

The old bells on the door jingled, startling her. She looked up to find an elderly woman shuffling in. She had a purple cane with a swirling pattern that matched her skirt. The woman peered over at Hannah and puttered over to her.

"My gracious me!" she said when she reached Hannah. "You've done gone off and got fancy on us." Her voice had that smooth southern drawl to it that made even her poor grammar sound like music. "The door said closed," she said, throwing a thumb over her shoulder, "but you're usually open at this time a'day, so I just tried the knob."

"Have we met before?" Hannah asked, the woman looking familiar.

"My name's Darlene Buxton. I've been friends with your gran since we were girls back in Kentucky." Darlene gave Hannah a direct but polite appraisal. "You're all your gran talks about, you know…" Her eyes squinted shut with her smile.

"I remember you," Hannah said with a tickle of delight, recalling Darlene and her grandmother dancing together in the shop.

"She was so apprehensive when you left to go to college in New York," Darlene said, tipping her head up to view the empty silver buckets near the ceiling. "She worried about you like crazy, all alone in that big city. It was so hard for her to let you go. But she told me once, 'Hannah wants a different life, and I know firsthand how that feels.'"

"I had no idea," Hannah said, thinking back to Liam's comment about how Gran had saved all her trophies because she'd missed her. Gran had always been so supportive. She hadn't given Hannah a single clue that she'd felt anything other than complete joy about her move to New York.

"Well, dear, I'm absolutely delighted to see you're taking over the shop for her since she can't be here to run it. I'm sure she's over the moon about it."

"Oh, I'm…" Hannah let the words trail off, the ever-present guilt surfacing. "I'm happy to do it," she said instead. No sense in getting into the details right now.

Darlene beamed. "The entire time I've known your grandmother, she was a different person among her flowers. How wonderful it will be for her to know that her memory and the memory of this place will go on for generations. I suppose that makes you the new Memory Keeper," she said with an excited grin. "That was what she always wanted. I'm proud of you for coming home to do that for her."

Hannah stared at her, speechless. Gran had wanted Hannah to run the shop? She'd never said anything of the sort...

Hannah's phone lit up with another notification from work. She clicked off the screen, her mind still going a mile a minute.

Darlene took in a long breath through her nose as she surveyed the rundown space. "I'm here to grab a quick bouquet for my book club. Something spring-like to give the ladies a touch of brightness to look forward to in these last few cold days."

"Of course," Hannah said, rushing over to the inventory boxes full of flowers. "I just got here," she explained. "I haven't whipped the shop into shape yet." Hannah grabbed a handful of pink tulips and white lilies that were still in good shape and set them on the counter, having absolutely no idea why she was pretending to keep the shop open.

"Oh, darling, I can't afford that many," Darlene worried aloud.

"It's no problem," Hannah told her. "It'll be my treat for not having the shop ready when you came in. I'll just charge you for a small bouquet."

Hannah grabbed a large glass vase from a box next to the counter and began to arrange the flowers, the white and pink color of them resembling a box of candy.

She trimmed a tulip stem and slipped it into place in the vase.

"Here you are," Hannah said, sliding the bouquet toward Darlene.

Hannah didn't know what she'd do if Darlene came into the shop again and found it in the same state, or what the fate of The Memory Keeper would be by next week, but what she did know was that her remorse had subsided when she'd told Darlene she was taking over for Gran.

"It's so beautiful," Darlene said, admiring her work. "I don't know how you can just throw flowers together and make them look like that." She turned the bouquet around to view it more closely. "It's a gift. I've only ever seen it in Faye and my mother before now." She looked up at Hannah. "And you have it too."

Hannah smiled.

Darlene paid for the bouquet. "Thank you for this," she said, the glass vase in one hand and her cane in the other.

"No problem," Hannah said. "Here, let me get the door for you."

As Darlene left, it all hit her: Darlene *Buxton*. Buxton Floral Company from Gran's journal. Darlene had known Gran since childhood... Hannah couldn't help but notice the coincidence that it had been Darlene who'd passed along Gran's idea that Hannah be the new Memory Keeper, when Gran herself must have gotten her start working under Darlene's mother.

Before she could spend too much time considering it, Hannah refocused on something else: Liam was walking up to the door.

He seemed just as surprised to see Hannah as she was to see him.

"I was walking by," he said tentatively, surveying the interior behind her tactfully.

"This is my gran's shop," she explained proudly, letting him enter to get out of the cold, even though the airy room was still a bit drafty. "It's pretty... um. Rundown." She was talking politely but the elephant in the room was hanging over her every word.

He nodded thoughtfully, running his finger along a half-empty display. "I see."

She walked behind the counter and scooted the stack of papers over in a feeble attempt to make things look better, but she knew it was a lost cause. "The rent's killing her, and we're trying to get her to close it."

Liam's eyebrows rose in interest.

Who was she kidding, even entertaining the idea that she could save this mess? She'd have to get Gran to sign the paperwork to relieve her parents from the lease. Then Hannah would pay off the bills, and in time, close the shop. That was really the only option.

"You look distraught," Liam noted, apology in his eyes.

"I am," she said. "Life is hard sometimes, and I just have to get my mind around that."

"Yes. Life is hard," he agreed, a weighty stare in his eyes. He opened his mouth to say something, but Hannah's phone went off on the counter.

"Sorry," she said, "it could be about Gran." She leaned over to view the caller. "Weird. It's work. I wouldn't expect them to call me direct unless there was something really pressing. Mind if I get this?" she asked.

"Not at all," Liam replied.

"Be right back." Hannah stepped into the hallway at the back of the shop and took the call.

"Hey, it's Amanda," her coworker said when Hannah answered.

As assistant director, Amanda had taken the reins while Hannah was out. Amanda had been passed over for the art director job when Hannah was hired and had been crushed, but she'd handled it kindly and professionally, even buying Hannah a paperweight for her office as a congratulations gift. Hannah knew that the only reason Amanda didn't get the job was because she'd never managed a huge project with a director before, so Hannah made sure that Amanda was right there with her now. She'd gone over her plan with Hannah before she'd left, and the entire project was in her very capable hands. Hannah wasn't worried a bit... until this call. Amanda never called her out of hours or on her days off.

"I'm so sorry to bother you on vacation, but we're having a major problem."

Hannah cringed, realizing that Amanda still thought she was on a beach in Barbados with Miles right now. "What is it?" she asked.

"Right after you left, the computer system at work crashed, and we've lost all the photography for the summer farmhouse spread."

Hannah's breath caught. "What?" she asked, barely even able to get the word out.

Hannah had traveled the country with the photographer personally, for every shoot, once a month, over the last six months, giving delicate direction on the content she wanted photographed. She had images of a farm family in their denim overalls, sitting on their weathered front porch after a day's work, the green harvester in blurry view in the wheat fields behind them; there was the shot with the old farm hound sitting next to a scarecrow at sunset... All the gorgeous, award-winning shots *lost*?

"We've been scrambling to recover them," Amanda told her. "The IT department has been working overtime. They think it had something to do with the file being open at the time of the crash. The damage to the hard drive caused a corruption of the software, and it's making it impossible to retrieve the files. They're still working on it, but I worry that by the time they do, it'll be too late. We're not going to hit deadline, and without the photos, we've got nothing. I tried to use old stock, but nothing is fitting the bill. Do you have the photos saved on anything at your apartment?"

"I don't think so. I kept them all at work, thinking the computer there was more reliable than my own." Hannah leaned back against the wall, the phone still at her ear, the enormity of this setting in. She'd just gotten this promotion and, her fault or not, it wouldn't look good if the first big project she'd been given failed miserably. If it didn't go well, she could be in real professional trouble. Without those images, there was nothing to put in the main spread with the deadline looming. She had to figure out how to fix this. "Oh my God."

"I know," Amanda said.

Suddenly, Hannah perked up. "What about on the camera itself? It should be in my office."

"Nope. I already checked. You wiped it clean, remember?"

Hannah tried to push through the haze of anxiety that was drowning her brain to remember wiping those photos from the device. "I did?" she asked weakly.

"Once we uploaded, you cleared all the photos because the tech department is always on our case about keeping images on the devices. You said yourself how annoying it was to sign out a camera, only to have it already full of some other project's pictures."

The misery of her attention to detail settled upon her. Amanda was right; Hannah *had* wiped it the day of the upload. "And the photographer? Does he have them, by chance?"

"Nope. We checked with him too. What do we do, Hannah?"

She squeezed her eyes shut and scratched her forehead. "Let me think for a second."

She needed to save the day. She just had no idea how. She racked her brain for anything, but the truth was that this was entirely the job of the IT department, and if they couldn't retrieve those photos, she had no idea what the feature of the magazine would be. They'd have to start from scratch, and they didn't have time for that.

"I'll think of something," she said. "Hang in there and I'll call you back when I've figured it out." Hannah said her goodbyes and ended the call, feeling like her head might explode.

"You okay?" Liam asked when she'd returned to the counter.

"Just work stuff," she replied, not wanting to get into it with him.

"I think you need something sweet and warm to clear your head—how about a coffee? We could go down the street to the coffee shop and grab one."

"I don't think so..." she said, not wanting to entertain any invitation from him at all.

"Can we just talk?" he asked.

She stood her ground. If he had anything he wanted to talk about, he could tell her right there.

"Hannah, I need you to hear me out," he said. "Then I promise not to bother you anymore. Please. Get a cup of coffee with me."

She deliberated. There was a terrible draft in the shop, and the warm coffee would be helpful. And delicious. Plus, it could take her mind off work for a while...

Hannah grabbed her coat as Liam opened the door, and the two of them stepped out into the sunshine. She locked up behind them, and they walked down the front path together, headed for Main Street. Hannah had no idea what she was doing, going for coffee with him, her future more uncertain than it had ever been.

Chapter Fifteen

"When does your mother arrive with Noah?" Hannah asked, unsure of how to have a conversation with Liam, given their new reality. She wrapped her hands around her warm porcelain cup of bergamot, espresso, and coconut milk as they settled in at a bistro table upstairs by the fireplace, away from the crowds of the coffee shop.

"About three o'clock," he said, looking at her as if a thousand thoughts were crossing his mind at once. "My mom's got a benefit she'd forgotten about in a few days, and she has to run out and find a dress for it as soon as she gets home, so it'll be just Noah and me tonight."

"Oh," Hannah said. She wasn't quite sure what to say. She leaned over her latte and took a sip, delighting in the warm, smoky sweetness of it. "Want to tell me why you really brought me here?"

He stared at her as if deciding where to begin.

Gently, she set down her mug, trying to stay calm. "You basically brush me off this morning, drop the bomb on me that you're married, and leave, only to show up again at Gran's shop and ask me to coffee. What's going on?"

"I'm sorry I did that," he said, shaking his head, remorse clouding his every feature.

"You're sorry you said you were married, sorry you kissed me when you were married, or sorry you asked me to coffee?" She didn't let him answer before she continued, "There's a lot going on here, Liam, and I'm not going to sit around and wait for you to figure it all out. Tell me right now whatever it is you have to say."

"You're dealing with so much…" he said, not answering any of her questions. He gritted his teeth as if he were scolding himself, and then looked her in the eye. "I'm not used to this."

She took in a steadying breath and waited patiently, giving him her full attention. It was clear that whatever he was trying to tell her was difficult for him.

"My wife…" Liam went silent and took a drink of his coffee. He swallowed and clearly attempted to regroup, clearing his throat. "Her name is Alison. *Was* Alison. She passed away of cancer two years ago."

Suddenly, Hannah's heart went from feeling icy anger to complete compassion for Liam. Liam was a single parent, trying to manage everything on his own. What must that have been like for the last two years? "Oh my God, Liam. I'm so sorry." All those thoughts she'd seen on his face now made complete sense. She put her fingers to her lips, breathless, trying to imagine the sorrow he must have felt.

"I haven't ever put myself in a situation where I could meet… someone else. I haven't gone on dates; my friends would want to set me up—no one compared to Alison." His fingers tapped nervously on the table and then stilled. "I travel a lot. I walk by hundreds of people every day, and their faces have no meaning to me. And then you just walked right out of my past and into my world. With a flower in your hair." He smiled at the memory. "I couldn't take my eyes off you."

"Wow," she said in almost a whisper.

"I remember feeling guilty that you'd stolen my attention—like I was being unfaithful to Alison's memory—so I pushed on toward the baggage claim. But our bags got tangled. And then I felt a wave of fear that my life was moving forward without my wife, and I wasn't ready. I'd gotten comfortable in my gray, empty world. I forced myself to let you go. When Georgia saw you, I wondered if I was getting a nudge to step out of my normal. When I woke up in the hotel room, kissing you, I wrestled with what to do, because I felt something for you that I couldn't deny."

Hannah could hardly breathe. "My goodness."

"When you asked me outright if I was married—it was the first time in two years that I'd considered what my answer to that question was. And I froze. Well, actually, I ran." He offered a weak smile. "I'm so sorry. I just don't know how to navigate the way I feel about you yet."

Hannah reached across the table and took his hand. "It doesn't have to be either-or," she said. "Alison is from a totally different part of your life. You're allowed to keep going and explore new friendships and relationships without her. You have to. It's why you're still here."

"I just feel like, after what you've experienced with Miles, you deserve to have someone who can give you their all, and I want to offer you that, but I don't know if I can yet. It's all so new."

"Let's just be who we are at this moment. We're friends. There's no rush to be anything more than that." She'd never felt more certain about that fact than she did at this moment. Neither of them was in any position to develop into something more than what they were right now. But they might just be the greatest of friends.

The world on her shoulders, Hannah walked back to Gran's house with shopping bags dangling from her fingers. After coffee, Liam had offered to drive her, but Hannah had wanted time alone to think. She'd stopped into a few of the boutiques and bought some clothes to get her through the rest of the week, the whole time lost in thought about everything. When she arrived at Gran's, she wasn't closer to having answers to any of it. She let herself in and walked into the kitchen.

"Hey there," her mother said when Hannah plopped down on a bar stool at the island. "How was Gran when you left?" Her mom's back was turned to Hannah while she pushed a wooden spoon around a large bowl cradled in her arms. She set down the bowl next to a greased cookie sheet and faced her.

"Good, I guess. She was sleeping."

Hannah peered into the bowl, excited to see a batter full of chocolate chips. Hannah had missed her mother's baking. However, even the cookies couldn't make Hannah feel better about what she was about to say.

"I'll help you get Gran to sign the forms for the lawyer," Hannah said, the reality of it causing a weight to settle on her chest. Everything inside her screamed that this was wrong, but the rational side of her didn't see any other possibility.

"You saw the shop, I take it?" Maura began rolling balls of dough and placing them onto the cookie sheet.

"Yeah. It's in rough shape." She rubbed the pinch that had formed in her shoulder, trying not to think about the disappointment Gran would experience when Hannah told her of their decision.

"Yes," Maura agreed.

"Those cookies ready yet?" her father teased as he came into the room. He patted the tops of Hannah's arms, before going around the island and giving Maura a kiss on the cheek.

"Doesn't matter," Maura responded playfully. "You aren't getting any. You're on a special diet—doctor's orders."

"I'll bribe you for them," Chuck said, nibbling Maura's neck, making her squeal.

"Must you two?" Hannah said with a laugh. But she was only giving them a hard time. They'd been together for forty-two years, and she'd never seen them argue. "I'm beat," she told them. "I think I'm going to go into Gran's room and take a nap or something."

"That sounds good, darling," Maura said. "I'll come get you when the cookies are ready."

Hannah headed down to Gran's room. When she got inside she crawled onto Gran's bed, promising herself it would be okay, that Gran would definitely be back home soon and she'd settle into life without The Memory Keeper. But her promise felt empty. Mentally exhausted and needing the peace that only Gran could bring, she moved the satin ribbon bookmark sewn into the binding of the journal and began to read.

April 7, 1943

My hands are so rough from the long hours at the factory. I help insert metal tubing into the guns, and even though I come straight home and wash with Palmolive soap, and then add a dab of Mama's lotion, they're still like sandpaper. I want to look nice when Charles returns home, but I'm going to be old and ragged. I've been tying my hair up at work, and it's dry and always lumped in the shape of the bandana I wear. I haven't done my pin curls in so long that I fear I've forgotten how. Ever since the war, I've had to do this awful job. It's not a place for someone like me. I'm not beneath it, but I want to create, take photographs, and drink a Green River at the soda fountain with a stack of books beside me. Will I ever get out?

With even more questions as to how her dainty, artistic, wild soul of a grandmother got out of working in a factory, Hannah read on.

May 12, 1943

Mama let me use some of the money we'd saved from working to visit my beautician, and I feel like a princess with my hair styled. The back is down and rolled beautifully and the sides are pinned up. Every strand is perfectly placed. I know I only have the one day off and I'll have to tie it back tomorrow at work, but today I put on a dress and took a walk through Louisville. I probably shouldn't have, but I went to Beaty's Drugstore and bought that Green River drink at the soda fountain. It was so fizzy that I got the hiccups. I met a very nice man there, too. He was reading a book on history when he caught me trying to see the cover. He introduced himself as Warren Townshend...

Hannah perked up. There he was—Pop-pop. Her heart filled with joy at the opportunity to read this moment as it had happened. She remembered her mother's photos of boxing what seemed like hundreds of history books when Pop-pop had passed. He'd loved to read Hannah bedtime stories about George Washington and Davy Crockett when she was young. Hannah ran her hand over Gran's words and kept reading, now dying to hear the whole story of how Gran and Pop-pop met.

He said he's twenty-one. He attends the University of Louisville. I told him about Charles and asked Warren why he wasn't in the war right now. He explained that he'd registered on his birthday, but he hadn't gotten drafted so far. Despite the possibility of getting called to fight in the war, he attended the university to study business. He asked if I'd be coming to the soda fountain again, and I told him I might.

Hannah placed the journal on her chest and closed her eyes, conjuring up a memory of her grandfather. When she was about six, Pop-pop had twirled her around and said, "You are an angel!" He took her hands, his giant fingers swallowing hers. "You know, I've only seen one other angel before you."

She'd been astounded that he'd actually seen a real angel. "You've seen one?" she asked innocently.

"Yes." Pop-pop gave her another spin. "I found her at a soda fountain."

"There are fountains made of soda?" Hannah had asked, making him laugh. "Did you ever see the angel after that?"

Pop-pop sent a fond glance over to Gran. "I see her every day."

He and Gran had found something amazing together, and Hannah could only wish she'd be that lucky one day.

Hannah was mindlessly clicking through TV channels in the living room when she got an alert that she had a video call from Liam. A video call? That was odd. She opened it and Liam's face slid onto her screen.

"Hi," he said. "Sorry to bother you, but it's just us boys here this afternoon and Noah asked if he could call."

"Noah wants to talk to me?" she asked.

Noah's face appeared on the screen, pushing Liam out of view. "Yeah," he said. "Can you tell me about the tire swing?"

"Oh, sure," she said, turning off the TV and folding her legs underneath her, getting comfortable. "It's on Mr. Abernathy's farm," she said. "Your daddy knows him—Emmitt Abernathy."

"Daddy?" Noah said. "Hannah wants to know if you know Nathy."

The picture wriggled and suddenly Liam's face was on the screen.

"Hi," he said with a grin.

"Hey," she returned. "How about instead of telling Noah about the swing, we show him? I'll call Emmitt and if he says it's okay, we could visit him tomorrow."

"That would be fun," Liam said. "We could go around ten o'clock."

"That works," she replied.

Noah cheered happily in the background.

"Excellent. Well, Noah, we should let this lady get on with her day."

"Okay. Bye, Noah!" she called.

A tiny voice from beside Liam filtered in. "Bye, Hannah."

"I'll see you tomorrow, okay?" she said.

"Okay!" Noah replied with a giggle.

Hannah ended the call and considered how lucky Liam was to have little Noah. He was such a light. Perhaps a day out with the two of them would lift her spirits.

Chapter Sixteen

After she'd gotten off the call with Liam and Noah, Hannah emailed Amanda to tell her not to worry about the missing photos for the rest of the day, that she'd see if she could find a backup file somewhere. It was more a way to give Amanda and the team a reprieve, and to save them from alerting the executives that Hannah wasn't there at the most crucial time in production. But Hannah knew she didn't have the files, and trying to convey the mood, message, and concept of the feature into imagery using old, unused stock photography would be nearly impossible.

She'd been so strung out over everything that she'd fallen asleep. When she awoke, her mother was in the kitchen, having an evening nibble of one of her chocolate chip cookies. Hannah came in and snagged one.

"You doing okay?" her mother asked, as she arranged a few of the cookies on a platter and set it in the center of the island.

"Not really," Hannah replied, picking at her cookie. She started filling her mother in about work and what Liam had admitted to her over coffee.

"Life can get absolutely manic sometimes," her mother said, shaking her head. "Hopefully, one day you'll be able to look back on this period in your life and understand what it was all for."

"Maybe..." she said, when her phone went off in her pocket. She hardly dared check it for fear it was Amanda, but regardless, she probably should answer. Hannah put down the cookie and took out her phone. "Hang on a sec," she said, confused. "It's Georgia, the girl I rode home with." She answered the call to Georgia's sobs.

"I need your help. Can you come get me?" she cried. "I didn't want to call, but I don't have anywhere to go," Georgia said, her breath heaving.

"Oh my gosh. Yes. Where are you?"

"I'm at the corner of Fourth and Church." She sniffled.

"I'm not far. Stay right there. I'll come pick you up."

"What's wrong?" her mother asked when Hannah hung up the phone.

"Georgia is all upset. She asked if I'd come get her in town." She stood up and went over to the coat closet, pulling out her coat and threading her arm into the sleeve. "May I have the keys to Dad's truck?" she asked.

"Of course," her mother said, digging the keys out of her purse and handing them to Hannah.

"Thanks. I'll be right back."

Hannah jumped in her dad's truck, which stayed at Gran's for when they visited from Florida and needed to run errands for her, and drove to get Georgia, the engine protesting from not being warmed up properly in the winter weather.

When she got there, Georgia and Jerry were on the corner in the freezing cold. Georgia climbed into the passenger seat, lumping her bags in with her and setting Jerry in her lap. "I'm so sorry to bother you," she said with red eyes as she fumbled to latch her seatbelt, her hands shaking, "but I've tried everything, and I didn't know where else to go. I've been sleeping in the woods since Liam dropped me off, and it's too cold to keep doing that."

"Oh my gosh, what happened?" Hannah asked.

"I had a lead for finding my parents from the agency where I was adopted. They gave me two photos: one of my parents and the other a baby photo that I'm assuming is a sibling. The back says, 'Franklin, Tennessee.'" She turned the photo over to reveal the name of their location in scratchy pencil. "So I thought this was the town where they lived. My father dropped the photos off to them one day about thirty years ago, and told them to give them to me if I ever came looking, despite the contact veto he'd signed. He confided in the agency that he was having second thoughts about signing."

"What's a contact veto?"

"It's a document that prohibits the release of information about my parents unless I agree not to contact them. I came to Franklin to do some research and see if I could find out who they are. I was just going to introduce myself, and if they didn't want anything to do with me, I'd leave. I came thinking I'd find them right away in such a small town. I hired an investigator here who was going to help me, but when I met with him, he said he needed more than unnamed photos with no other identification. He's going to guess the age of the child and see if he can find birth records, but it's a long shot. I've shown them to everyone, and I have no leads. I really thought I'd find them, but I guess I was wrong."

"Why didn't you call me sooner?" Hannah asked.

"I didn't want to bother you with everything else you've got going on, but when the investigator told me he had no leads, I just crumbled. I spent my last bit of savings on the trip here, and I have no job, no money—nothing. I wanted to find my family, and now I just feel lost."

"Stay with me at my gran's. There's plenty of room," Hannah offered, rounding the corner, and making her way toward Gran's house.

"You sure it's okay?" Georgia asked.

"Of course it's okay," Hannah replied. She actually liked the idea of having Georgia around. Perhaps she could help her new friend in some way.

"I think he likes that, Dad," Hannah said, while Chuck rolled the old tennis ball he'd found in the shed across the floor.

He let out a loud guffaw when Jerry sprinted after it, his little paws tip-tapping while he growled and tried to bite it, his tail wagging a mile a minute.

"Watch this," her father said with another chuckle. He walked over, took the ball off the floor, and sat down with it.

Jerry ran over and planted himself in front of him, staring up at the ball, his tail wagging back and forth over the carpet. Chuck rolled the ball gently across the floor and Jerry tore off after it, barking and sending Chuck into fits of laughter.

"I needed this," her dad said.

"We'll have to get him some toys," Maura suggested with her hands on her hips, the dish towel she'd been using to clean up dangling from her fist. "He's too cute." She shook her head fondly at the dog. "Georgia, come on to the table. You need some good ol' southern cookin' after the night you've had."

"Mama never misses an opportunity to cook," Hannah told her friend.

When she'd explained Georgia's situation to her parents, Hannah's mother had immediately taken Georgia and Jerry under her wing, changing the sheets in Hannah's old room, and making a big dinner for everyone. She'd even scraped together some leftovers for Jerry, despite Georgia's promise she had enough food for him. Jerry had been more than excited about his meal, nearly throwing himself into the food bowl.

"I hate staying here and not doing something to pay y'all back," Georgia said, taking a seat at the table. "I'll work for free if you have anything you'd like me to do."

"You are as sweet as you can be," Maura said, setting a plate of chicken casserole in front of Georgia. "Tea or lemonade?"

"Tea, please." Georgia turned to Hannah who had taken a seat beside her. "I'm not kidding. It would make me feel better to help in some way."

"Y'all could clean up Gran's shop, Hannah," Maura said. She handed Georgia a tall glass of iced tea with a lemon wedge on top. "We'll have to leave it clean and painted when we move out. I know it's not very glamorous, but it *would* be a great help to us. We could probably even pay you, Georgia. We've still got the extra help factored into the budget."

Hannah knew that they really had no budget; it was her mother trying to help Georgia. Something she loved to do—helping others. It was what she did best.

Georgia said, "I'd be happy to help. Anything. Just tell me."

"I'll put you on the books then." Maura offered her a big smile.

Georgia folded her hands, looking delighted. "It'll feel so good to be needed. Thank you."

"Why don't y'all go over there tomorrow after you see Gran?" Maura proposed.

"Sounds good to me," Hannah replied. "Though does that mean *I* have to take the papers to her?"

"We don't have to bombard her with it first thing," her mother replied. "We can hold off for the time being…"

Hannah was happy to be able to help Georgia, even if it was only short term. And a tiny part of her couldn't wait to get back to The Memory Keeper. Perhaps cleaning it up would keep her mind off her uncertain future for a while.

Chapter Seventeen

The whole house was still sleeping when Hannah awoke in the morning. She'd taken Gran's journal with her to make a cup of coffee, quietly turning on the morning news on the TV in the kitchen. She watched long enough to catch the weather. A warm front was moving in.

Now she sat at the table in the silence of daybreak, peering out the window at Gran's rocking chairs on the porch. Gran used to sit in one of those rockers every summer. It would be so nice to have coffee with her grandmother out there when the weather got warmer. Would she ever be able to do that again?

Hannah tried not to contemplate the question. Instead, she decided to read the next entry in Gran's journal.

June 5, 1943

Charles is missing. No one has heard from him since his last letter in March. I'm worried sick. There have been rumors of a battle that took place around where he'd told us he was stationed, but no one can find him or his friend Alvin. I never knew he had a friend named Alvin—his mother told me that Alvin had been his bunkmate. I go to work every day and I am thankful now for the long hours James Williams gives us, because then I don't have to be alone in my

*room to ponder all the possibilities of what might have happened
to Charles. The not knowing is causing me to guess at what might
have transpired over there, and my mind is running wild, keeping
me up at night. I pray for his safe return.*

Hannah considered the reality of how it had probably come to be
that Gran had ended up with Pop-pop, and her heart sank for Charles.
She knew the outcome before she'd even read it.

Jerry trotted in and jumped up, putting his paws on her leg. Hannah
closed the journal and stroked his head.

"Morning," Georgia said, padding into the room with a bag of dog
food in her hand. She'd donned flannel pajamas and her hair was in
a messy ponytail, not much different from her regular style. She set
the food bag by the wall and opened the back door in the kitchen to
let Jerry out.

"We don't have a fence for him," Hannah warned.

"It's okay. He won't go far. He does his business before breakfast
every morning… Is that coffee?"

"Yeah. Cups are in the top cabinet to the left of the coffee maker."

"I *love* you," Georgia said, heading over to make herself a cup. Once
she'd made her coffee, she joined Hannah at the table and peered out
the window at Gran's rocking chairs. "Those are nice," she said.

"Maybe we'll be able to sit out there soon. The weather's supposed to
be warming up… Unless you find your parents before then." Hannah
put down her mug. "Would you show me their photo?"

"I'll go get it." Georgia let Jerry in and then went back to her room.

Jerry sniffed around by the dog-food bag, seemingly out of sorts
because his breakfast wasn't ready. He peered up at Hannah.

"I've got nothin'," she said to him, putting her hands in the air.

Georgia returned with the photos, setting them in front of Hannah.

Hannah peered down at the one of Georgia's parents. "They look like a nice family," she said, as Georgia poured some dog food into a bowl for Jerry. "And the baby is adorable." Hannah ran her finger over the blue blanket with miniature anchors on it in the baby's arms. "Who were your adoptive parents?" she asked.

"A woman named Betty and her husband Paul. They were great people, but I never really felt like I fit in their family. They were incredibly... traditional," she said, sitting down with her coffee. She dragged the photo of her birth family over to her with a finger and gazed at it. "I was their 'wild child,' as they called me. For years I thought I *was*, but the older I got, the more I realized that I wasn't rebellious, I just saw the world differently. While they wanted me to learn chess, I wondered what it would look like to paint my room in vibrant patterns. They signed me up for the science club in school, and I wanted to take dance. Stuff like that."

"That had to be hard," Hannah said.

Georgia kept her gaze on the photo. "I wondered over the years if my birth parents were creative like I am."

"Hopefully, you'll find out one day." Hannah sipped her coffee, feeling blessed to have had her family to support her. "What made you start looking for them now?"

Georgia held her mug in both hands and peered down into the brown liquid. "You got time for a long story?"

"Of course," Hannah replied.

"All right, then. I first started thinking about them at eighteen, when I got pregnant," she said.

Hannah stopped mid-sip, her mug dangling from her fingers in front of her. She realized the coffee was about to spill, so she righted it.

"Paul and Betty were no-nonsense about it. They told me that if I was grown up enough to make that happen, I had to get a job and figure out how to be an adult. I had no idea what to do, but I knew what I *didn't* want to do, and that was to be sloggin' it somewhere in a nine-to-five job. I started takin' photos and hangin' 'em up in the grocery store. Every now and again, I'd sell one. The biggest one I ever sold went to a guy named Brent Silva. He was passin' through and, after a night out at the bar, he offered to give me a ride to Chicago. We dated for a while.

"Before I knew it, I had a tiny apartment on the outskirts of the city, and I was waitressin' at the local bar and grill. I'd get so tired by the end of my shift that I could hardly see straight, and I questioned whether I'd have enough energy to come home and take care of a baby. Brent and I split up, and I wondered if it would be better for the child if I gave it up for adoption like my parents had."

"Did you?" Hannah asked.

Georgia shook her head. "Naw. I lost it. It was God's way of saying, 'Not yet.' But by then I liked the freedom of being on my own, away from my parents. I began to see that all the things I'd done 'incorrectly' according to them were actually just creative—different. I'd spent my whole life trying to be the wrong thing and feeling like a failure, when I wasn't. I just couldn't see that until I got out on my own. I got rid of my apartment, bought a tent to live in so I could travel easily, and started taking photos full time for about a year all over the country.

"I used what I earned, went back to Chicago, and took some classes at the local community college at night whenever I could afford them, and I ended up transferring to a four-year school on an art scholarship—I only took a couple of classes at a time, just what I could afford, since books and stuff were so expensive. After about six years, I had an art degree, and I took a position as a creative associate at a boutique media company in the city. I barely made anything, but I got another apartment. I had to waitress on weekends and twice a week in the evenings to make rent in downtown Chicago, but I felt like I was going somewhere."

"That's wonderful," Hannah said.

"And then it all came crashing down when I met Jackson Reuttiger."

"Who's that?" Hannah asked.

"My ex." She took a long drink from her mug and swallowed. "Jackson was different from anyone I'd ever dated. I met him at the bar and grill where I used to work those extra hours. He had some big job in the city—I never really figured it out, but whatever it was, he wore expensive button-down shirts and Italian leather wingtips. We dated up until a few weeks before this trip. I was on cloud nine most of the time during our relationship. I remember thinking how far I'd come when the two of us walked into the bar where I had worked and had a beer together. I had people waiting on *me* for a change."

Hannah smiled.

"But one night when we'd gone to get a drink, I got that vaguely familiar queasiness in my belly, and I told him I just wanted water, that I didn't feel well. I saw the fear in his eyes, as if his future with me flashed before him and terrified him to the very core. And I knew that he was not the person I wanted to be with me and my child." Georgia's eyes got misty and she cleared her throat. "He didn't have to worry though, because I lost that baby too."

"Oh, I'm so sorry." Hannah covered her mouth, and then it hit her. "Did you lose the baby recently?"

"Yeah. About four months ago." Georgia's voice broke.

Hannah reached over and gave her a hug. The tightness of Georgia's squeeze surprised her, and Hannah knew that Georgia just needed someone to listen to her.

"So that prompted you to find your parents?"

"I just felt like no one understood me—not my adoptive parents, not Jackson... I want to find my people, you know? No hard feelings, no strings attached. Just people like me." She gathered up the two photos and held them in her hand. "I hope I can find them."

"Me too," Hannah told her.

Her heart ached for Georgia to find the people who would take her for who she really was and lift up her talents. There was no telling what she could do if she had that support in her life.

While they were finishing their coffee, the investigator called Georgia and asked her to meet him to hear some more ideas he'd had about finding her parents, so Hannah had dropped her off in town, then headed to see Gran at the hospital for a quick few minutes before meeting Liam and Noah.

"I read about Charles going missing," Hannah told Gran.

A nostalgic look came over Gran's face, and she lifted her bruised arms to fold her hands together, the IVs pulling tighter with every movement. "There are two sides to every coin," she said with intensity in her eyes, as she looked at Hannah.

"What do you mean?"

"I'll come back to Charles. Let's talk about your own life for a minute."

Hannah scooted her chair closer when Gran reached for her hand.

"I'll tell you what I know from years of experience: There are people in life who allow you to do your own thing, roaming free like a caterpillar just walking along its path. There's nothing wrong with that—there's something to be said about the love and trust that creates that kind of freedom. But there are others who can affect you in such a way that before you've even realized it, you've become a butterfly, soaring on brightly colored wings you never knew you had. When you meet *that* person, you might look back on the version of you who was with Miles and not even recognize her."

Hannah nodded, Gran's wise words were always so inspirational. "So are you saying that Charles was your Miles?"

"Mm," she said, her thin lips pressed into a weak smile. "Charles was nothing like Miles. I adored him. He was a charming man. I still love him now. Our story was tragic, as it had to be. God puts people in our lives in mysterious ways…" Her eyes glistened with tears, and she blinked them away.

Hannah nodded, considering this.

"If Charles had lived through the war, who might I have become?" Gran asked. "Or more importantly, who might I *not* have become?"

"I wouldn't be here," Hannah said. "Because you and Pop-pop would never have had Dad."

"That's right." She squeezed Hannah's hand. "I might have never had my flower shop. It has defined me for so many years. I just know that it could be amazing again," she said, switching gears—Gran's mind was always on that shop. "How's business been the last few days?"

Hannah let go of Gran's hand and leaned toward her. "Gran, you must know how dire things are with The Memory Keeper. You *have* to be aware, right?"

Gran pursed her lips. "I won't give up on it," she whispered stubbornly.

"Pop-pop would be okay if you let it go. I'm nearly sure of that. He'd want you to rest, Gran. Your heart can't take the day-to-day stress of the job anymore."

Gran closed her eyes, clearly exhausted, and murmured, "Without The Memory Keeper, I have no heart at all. I built it from nothing. But it built me as well." She waggled a shaky finger at Hannah. "And I know your parents are trying to close it down again. I told them a few years ago that I wouldn't do it, and I won't do it now."

"But it's putting Mama and Daddy in financial trouble, Gran. I know you wouldn't want that for them."

Her eyes misted over. "I suppose I was hoping someone would save it, the way it saved me."

A tiny plume of guilt swelled in Hannah's stomach because, after what Darlene had told her, she knew Gran meant Hannah was the *someone.*

Gran swallowed hard and looked Hannah in the eye. "I was a naive child when I started that shop. But making bouquets for people, I learned about the world. I met people who were grieving, I went through more wars, I participated in celebrations, and I saw happy parents with their newborn children... Everyone I met through The Memory Keeper was a chance to learn about people and myself. By learning about the world and who was really in it, I was a better wife, a better mother, and a better grandmother."

Hannah compared this to her own working life. She thought about Amanda, the person with whom she worked so closely. She didn't know what Amanda liked to do for her birthday or who was in her family. She had no idea where Amanda had grown up. She didn't know that kind of information about anyone in New York at all. And yet she'd called them all friends. This whole time, she'd thought that she'd become a more well-rounded person if she got out of this small town, but perhaps she'd have learned more staying right here.

Chapter Eighteen

"Hannah!" Noah called, breaking from his dad's side, and running toward her down the dirt path to Emmitt Abernathy's cottage, where Hannah had asked Liam to meet her. Noah wrapped his little arms around her and squeezed her waist.

"Hi," she said with a chuckle, his embrace surprising her. "Are you ready to swing really high?" she asked him, waving to Liam who was partway down the dirt road, catching up.

"Yes!" Noah took her hand and looked up at her from under the stocking cap that had slid down his forehead. He pushed it into place with a mittened hand.

"Well," she said as Liam joined them, "I called Mr. Abernathy and let him know we might be stopping by. He said we were welcome to swing, and we could even pop in to see him for some hot cocoa if we get cold."

Noah's eyes grew round. "I'd love to have some hot cocoa."

She leaned down and whispered, "He said he keeps a secret stash of peppermint balls in his cabinet, and sometimes he'll slip one or two into the hot cocoa."

"Can we get some now?" Noah asked.

Hannah laughed. "Let's swing first." She led him toward the old tire swing.

"Hey," Liam said, stepping up beside her.

"Hi," she returned, as they walked over the hill that ran next to Emmitt's cottage.

Emmitt had a modest A-line home on his farm with a small front porch and two rocking chairs out front. A yellow glow came from the windows, giving the home a kind of warmth she'd only ever seen in her childhood. They passed two oak trees that had a hammock strung between them. It was full of fallen leaves, the canvas sagging with their weight.

In the summertime, Emmitt had always allowed the kids in town to walk along the side of his house and use the tire swing that hung from a huge maple tree, offering a gorgeous view of the river along the back of the property. He had a grandson their age named Tommy, but even if Tommy wasn't there, Emmitt always welcomed them on his farm. They'd go all the time, and in the evenings, they'd see Emmitt and his wife Sue waving from their porch. They didn't care at all that there were always kids on their land. Instead, it was like a big family.

"I haven't ever been here," Liam said, looking around. "Tommy and I played baseball together when we were young."

"I'd forgotten you both played baseball," Hannah told him. "Emmitt lives here alone now—Sue passed away a few years ago and Tommy's in the military, stationed in Arizona."

"Wow," Liam said. "How life has changed for us all, right?"

Hannah nodded, understanding the truth of his question.

The cold grass crunched under their feet as they made their way down the other side of the hill to the swing in the middle of the yard.

"Emmitt was delighted I'd called," she told Liam as they continued on through the vast property. "I had to get his number from Gran right before I left her today. It's been so long since I've spoken to him." She swung Noah's arm back and forth playfully as they talked.

"Is that the swing?" Noah asked, pointing to the old tire suspended by a thick rope from a towering maple tree. It twisted around in the wind.

"Yep!" Hannah said, remembering all the times Gran and Pop-pop had brought her here to swing when she was about Noah's age. She'd stayed outside for hours on end, swinging, and catching lightning bugs at the riverbank while her grandparents had chatted with Emmitt and Sue.

When they reached the swing, Hannah held it still so Noah could thread his legs through. "I like to hold on to the rope," she said, "but some of my friends used to hug the tire—whichever feels more comfortable to you."

"I want to hug the tire," Noah said with an enormous grin on his face. "Don't push me too high at first."

Hannah grabbed the tire and pulled it toward her, Noah's sneakers dangling above the cold ground. "This good?" she asked Noah. "Or higher?"

"A little higher," he replied.

She pulled the tire to her chest and then let it go, Noah sailing into the air as smooth as if he were gliding on a sheet of glass. The arc of the swing paralleled the riverbank, Noah's head tipping back, his whole body jiggling with his laughter.

"Do it again!" he said, kicking his legs. "But this time, higher!"

Hannah got hold of the tire and pulled it almost to eye level, letting it go. Noah squealed with delight as he flew through the air over the lush grass of the yard.

"That tickled my tummy!" he called down to her. "Go higher!"

"I think if you want to go any higher, your dad's gonna have to do it."

The tire swing twirled as it sailed past them. "Will you please push me, Dad," Noah asked, but she could hear in the little boy's voice how differently he approached his father compared to herself. He was more reserved, unsure. And so was Liam.

Hannah stepped aside to allow Liam to move into position. He reached out and caught the tire, pulling it up above his head and then letting go. Noah and the tire catapulted downward and then back up toward the trees, the little boy alternating between screams of excitement and fits of laughter.

"Wow! Who knew your dad could push tire swings like that!" Hannah said, grinning at Liam.

Liam's shoulders relaxed and he caught the swing again, sending Noah through the air once more and making his son hoot with the thrill of it.

"Don't stop!" Noah cried. "Keep going, Daddy!"

Noah's encouragement seemed to affect Liam, and he broke out into an enormous, doting smile at his son, pushing him again and watching him fly. Hannah felt a buzz of pleasure, seeing the exchange. It was the first time she'd ever witnessed real closeness between them, and she couldn't get enough of it.

"Hello-o!" a voice called from the cottage. Emmitt was in his denim overalls, waving a weathered hand at them from his back porch.

"Hi, Emmitt!" Hannah called over to him.

"Are y'all blocks of ice yet?" he asked. "It's still chilly in the shade, ain't it?"

"It's a tad chilly, but we're having a blast," Hannah replied.

"Glad to hear it! I've got cocoa ready if y'all want to warm up."

"Oh!" Noah said, dragging his feet on the ground to slow himself down. "Can we have the peppermint balls?" he asked Hannah.

"We can go see! Want to take a break and get some cocoa?"

Liam leaned over and held the tire swing steady so Noah could get off. Noah reached out for Liam's hand. Hannah could tell by the surprise in Liam's face that Noah reaching for him wasn't something he was used to. Liam regarded his son curiously as the two of them walked hand in hand up the hill.

"Daddy, you didn't get to swing," Noah said, looking up at his father.

"That's okay," Liam told him.

"Maybe after we have our cocoa," Noah offered, breaking free from Liam's hand, and running up the steps to meet Emmitt.

"Good Lawd in heaven," Emmitt said when Hannah and Liam ascended the steps. "You're all grown up. How in the world did that happen?" he teased Hannah. "Last time I saw you, you were a lanky teenager headed out into the wild blue yonder."

Hannah smiled and gave him a hug. "It's been too long," she said.

"Who's this you brought with ya?" Emmitt asked.

Hannah introduced Liam and Noah.

Emmitt bent down to be at eye level with Noah, stroking his gray beard. "I hear somebody wants some hot cocoa. But ya gotta pass the test. You know what that test is?"

Noah shook his head, his eyes wide.

"You gotta take off your gloves there 'n' show me your hands."

Noah did as he was told, holding up his little hands, his fingers spread wide.

"Yep. Definitely hot cocoa time. Your hands look colder than a frosted frog."

"A frosted frog?" Noah asked, scrunching his nose with a giggle.

"Yep. Never seen one myself—it could be that the ones around here are so smart, they don't get frosted. What do you think?" Emmitt led Noah across the uneven hardwood floor into the kitchen, and sat him down at an old Formica table. He pointed to a bowl in the center that was full of his famous peppermint ball candies. "Would you like one of those?" he asked, pointing to them.

"May I?" Noah asked.

"Of course." Emmitt pushed the bowl toward Noah.

The little boy got up on his knees and popped one in his mouth.

"Have as many as you want," he said.

Just then, the kettle on the stove whistled. Emmitt pulled four mugs from the old wooden cabinets and filled them with the hot water, spooning in a chocolate powder mixture from a mason jar.

"It's so nice to have you all visit," Emmitt said. "It's been a while since I've had youngsters come over." He dropped a couple of marshmallows on the top of each mug and handed them out, before taking a seat. "How's your daddy doin'?" he asked Hannah, before blowing on the steam rising from his mug.

"He's doing well," she said. "Just taking it easy, you know?"

Emmitt gave her a knowing grin.

Hannah shrugged off her winter coat and took a sip of her hot cocoa, the warm, sweet liquid soaking down to her bones.

"And how about you, sir?" Emmitt said to Noah, who'd handed Hannah his coat and hat. "How was the ol' tire swing?"

"It was fun!" Noah said, pushing his marshmallows around with his straw. "My favorite was when Daddy pushed me."

"Daddies are good at that kind of stuff. They always get to do the fun things."

"Like what?" Noah asked.

Emmitt scratched his wiry beard. "Well, when my boy was young, I took him fishin' or we built things together. Sometimes we played sports, even though he got way better than I ever was at hittin' a baseball."

Noah looked over at Liam, clearly attempting to process this information. "Daddy, can we play baseball sometime?"

Liam seemed surprised by his son's question and interested at the same time. "Of course we can," he said, but his answer seemed slightly hesitant. What was holding him back?

"Could Hannah come too?" Noah asked, that uncertain look he got whenever he spoke to Liam coming through.

"If she wants to," Liam replied.

Hannah leaned on her elbow, her eyes on the adorable boy. "I'd love to play baseball with you two," she said.

Emmitt sat back and folded his arms, content. "You know," he said, "in all the years I've been around, I couldn't train somebody anymore at my old job if my life depended on it—I've forgotten it all—but I can list all the great hits my son did during his little league baseball games, all the way through to his senior year on the high school team. I remember each one of 'em like they were yesterday."

Emmitt had never missed a moment with friends and family, and Hannah could only hope that one day, she could have those kinds of memories to keep her warm on the cold days.

"Any luck?" Hannah asked Georgia when she picked her up from the investigator's office later that day.

"Maybe. It's a long shot, but he suggested I visit the local public records office to have a chat with the people in there. Think I could stop by there first for a bit, and then we can go over to your gran's shop?"

"Of course." She made the turn headed for the office. "I'll just wait at the house until we go to the shop. Anything you need me to do with Jerry?"

"You could let him out. That would be awesome. Then just put him in his crate if you need to have him out of your hair."

"Sounds good. Text me when you need me to come get you."

Hannah drove Georgia to the office and let her out.

"Fingers crossed," Georgia said as she got out of the car.

"I'll have everything crossed for you," Hannah told her.

"You're an angel. Thank you for doing this," Georgia said.

"No problem at all."

When Hannah got home, she found her mother and father on Gran's sofa in the living room with Jerry in her mom's lap.

"Where's Georgia?" Maura asked, stroking the dog.

"I dropped her off at the records office. She's looking for a lead to find her birth parents."

"Oh, I hope she finds something. She's such a sweet girl." Her mother smiled. "How was Gran this morning?"

"Okay," Hannah said. She sat between her parents, disturbing Jerry who crawled off her mother's lap and found Hannah's. Hannah scratched his head.

Hannah's phone interrupted the conversation, pinging with an email. She handed Jerry to her father and pulled it out of her pocket to check the message. "It's Amanda at work. I should probably get this," she told her parents, peering down at the sender. "She's been looking for some images she needs. Maybe she found them."

"All right, honey," her mother said.

Hannah went to Gran's room to go through the entire email. It read,

I know you said not to worry, but IT's wondering if you and the photographer emailed the images at all. They might be able to see if they can sift through download files to find them. But it would be a big project, so they want to get confirmation that you may have emailed the images first. A.

Hannah racked her brain to remember if they'd shared any emails at all, but sadly, she didn't think they had. She responded, "I was with the team on the photo shoots and I took the company camera that was used back to the office, so no, I don't think I downloaded any images. Good thinking, though."

She clicked off her phone and flopped down on Gran's bed. What was she going to do about these photos? She checked the calendar on her phone, her heart thumping. There were only about two weeks remaining to finish the project and get it to production.

She sat in Gran's room and thought for a second. The writers were already in edits, certainly. Could she get any photos around town to replace them? She considered Ardy Wright's farm, but it was too small and had neighborhood homes surrounding it...

Hannah fired off a quick email to Amanda to ask to read the articles once they were ready to go, so she could see the angles the writers were taking. Then she sent another email to the photographer, warning him that they may have to go in another direction. The worries and problems kept going around in her head, consuming her.

Then, all of a sudden, something clicked. She realized that she was closed up in Gran's room, fretting about work, when she had other things she could be thinking about. Hannah set down her phone and grabbed Gran's journal, opening it up to the next entry to get work off her mind for a while.

June 10, 1943

Still no word from Charles. I went back to the soda fountain yesterday to see if Warren was there. He was so lovely to speak to, and I know he understands the way this war can worry someone so. My parents

won't speak of the war in any way, and just the mention of it sends
Mama into a fit of tears, so I don't bring it up. I'd really love to talk
to someone about it before I explode. I noticed the Buxton Floral
Co. has advertised a small bouquet for grieving families who have
lost loved ones. I offered to help the floral company deliver those
arrangements in the evenings after my shift at work. It makes me
feel like I'm helping to spread a little joy in this awful time.

Hannah brightened. Perhaps Gran could close the shop and volunteer a few hours a week at another florist's somewhere else. The only problem was, there wasn't another floral company within walking distance so someone would have to drive her… With a deep breath, she read on.

June 12, 1943

I had a long talk with Minnie Buxton who runs the floral company this
evening, when I went in to pick up my deliveries. She was worried about
her ability to offer the low price on the grievance bouquets after the summer
months, as the cost of flowers will go up when the weather turns colder.
She's making so many and charging so little that she fears she wouldn't be
able to continue. But I had an idea. I explained how adding more baby's
breath and switching out the daisies for carnations could retain the shape
and color of the bouquet. She let me make an arrangement to show her,
and she was so excited by my creation. We danced around the shop in
relief. That was the first time I've felt real joy in so long.

It was just like Gran to have a suggestion for how to save a little money on the arrangements by thinking outside the box. She read the last two sentences again, her own memories of dancing with Gran in The Memory Keeper to songs from the old record player surfacing. Hannah turned the page and scanned the next entry.

June 18, 1943

I haven't been sleeping very well lately. I keep thinking about the grievance flowers I've been delivering—there are so, so many... My evenings stretch all the way to nightfall, delivering to family after family, and knowing that all of them have lost someone important to them. I am met with tears over and over, and it's terribly taxing. But I love working in the flower shop so much that I've been asking around to see if I can find a place in a nearby town where I could open my own business. The idea seems too daunting at times, and it's probably never going to happen, but I feel something niggling in my gut, telling me that my frustrations about the life I'm leading right now are the whispers that I'm not where I'm supposed to be yet.

Hannah read that last line again, the hairs on her arms standing up. She'd never considered that before. Gran had gone on to open that flower shop she'd thought about, and all her talk about being on the right path was starting to hit home.

Hannah's phone sounded with a text. Georgia was asking to be picked up at the records office. She closed the journal and headed out of the room, taking the journal with her. She couldn't wait to hear how Gran had gotten from Kentucky to Tennessee, where she'd open her own floral shop. It all gave Hannah hope that there might actually be another path waiting for her in life. And if so, could she find it?

She got into her dad's truck and drove across town to the public records office, where she reached across the seat to unlatch the door for Georgia.

"Find out anything new?" she asked.

"Nope. Nothin'," Georgia said. "I feel like they're so close and yet so far."

"I'm sorry," Hannah said. "Give it time. Someone has to know them. Maybe I can show Gran your photos when I go to see her again."

"Yeah," Georgia agreed, but the disappointment on her face was clear.

They drove to The Memory Keeper. It was time to get the shop ready to close. As Hannah made her way there, she knew that, just like Georgia's nameless photos, there was no easy answer for The Memory Keeper or Gran.

Chapter Nineteen

"What's that going around the ceiling?" Georgia asked, pointing up to the lone rail that lined one wall of The Memory Keeper.

"I'm not sure," Hannah replied. "As a kid, I never really noticed it. I'll have to ask Gran."

"Hm." Georgia gazed up at it.

Hannah went over to the counter and dropped a new box of file folders and the journal onto it, taking a sip of her to-go coffee they'd gotten on the way and assessing the mess.

"I suppose we should start to get rid of what we don't need and pack up the rest," she said, overwhelmed by the task at hand. "We'll get the shop looking as good as it can be while it's still open, but keep the inventory minimal. Then when we finally close, we'll have less to get rid of."

"Sounds good," Georgia said. "Where do you want me to start?"

"Let's sort all these papers. I'll label the files and put them over against the wall, then hand you a document and tell you which file to put it in. Once we get all this organized, we can start cleaning and painting."

"Yes," Georgia said. But then she stopped, running her fingers over the journal. "Whose is this?"

"My gran's. She gave it to me to read for my birthday."

"Have you started it yet?"

"Yes. It's really interesting. Her boyfriend is missing in the Second World War, and she's working at this factory she hates and delivering flowers in the evening."

"Wow. Sounds like she's had an interesting life."

"Should we read an entry before we get started?" Hannah asked, dying for any chance to procrastinate and dig back into Gran's life.

"Absolutely!" Georgia hopped up on the counter, scooting the papers out of the way, and sipped her coffee.

Hannah picked up the journal and opened it. She began to read.

June 23, 1943

It was incredibly hot yesterday. But I didn't have to worry. Mama got together with her friends in the neighborhood last week, and they all sewed us new clothes. Mama used the pillowcases we have to make us all shorts for the summer as a surprise. She even reused the lace and sewed it to the collar of one of my shirts, creating a matching outfit that is just tops. It felt so light and airy that I asked if I could take a walk down to the soda fountain yesterday, and I saw Warren! I hadn't planned to stay so long with having to go to work the next morning, but I told him all about Charles, and it was so nice to have someone who understands and listens. I confessed to him how much I hate working at the metal factory and how it really does get my spirits down, even though I'm so thankful to have employment. Warren asked me if I'd come back tomorrow. He said he'd buy me a Coke.

"Who's Warren?" Georgia asked.

"My Pop-pop."

"Oh," Georgia cooed. "The plot thickens! Read some more. Pretty please?"

"We have to get some work done!" Hannah laughed, but she wanted to read more just as badly as Georgia did. "But you twisted my arm," she teased. She grabbed her coffee and turned the page.

June 27, 1943

I really enjoy my talks with Warren. I've visited with him at the soda fountain every day for the last four days. I teased him that he was going to use all his student funds buying me sodas, but he dismissed it completely and bought me one anyway. Today, he read me some of his history book and we discussed the differences between the two world wars. It was fascinating. He's a very serious man. He talks about things I've never thought of before, but sometimes I can make him laugh. I do find that as exciting as when I made the bouquet for Minnie.

"Warren is Casanova!" Georgia said with a laugh. "He's totally moving in on her! And while she has a boyfriend too?" She pursed her lips playfully and shook her head.

The idea that Pop-pop had any dating game whatsoever made Hannah laugh out loud. He'd never try to steal another woman on purpose. "I do think he was smitten with Gran, but he'd never have made a move until he knew she wasn't taken. He was too good a man."

"Read another entry!" Georgia said.

Hannah didn't mind the request at all. The mess in the shop would still be there when they'd finished reading, and she was enjoying herself. "Okay, one more and then we *have* to get some work done."

"Of course," Georgia agreed.

July 2, 1943

I got a letter from Charles!

Georgia gasped. "This is like a movie!" Then she mimed buttoning her lips shut and said, "Sorry," with them pressed together. She ran her finger in circles in the air to gesture for Hannah to keep going.

Hannah continued.

In my hand, I'm holding the battered envelope addressed in his handwriting, trembling with excitement. I can't wait to open it! I'll write down everything he says on the lines that follow so I can keep it in this journal forever. I'm opening the letter now. Oh, I can see more of his lovely handwriting! He says—

Hannah stopped reading.

"What does it say?" Georgia leaned over the journal, trying to view the last sentence.

"There's nothing there," Hannah said, showing it to her. "It just stops, mid-sentence."

"Well, turn the page! You can't end like that!"

She peered down at the half-sheet of empty lines below that last word. Confused, Hannah turned the page.

July 3, 1943

I am writing through my tears. I've cried all night and Mr. Williams has threatened to fire me for not giving notice, but I couldn't go to

*work today. I can hardly move. I wasn't able to write it before, and
I can hardly do it now, but Charles's letter said:*

    My dearest Faye,

    *If you're reading this, then they've found me in the fields and sent
my final goodbye to you. I'll keep this letter in the pocket of my jacket
every single day I have to go into battle, so that no matter what, I'll
get to say I love you. I hate this war and the time it has stolen from
us, but I want you to go on and be happy. Do the things you love.
Don't waste time doing anything else.*

All my love,
Charles

"Oh, that's so sad." Georgia's face had dropped, her body still.
"What a terrible thing to have happened."

"Yeah…" Gran's comment about the two sides of the coin came
back to Hannah, and it really hit her how different Gran's life would've
been if Charles had survived the war. It was bittersweet to believe that
things had happened for the best, the way they were meant to happen.
For Hannah to have been born and have a life, Charles had to pay
with his own.

"That's a somber note to start cleaning on. Can we read just one
more?"

"It might depress us even further," Hannah said, still lost in thought.

"It's worth a shot."

"All right." In an odd way, the journal was helping her see her
priorities more clearly. It spoke to her. She moved on to the next
entry.

August 15, 1943

We had a summer thunderstorm all day today, and then the sun shone so brightly afterwards that I could hardly see when I walked to the floral company. On my way, a rainbow arched over the flower shop and I couldn't wait to get inside to tell Minnie. She told me it was a sign that happiness is all around us, if we just pay attention and look up instead of down. Then she put a record on her RCA turntable, grabbed my hands, and we danced. I laughed so hard and it felt just glorious. While my grief still comes in waves, I promised myself more moments like that one. It was then that I realized I hadn't been to the soda fountain in a long time. Minnie said she'd deliver the bouquets for me tomorrow afternoon, and she even gave me a nickel to get a soda.

"Perfect entry to end on! And I've got something to lift our spirits that fits right in." Hannah set the journal on the counter and went to the back corner of the shop, where Gran kept her old record player. She pulled out the "Rockin' Robin" record and put it on, turning the volume up.

"I never knew that it was Minnie who first danced with Gran. What a wonderful woman she seemed to be for my grandmother. When I was a little girl, Gran and I used to dance around the shop to this song. I guess I can thank Minnie for that."

Chapter Twenty

Hannah and Georgia closed up the shop and headed home in the dark of night. They'd worked like crazy to get everything straight, and The Memory Keeper was as neat as a pin and ready for cleaning and painting tomorrow. They had organized the paperwork, called a landscaping company who'd be there tomorrow, researched a couple of painters to get quotes, and weeded the sidewalk outside. While they were out there, they'd spent a long time planning other ways to spruce up the exterior.

When they'd gotten back to Gran's house and had dinner, Georgia took Jerry outside, and Hannah was just helping her mother finish cleaning the kitchen when her phone lit up with a text from Liam: *Sorry it's so late. I was wondering if you'd talk to Noah. Could you do a video call with him?*

She texted back: *Of course.* Although it was an odd request at such an hour—it was nearly 8 p.m. After a very long day, she was ready to shower, get her pajamas on, and settle in for the night.

Her phone vibrated, so she answered it as she made her way back to Gran's room. Liam's face surfaced on the screen. "I'm sorry again, but my mom's gone out tonight for the benefit I told you about. It's just Noah and me. He doesn't want me to read his bedtime story. He said he wanted me to call you and have you read it."

"What?" The idea of Noah asking for her gave her an unexpected flutter of happiness.

"He's actually teary-eyed over it. If I text you the words, will you read them to him while I turn the pages?"

"Bedtime stories can't be read over a phone," she said. "Why don't I just come over and read it to him?"

"You sure you wouldn't mind?"

"Not at all. I need to jump in the shower really quickly, though. I've been cleaning the shop all day."

"No problem. I'll text you the address." His face turned away from the screen. "Noah, Hannah's coming over to read your story to you, okay?" He turned his phone to show Noah, whose bottom lip was wobbling.

"I'll be there in just a bit," she told him.

Noah nodded.

"See you soon," Liam said.

Right when she ended the call, an email came in from Amanda. *Here are the articles for the spread…*

Hannah ignored it for the time being, and after a quick shower she headed off to see Liam and Noah.

Taking stock of her surroundings, Hannah pulled her dad's truck onto the shoulder of the winding country road and checked the navigation one more time. There was nothing but farmland on either side for as far as she could see, but the navigation kept telling her she'd arrived at her location.

She looked ahead of her, and way down the street she made out a lone mailbox. Could that be it? Hannah put the old truck in gear and headed down toward it. When she arrived at the mailbox, she put down the window, the cool air rushing in, and squinted to see what was at the end of the single-lane dirt drive, but it was so dark that her headlights didn't give her enough light.

She put the truck in park and tapped on her phone, describing where she was and asking Liam if she was at the right place.

He returned, *You're here. Come on down the drive. The house is a couple miles off the road.*

Hannah turned in and bumped her way down the long lane, past the fields and through the trees, slowing to look at their massive trunks stretching into the heavens, their barren branches like arms reaching over her. Rows of crops lined the path for as far as her headlights could reach, each field boasting its wares with adorably painted wooden signs on the edges—lettuce, cauliflower, pumpkins, cucumbers... She continued all the way to a mass of gorgeous ancient oak trees that picked up where the fields left off, lining the path in single file. At the very end, she thought she could make out the hint of an old farmhouse. She was willing to bet that with the coming spring, the leaves would create a shady canopy above the path. Eventually, the colossal farmhouse came into view and Hannah gasped.

The stunning structure was obviously historical, with two chimneys on either side of the tin roof. Rocking chairs dotted its wide front porch that wrapped around three sides of the house, and all she could think was how much Gran would love this old house... Could she use photos of it for the magazine?

The front door swung open and Noah came out, standing on the porch in railroad pajamas and sock feet. As Hannah shut off the engine and got out, Liam joined Noah to greet her.

"My goodness, I'm cold just looking at you in your socks out here on the porch," Hannah teased the little boy, dropping the keys into her handbag as Liam opened the door wider to allow her inside.

The interior of the home had been renovated—no house built in that time period had an open floor plan with a wall of French doors leading to a covered back porch capped by a stone fireplace. The ceilings in the main room that housed the kitchen, den, and dining areas were vaulted and striped with exposed beams jutting from one wall to the other.

The kitchen matched the living area—everything done in white-washed wood with dark-blue accents. An old metal retailer sign listing various vegetables and their prices leaned stylishly against the corner next to the oversized farmhouse table.

"Ready for your stories?" Liam said to Noah. "We need to get you in bed. It's way past your bedtime."

Noah took Hannah's hand and walked with her down the hallway.

"I didn't know your grandmother was a farmer," she said to Noah, wondering how one woman could take care of this whole farm all by herself.

"Yes. She grows lots of stuff for the shops and the farmer's markets," he told her as they walked. "I get to have all the strawberries I can eat." They stopped at an open door. "This is my room when I'm at Grandma's house."

Hannah stepped inside. A model train and track circled the ceiling and there were more locomotives on the bedding. "Do you like trains?" Hannah asked.

"Yeah," Noah replied. "My grandpa used to collect them." He grabbed a book and held it out to her before crawling under his covers.

"Oh, that's nice." She kneeled down at the side of his bed and opened the book. As Noah snuggled under his blanket, Hannah started to read.

Noah looked at her with sleepy eyes, complete innocence in them, and her heart wanted to burst. Suddenly, she longed for moments like these, building her family, and spending precious slips of time knowing that it was about so much more than just the story she was reading. Before she could even get the book finished, he was asleep.

She realized Liam was watching her intently, curiosity in his eyes, and a fond smile on his lips.

"He was tired," she whispered to him as they left the room.

Liam closed the door, latching it quietly. "He was exhausted. It took all his energy to stay up until you arrived. Sorry you had to come all the way out for that."

"It's no problem," she said. "I enjoy being with him."

Liam smiled. "We went round and round about reading his stories until he asked to call you. He didn't want me to do it."

"Don't you normally read him his stories?" Hannah asked.

A guarded look came over him. "His nanny reads them usually," he said. "She's typically the one there with him when he goes to bed."

Hannah nodded. "That has to be difficult for you, not to see him before he goes to sleep," she said, as they walked together back down the hallway to the living area.

"Yes. It's... hard."

Hannah understood grief and how it could ravage the mind and heart. As much as a month after Pop-pop's funeral, she could be going along with her normal day and still burst into tears over him, the finality of him being gone totally overwhelming her.

"While you're here, can I ask a totally random favor?" Liam asked.

"What's that?" she replied.

"My mom needs a dish to take to her book club tomorrow, and I told her I'd help her make one, since she'll be out so late tonight."

"That's nice of you," Hannah said.

"It was the least I could do to repay her for watching Noah for a week, and having to rush home to get to her benefit with him in tow."

Hannah stepped up beside him. "What are you going to make?"

"That's just it. I have no idea. I'm not really a cook…"

She laughed quietly so as not to wake Noah. "So you want me to think of a dish and help you make it?"

"Pretty much."

"Well, you've got the right person," Hannah told him. "I love cooking and I don't get to do it enough." She took him by the arm. "Take me to your kitchen, sir," she teased. "Let's see what ingredients you have."

"I think my mother was scared to see what I was going to come up with—I could tell by her face," Liam said. "I'm sure she's expecting a bag of chips and peanut butter sandwiches."

"She'll be very surprised then. There won't be a peanut butter sandwich in sight," Hannah said as she peeked into the fridge. "She's got a great array of vegetables… And what's this?" she asked, pulling out a large tub and removing the covering. "Oh! Chicken—that works." She handed it to Liam who set it on the counter. "Do you have a deep dish I can use to make a casserole?"

Hannah washed her hands, drying them on the kitchen towel while Liam pulled a baking dish from the cupboard and set it next to the chicken.

"What vegetables do we need?" he asked, as he got out a bunch of carrots and an onion.

"Definitely grab the broccoli. Do you have any other vegetables in the freezer? Oh, and I'll need a few large bowls for combining ingredients."

While he opened the freezer door and took a look, Hannah asked, "Who cooks for you at home in Charleston?"

"I just order prepared food—I usually work through my mealtimes. Elise, the nanny, cooks for Noah."

"When was the last time you sat down at a table and had a nice dinner?"

He stopped and turned toward her, homing in on her. "At your grandmother's with you."

Hannah's cheeks flushed, and she took in a breath to keep the flutter that the memory had caused at bay. "I meant before that," she said, but he was already remembering that night again too, she could tell.

Then, all of a sudden, he closed right up. "I don't recall," he answered. He pulled a bag from the open freezer. "Mom has these mixed garden veggies. They're already diced—"

"What's wrong?" she asked bluntly. She took a step toward him. "You can tell me. We're friends, remember?" The word "friend" felt odd on her lips, like it didn't fit who they were.

"I haven't had a regular dinner since Alison…" he admitted. "And then you." His eyes met hers again, uncertainty swimming around in them.

"Have you eaten tonight?"

"Not yet."

"You didn't eat with Noah?" she wondered aloud.

He shook his head. "Well, I did nip a chicken finger," he said with a smirk in her direction. "But that's long gone."

She grinned at him, thinking. "We should double the recipe then." She hadn't planned on eating, but maybe she could get him to open up about his relationship with his son. She flicked on the radio in the corner of the kitchen, turning the volume low, the tunes filtering into the air around them. "Are you free now?"

"I am," he replied.

"Perfect," she said. "We could find some matches and light that candle over on the table? That would be nice."

Liam pulled a lighter from the drawer and went over to the candle.

"How about herbs—got any of those? We need parsley, salt, pepper, and chives if you have them. Oh! And I saw some cream and butter in the fridge. If you have flour and baking powder, we can make a dish that will set your world on fire."

"What's the dish?"

"It's my gran's famous Buttermilk Chicken Pickin'."

"Now that sounds like a dinner I'd like to dig into," Liam said. "The ingredients alone sound terrifyingly delicious." He handed her a bowl from the cabinet.

"Does your job require so much of your time that you have to work through your meals?" Hannah asked, curious, getting the flour and then measuring out what she needed.

"Yes," he replied. "My dad always wanted me to do what I love—he told me that all the time. So I'm using my inheritance to build my company. My partner and I started small, but now I want to invest my inheritance money in the business to expand." He handed her the baking powder as she reached for it.

She tried not to focus on the glaring warning sign—he was building a company that took up so much of his time that he ate at his desk and left his son with a full-time nanny. "What's the business?" she asked.

"I acquire parcels of land, and either renovate or build large retail and business developments on them, and then sell them. I've actually just acquired the vacant shops on the corner of Main Street and Ivy Lane downtown."

Hannah knew those streets. That was the strip of shops currently blocking The Memory Keeper from the view of Main Street. "Oh, do you know what shops are going up there yet?" she asked. If the right retail came in, people might venture down Ivy Lane and find Gran's shop.

"I've got a company renting that development which plans to bring in a bookstore and a couple of clothing boutiques."

"Oh, a bookstore would be amazing," Hannah said.

Liam smiled. "My mother would agree."

"Yes, right!" Hannah refocused on the task at hand. "We've got some biscuits to make."

The buttery aroma in the kitchen smelled divine, both casseroles now in the oven, baking. The music was playing softly on the radio, the candle flickering between Hannah and Liam at the table.

"So tell me about *your* job," Liam said, as he poured Hannah a glass of white wine.

"I'm an art director for a magazine," she told him.

"I remember you wanting to do something like that when we were kids," he said. "You were so excited to go off to college. So you must love what you do." He handed her the glass.

She considered his observation. "Honestly, I used to, but now I'm not so sure. And I'm having some trouble at the moment."

"What is it?"

She explained the situation with the lost photos. "The title of the spread is 'From Our Homes to Yours,' and it was supposed to be a collection of farm life from around the country. I've got the articles sitting in my inbox right now, but I haven't had a chance to look at them yet. I'm hoping they'll give me some inspiration for a new shoot."

She considered asking Liam if she could photograph the farmhouse, but decided against bringing it up right now. The last thing she wanted to do was to get caught up in a lengthy conversation about work.

The oven timer went off. "Looks like dinner's ready," she said. "I'll bring it over."

"I've got it," Liam said. He stood up and grabbed the blue-and-white checkered kitchen towel from the sink, then pulled the casseroles out of the oven, bringing one of them to the table and setting it on a trivet.

"It looks delicious," she said, peering over it. The vegetables were bubbling up through the browned biscuits that had formed a fluffy crust on top, more vegetables peeking out from the edges.

Liam dished out the casserole, dropping a large, piping hot square in the center of the plate and handing it to her. Then he filled another plate for himself.

"How's your grandmother?" he asked.

"She's doing okay, I guess." Hannah set her napkin in her lap. "I hate that she might be spending her final days in the hospital. Life can be so fragile; it can change in an instant. It makes me want to seize the moment, any chance I get."

"So. If this was, in fact, your last day, and you knew that, what would you do?"

"That's a tough question," she replied. "It's easy to say I'd run off into the sunset, but life isn't that simple when there are things out of my control, like Gran being sick. I suppose I'd spend the day with the people that mean the most to me. How about you? Is there anything you've always wanted to do?"

He took a drink of his wine, his expression making him look like he was solving some sort of algebra problem. Then he set his glass down and pushed back his chair, standing up and walking to Hannah's side of the table. He took her hand, gently pulling her to a standing position. The only sound between them was the radio playing softly. He put his arm around her and held her hand, swaying to the slow music. "If today were my last day," he said, looking into her eyes, "I'd dance with you."

She peered up at him, surprise washing over her like bubbles in champagne. "This is what you'd want to do on your final day—dance with *me*?" she asked.

"One time, at the bonfire in the field, when we were kids, you and Morgan were dancing in the headlights of one of the trucks. I still remember your long hair falling down the back of your sundress and your hands above your head. The other guys were hooting and hollering, but I thought, 'I wish I could dance with her.'"

"Why didn't you?" she asked.

"When I finally got the nerve to jump down from the back of the truck, Ethan had pulled you aside and asked you to go home." Out of nowhere, Liam dipped her, making her laugh. He pulled her upright. "I think my final day would be about... taking chances." He twirled her out and then brought her back in to him, making her smile again.

"Can I dance, Daddy?" Noah's groggy voice came from the doorway, causing both Hannah and Liam to start. "I woke up," he said, his eyes heavy, a pink line on his cheek from the sheets.

Hannah walked over to him and took his hand. "Of course you can dance," she said. "I'll tell you what. I'll show you how I learned to dance. Your dad has bigger feet than I do, so he'd be the best to do this." She turned Noah toward Liam. "Step up on your daddy's feet and hold on to him." She twisted the knob on the radio slightly so they could hear the music better. "Now, Liam, dance like you were with me, and Noah will learn your steps."

Liam began to move his feet, Noah gliding along with him. Noah broke out in a look of pure sleepy happiness as he peered up at his father.

"Hannah's a good teacher, isn't she?" Liam asked Noah.

"Yes, but you're good too," Noah said, wriggling his little toes on Liam's feet.

Liam lifted him up into his arms. Without warning, Noah put his arms around his father's neck and gave him a big squeeze. Hannah's heart pattered. If this were her last day, that, right there, would be on her list of things to see.

Chapter Twenty-One

The next morning, Hannah and Georgia had gotten to The Memory Keeper early.

Georgia sat cross-legged in the empty display window. "What if we could make this place great again?" she offered optimistically. "What if we could get enough sales to pay off the debt and turn the shop around?"

"I have to admit, I thought that too after hearing about the new shops Liam's bringing in." Hannah opened the back door and set a bowl of milk out for Speckles, although she still hadn't seen the cat. "But where could we even start?"

Georgia hopped off the window and came up behind her. "You're too involved in the situation," she said. "Close your eyes."

Glad for the distraction, Hannah complied.

"You work at a magazine, right? You're doing a magazine spread on flowers, and this is a blank page. Just one giant, three-dimensional canvas. What do you put on it?"

Images began filtering into Hannah's mind. Painted, curling letters in cursive script spelling out "The Memory Keeper" slid onto the back wall in blues and greens like vines, with pink, purple, and yellow bunches of flowers along the tails—all of it swirling over a mural of some sort. The old counter at the back became an oversized whitewashed antique dresser with a marble top, the old record player cornered on it, and cut-glass antique vases of flowers sitting on light disks illuminating the back wall with shimmery sparkles.

Hannah suddenly thought back to what Liam had said about taking chances, his suggestion giving her new perspective. What if she could make a different kind of shop here? If they could make The Memory Keeper inviting for new customers by bringing it into the present, they might have a shot at turning things around.

"We have to paint anyway at the end of the lease," Hannah said, still thinking about the possibilities. "We need the brightest white paint possible." She opened her eyes. "The flowers will provide the color."

"Yes!" Georgia agreed, beginning to bounce around the room. "See all those silver buckets? Let's replace them with new ones and fill them with flowers from floor to ceiling."

"But how will we get to them?"

Georgia's gaze landed on the track at the top of one of the walls. "I'll bet there was a ladder that used to slide across that wall."

"Oh, you could be right."

"Wouldn't it be gorgeous if we replaced it with a wide, substantial, wooden ladder in a thick gloss of stain?"

"That would be gorgeous! I'll take measurements for it right now." Hannah and Georgia had a vision together that was shaping up beautifully. Their creative sides connected easily, and Hannah was so glad Georgia had been here to offer her suggestions. It was still a long shot, but what if it actually worked? "So how do we replace something like the ladder? It would have to be specially made."

"We can ask around to see if anyone knows a woodworker in town who could make it. I'm sure there's someone."

"I think I'd like to have these wood floors buffed and sanded too, and then put on a thick coat of clear sealer to shine it up and make it match the ladder. Its imperfections and the light wood color would make a nice canvas. We could hang some chandeliers where those old lights are. Plunging, crystal ones. And then we can stain the old wood cashier's counter." She turned to the long blank wall to the left of the door. "What if this wall was filled with some sort of artwork? Then, in front of it, we could put a line of rocking chairs with coordinating pillows."

"That sounds stunning." Georgia danced over to the display window. "I can see this window dressed in elegant satin curtains, drawn back at the sides here with curtain pegs. And in the window area, there's room to use varying heights of antique furniture—whitewashed like the others you mentioned—to showcase the current displays of floral arrangements for the season. I've walked past about three antiques stores in town. There's no shortage of furniture."

Hannah put her hands on her hips, thinking. "We're talking a lot of money for a renovation like that..." she told her, the idea settling in. "What if we can do it on a shoestring budget? Do it ourselves and only hire for the things we absolutely cannot do."

"Of course! We could get it done in a week if we really push through."

"I think we could too," Hannah said, as she took in the gloomy walls in their current state. The idea of surprising Gran with this made Hannah come alive. She cringed at the thought of asking for more time off from work, but perhaps she could explain the health of her grandmother. She'd have to figure that out later. "The inside is easy," Hannah said. "But what do we do with the outside?"

Georgia leaned on the wide display shelf to peer out of the large storefront window. "That big section of brush has to go," she said.

"Definitely," Hannah agreed. "We need to totally gut the yard and replace it with sod and new mulch beds. The exterior clapboard siding could be a bright white as well. But I know that's a lot..."

"We could clear most of the brush ourselves, and do our own landscaping."

Hannah chewed on her lip, calculating the numbers. "If we do everything inside ourselves, I think I could afford to pay for most of the outside... Oh, I just thought of something!" she said, coming over to Georgia. "What if we made the outside super inviting with flowers, painted the current seating areas, and added some brightly colored umbrellas? We could have water bowls for customers' dogs, bird feeders, and bowls of milk for cats—Gran would adore that. If people know they can sit down and relax here, 'make memories,' they'll think of us first as the place to go when they need flowers."

"I love that," Georgia said, clapping her hands with excitement. "We could even partner with the local bakery and do things together for the major holidays."

Hannah could feel the anticipation building. "You know, my gran used to always offer shoppers lemonade or iced tea. We could have a lemonade station and silver tea service."

"Now you're talkin'," Georgia said with a giggle. "I'd love to design the exterior for you. I could draw up some sketches."

"That would be amazing! I think I know the perfect person to paint what we want on the interior as well... I wonder if we could get it done in time. It would be amazing to surprise Gran when she gets home from the hospital."

Hannah's dreaming about the shop had carried over to the idea that Gran would walk out of the hospital one day. That she'd be back to her busy self, strolling into town every morning and chatting with the locals. Even though Hannah knew there was a possibility that Gran's future had other less favorable outcomes, she wanted to hold on to her faith for just a while longer. And fixing up the shop would help her do that.

"Miss Hannah Townshend—our own town beauty queen returns!" Ethan's father Ardy said, wiping his hands on a grease-streaked shop towel. His hair had grayed on the sides, and his potbelly was bigger than she remembered, but his smile was just as warm.

"Beauty queen?" she laughed. "It was only the once, and I was Watermelon Festival Queen. Hardly the town's beauty queen when it was only me and three others in the running."

"You wore that crown well." He stepped up to her. "I'd hug you, but you don't want to get dirt on those fancy clothes of yours." He offered her a big smile. "You lookin' for Ethan?"

"I am," she replied.

"He's on lunch break—" Just then, the door to the shop opened. "Well, look at that. Speak of the devil."

"Somethin' wrong with your daddy's truck?" Ethan asked, coming in and giving her a playful once-over, clearly wondering why she was there. He loved giving her a hard time, and she didn't mind at all. It was Ethan's way of showing affection.

"Ethan, I just wanna make sure you're gonna be home—" A woman with wispy brown hair and an unfussy appearance came in, a young toddler on her hip, still chatting up a storm to Ethan before she stopped, catching up to the situation, her gaze landing on Hannah.

Ethan turned around, and the atmosphere became notably uneasy, to Hannah's confusion. "This is my wife, Christie," he said, introducing them. "And my son Wesley."

"You have a son?" Hannah asked, taking in the child's familiar blue eyes.

"I do," he said quietly. Ethan gestured toward Hannah. "Christie, this is—"

"I know who she is," Christie cut him off. Her words were more guarded than angry, but they gave Hannah the feeling that she wasn't very welcome in Christie Wright's presence. "Come on home right at five, please. You need to watch Wesley for me."

"I will," he said.

Christie gave him one final lingering look, and then left, the mood lighter once she'd gone.

Ethan jammed his hands in the pockets of his jeans as he shared a quick glance with his dad.

Hannah stood between the two men, waiting for some explanation.

"I've gotta get back in there," Ardy said. "Got a transmission that's givin' us all fits. It's great to see you, Hannah."

"See ya," she said, still waiting for Ethan to give her some idea of what was going on, the confusion eating away at the excitement she'd had when she'd first arrived at the body shop looking for him.

"So, what's up?" Ethan asked Hannah, as if nothing was wrong.

"I'm not really sure," she answered honestly. "What just happened?"

"She's just testy, that's all."

"Testy." She said the word like a statement, but he knew full well it was a question. "And you have a son?" Hannah felt her tone soften at the memory of those rosy cheeks and blue eyes. "Why didn't Gran tell me? Surely she knew."

"I don't see your family anymore, Hannah. I went on and had my own life after you left. I sank myself into work and focused on raising my family," he said. "Like I told you, there's a lot you don't know about me these days. I've gotta clock in." He went over to the computer and typed in something. "You just droppin' by to say hey, or are you in the market for an oil change?"

"I need your artistic skills," she said, finally allowing a warmhearted smile to settle on her lips. She knew that would get him.

"I don't do art anymore," he said. "Look, I gotta get to work."

"Wait, what?" she said, grabbing his arm to stop him from going toward the door to the garage.

"My painting days are long gone."

Hannah was sure a whole lot had transpired in the years she'd been away, but this was a complete and utter shock. "You don't paint anymore at all? Not even in your free time?" Her words withered on the air, her disappointment clear.

He shook his head, something more in his eyes than what he was telling her.

"You could start again," she suggested. "You're the best, and I need you."

"Sorry, Hannah. You'll have to find someone else."

"It's for Gran."

Surrender slid down his face.

"Could you just come to The Memory Keeper after work and see what I need?"

His chested puffed out with an inhale that he then blew through his lips in frustration. "I can't tonight. I've gotta get home to watch Wesley."

"You could bring him," she suggested. "Maybe we could take him for ice cream after."

"I can't."

"What's going on?"

"Ethan," a man said from the door to the garage. "We're shorthanded in here. Wanna finish up that marathon lunch break and get to work?"

"Yeah," he said. "Sorry. On my way." He addressed Hannah. "Look, I gotta go. I'll catch up with you later, okay?"

"Ethan!" the man called, causing Ardy to leave what he was doing and walk over with an expectant shrug.

Ethan went into the garage, the door closing between them, leaving her in the waiting room alone. Stunned, she turned around and walked out, feeling anxious. Ethan had been so adamant his whole life that he'd never end up working at Ardy's body shop, and there he was, clocking in.

And why had Christie been so standoffish? Hannah had never met the woman in her life. What had she ever done to her? She remembered what Ethan had said about Christie worrying he'd want to see what was out there in the world, but Hannah had come into *their* world. So what was with her?

Ethan was right about one thing: things had definitely changed. In fact, nothing at all seemed the same anymore. She wanted to talk to Gran. Maybe she could swing by the hospital for a visit after she and Georgia finished at the shop. She got into the truck and headed back.

Hannah had left Georgia in her room, searching online for leads on her parents.

Hannah had attempted to see her grandmother on the way home, but Gran had been asleep when she'd stopped by, so Hannah didn't stay. Her mom and dad were out getting groceries, and Hannah found herself alone. Needing to hear Gran's voice, she pulled out the journal and settled in.

August 16, 1943

I couldn't believe my eyes when I walked into Beaty's Drugstore after so long. Warren was sitting at our usual spot at the soda fountain, reading his book with two Cokes in front of him. I surprised him, coming up behind him. "Thirsty?" I teased, while also wondering for whom he'd bought the second Coke. When he turned around, I could hardly breathe when I saw his smile. No one has ever smiled at me like that before. It seemed as though he were going to jump up and hug me. The soda clerk made Warren's cheeks go pink when he told me that Warren had bought two Cokes every day for the last month and a half, waiting for me to come back. We talked forever. I told him about Charles because I knew he would understand. I also told him about dancing with Minnie and how it lifted my spirits so much. We talked so long that I drank the Coke he bought me and even used Minnie's nickel for a second!

August 18, 1943

I've been learning how to make all kinds of beautiful bouquets with Minnie. I meet her before I go to work at the metal factory and we make all the bouquets for the day together. She says I surprised her with how well I could choose flowers and that one day I will end up putting her out of business. I'd never do that.

It was so great that Gran had found out what she was good at doing at such a young age, and that she'd had a mentor in Minnie. Hannah had learned the ropes all by herself—no one understood her job, and sometimes it did feel lonely. She definitely didn't dance around her office, that was for sure. The deadlines could be taxing, and she couldn't always get her colleagues to see eye-to-eye with her, but she enjoyed the creativity of it.

Her phone pinged with an email. It was Amanda. If only the magazine spread could be as uncomplicated as making a bouquet of flowers. She opened the message to read: *Hi Hannah, sorry to bother you again but Rich is asking to see the draft layout… Help!*

Rich Baldwin was Hannah's boss. She set down the journal and decided it was time to read the articles Amanda had sent over, and figure out what to do. She knew it would only send her into hours of thinking and puzzling over how to make everything fit, but she had to face it. Hannah opened her laptop and pulled up the articles for the feature.

She began to read, and as her eyes moved along the words on her screen, relief like she'd never felt before washed over her. "These are all talking about families and the culture of farm life," she said in a whisper. "So I need to get photos of a family…" Hannah needed a professional photographer quickly, and she needed a family. She looked up from her computer, knowing exactly where she could get both and wondering if it could be possible. She sent an email to Amanda: *I've got an idea for the spread! Sit tight!* Then she pulled out a pad of paper and got to work.

Chapter Twenty-Two

The southern weather at this time of year could tantalize with a warm day of mild breeze and spring-like sunshine, and then snatch it all away the next day with gray tormenting skies and a debilitating snowstorm. This morning was one of the good days. The sun was bright in an electric-blue sky, melting the snow and making everything feel like magic. Hannah had gotten up early and was already at The Memory Keeper, on a ladder, putting the finishing touches on the freshly painted white wall as a beam of sunlight stretched across her path.

"Wow, you move fast," Georgia said, walking through the door with two cups of coffee and a paper sack from the local coffee shop in each hand, and Jerry in her shoulder bag.

Georgia had planned to do a couple of interviews with town historians to see if they knew anything about her parents, but she'd come to The Memory Keeper first with Hannah.

"When I left, you'd just started painting, and now you've almost finished that wall."

"Just the one coat," Hannah said from atop the ladder. She'd decided to paint all the walls bright white and then add color using flowers, just like she'd envisioned when she and Georgia had first discussed it. The more time she spent in the shop, the calmer she felt. It was definitely a challenge, but working there was peaceful and comforting.

"It already looks so much fresher and newer in here." Georgia set the coffees down on the clean counter in the center of the room and let Jerry out of his bag. He pitter-pattered across the shop floor, sniffing the boxes of flowers.

"I know." Hannah leaned back and admired her work.

As she climbed down the ladder, she caught sight of something black darting past the back-door window. She paced over quietly and looked out, hoping it was Speckles. She'd love nothing more than to see the jet-black cat, lapping up the milk she'd put out for it. But when she got to the window, whatever it was had gone, the milk still there.

"I haven't seen the stray cat Speckles that Gran has befriended at all since I've arrived home, and I know Gran's going to ask," she worried aloud. "I want to be able to tell her she's just fine. It would be such a good feeling."

"Wonder where she's been this whole time?" Georgia asked.

"No idea." Hannah left the door and checked the names written on the side of the coffee cups Georgia had set on the counter, grabbing hers. "What kind did you get me?" she asked.

"Honey and almond milk." She lumped the sack on the counter. "I got us muffins too. I ate mine already."

"That sounds delicious," she said, wiping her forehead with her paint-streaked arm. She checked her phone and there were no new messages. She'd texted Ethan this morning to ask again if he'd stop by, but she hadn't heard from him. She'd told him she'd be there all day.

"Need anything else before I head out to my interviews?" Georgia asked.

"I think I'm good here," she replied.

"Jerry, come!" Georgia called, scooping up the Chihuahua into her arms. "You sure your dad's okay with me taking the truck?"

"Yes, he's totally fine with it."

"And you'll be all right here at the store?"

"Of course. I'm painting all day, and even if I have to walk home, it's totally doable. Gran does it all the time. The weather's going to be halfway decent today, so the walk should be nice."

"Text me if you need me." Georgia grabbed her coffee, slipped Jerry into his bag, and walked out into the sunshine.

Hannah felt a swell of optimism as she walked to the back of the room and turned on the old record player. "Rockin' Robin" began its tweedle, causing her to spin around, forgetting about everything for a minute. She closed her eyes and twirled, letting the sound take her back to simpler times. It was the most cheerful she'd felt in a long time, until the bells on the door jingled.

Christie stood inside, the door swinging shut behind her.

Hannah jogged back to the record player and turned it off with a scratch, before going up to the front to greet Christie. "Hello," she said, approaching her cautiously.

"I was just wonderin' if you were here for Ethan," she said, squaring her chin proudly even though she seemed anxious.

"What do you mean?"

"Because if you are, I need you to let us be." She ran her hand nervously through her wind-blown, wispy hair. "I'm askin', woman to woman, for you to back off."

What was she talking about? "I came home because my gran is sick in the hospital," Hannah said. "I've been in touch with Ethan because he was my *best* friend. And I'm not taking him anywhere, so you have nothing to worry about."

"I'd like you to leave us to our life together. It's already hard enough without you interferin'. I came in to tell you—please—don't ask him to paint anything. He said you wanted him to paint somethin' in here."

"Why shouldn't he paint?"

"Because it puts these big ideas in his head."

"What's so wrong with big ideas? He's very talented."

"He's got commitments now." She pursed her lips in disapproval. "Look, when we started datin', I got pregnant, and he had to go to work for his dad. Paintin' reminds him of everything he gave up to be Wesley's father. And he confessed to me once that he feels guilty for ever wantin' any life other than the one we've got, so I know he thinks about it."

"He can have both. He doesn't have to give up painting," Hannah said.

"I think he's afraid of where it might take him if he were to give it his all."

"What do you mean?"

"If by some miracle he were to break out of this town, it would eventually take him away from us. What if he ended up in some art gallery in New York City, or somethin' like that? We wouldn't know what to do up there. He and I would drift apart, and the next thing I know, Wesley wouldn't know his father or have anything in common with him. And that's best-case scenario."

"What's worst case?"

"He'd waste his whole life tryin' to be somethin' he's not. Me gettin' pregnant changed things for him, but I think it just made him finally grow up."

Hannah thought back to all the times in high school when Ethan had been frustrated with her for planning to leave. But now, she wondered if it was because he too wanted to follow his dreams, and for some reason he didn't feel that he was capable of doing it.

"Chasing your dreams isn't only a childhood endeavor—it shouldn't be something he has to 'give up.' And there's art here too, you know. He could stay close to his roots and paint around town and in Nashville, like he'd been doing."

"But eventually, he'd move on," Christie said, her face worried.

"So you're saying that Ethan isn't using his God-given talent because of fear that it might give him success? That doesn't make any sense at all. I think the fear here is yours—you worry that you're a second choice in his life, and I doubt that very seriously."

"Sometimes you just gotta live the life you're given, ya know?" She gritted her teeth. "You roll into town with these grand ideas, puttin' thoughts in his head, confusin' him. Just let him be. We were all just fine before you came."

"Were you fine? Because that kind of thinking doesn't seem fine to me." She shook her head. "What about *you*, Christie? What are your dreams?"

"Me? Oh, I can't paint or anything. And I don't live a fancy life like you do. I just work up at the supermarket as a cashier. It's good pay and they let me work during daytime hours so I can find childcare, and that's nice of 'em."

"But when you were a little girl, what did you want to be when you grew up?"

Christie's dubious stare hung between them before she answered. "That's just it, Miss Townshend—those were my childhood *dreams*; not talents, not reality. That's what I've been tryin' to get through to you and Ethan both."

"Okay," Hannah said, switching tactics. "What was your childhood *dream* then?"

"To be a dancer. That should prove what I'm sayin', right there."

"Why should it prove anything? If you want to do that, you can. Do you remember when you stopped wanting to be a dancer?"

"I've never stopped, but it makes no sense to think I'd ever be a dancer. I'm five foot three." She laughed incredulously.

"However, if you had pursued it, you could be in New York dancing while Ethan paints. Now wouldn't that be something?"

Frustration showed on Christie's face as she put her hands on her hips. "People like Ethan and me don't live in a big city. It's not who we are."

"Then don't live in the big city. But I do think you should give yourself permission to follow your dreams."

"Let's agree to disagree."

Hannah grinned at her. "I'm gonna get you dancing," she said.

Christie looked at her like she'd lost her mind. "What?"

"I am," Hannah declared. "I'm going to get you dancing and Ethan painting, and I guarantee it'll change your life."

"Miss Townshend, I think you might be a little crazy." She said the words, but Hannah noticed the interest in her stare. Perhaps Hannah had offered some faith in the possibilities when Christie hadn't thought there was any. She definitely didn't look convinced, but she seemed contemplative.

"I probably am crazy," Hannah said. "But I've never missed an opportunity."

"This talk has been… interesting," Christie said, turning toward the door. But as she left, she said quietly over her shoulder, "I'll send Ethan by to take a look at what you need done."

"Christie, you're fabulous!" Hannah called as the door shut behind her. When Christie walked past the display window, Hannah almost swore she could see the makings of a smile on her face.

"Have you completely lost your mind?" Hannah's mother asked on the other end of the line, as Hannah stood in the middle of The Memory

Keeper. "You're going to throw all your money into the shop, and for what? We have no way to keep it going, nor has anyone proven that it can be successful in this day and age. We've already sunk so much into that place; I just can't, in good conscience, allow you to spend your hard-earned money on this…"

"I'm an adult, Mama," she said. "I'm not going to be reckless, but I have to try. I'm wiping the bills—that's final. It's important to me to make it work."

"Why, Hannah?" her mother asked.

She tried to figure out the answer, and while she wanted to say that it was for Gran, something inside her told her it was more than that. She wanted to make memories too, and she truly felt like this was something she should do. She wanted to look back on her life and know she'd made a difference. "I want to see if I can make it successful," she said.

"How? You'll be in New York."

"I know. I haven't figured everything out yet, but the one thing I'm sure about is The Memory Keeper. I can't let it go."

"You've always been strong-willed," her mother said, "but you've also been great at everything you do. Let's see what you can do with it."

"Thanks, Mama. I love you."

"Love you too."

Hannah looked around Gran's shop with a new sense of purpose. Time to spread her wings.

"How did the interviews go?" Hannah asked Georgia when she came into The Memory Keeper. She stepped down off the ladder, having finished the wall.

"I met a great news reporter who's gonna look around to see what he can find, though the historian had no leads at all." Georgia let Jerry out of her bag. "But my conversation with the reporter wasn't entirely about me."

"Oh?" Hannah beckoned Georgia to the back, as she went to the kitchenette to wash the paint off her hands.

"I hope you don't mind. I was telling him about The Memory Keeper. He wants to do a piece on the revitalization of it."

"What?" Hannah asked, flicking the water off her hands, and drying them on a paper towel.

Georgia stepped up next to her. "Yes. It would be part of a series the paper's doing on historical properties, and it would be featured on the front page next to the town's Spring Festival."

Hannah threw her arms around Georgia. "That's amazing! The publicity would be incredible..." She clapped a hand over her mouth in excitement. "When would the piece run?"

"He wants to do it as soon as we're ready. Here." Georgia reached into her pocket and pulled out a business card. "It's got his name and number. I could definitely help with the photo shoot of the shop..."

"I've got to get Ethan in here, like, now. Do you have the keys to the truck?"

Georgia handed them to her, a buzzing glimmer in her eyes.

"Man the fort. I'll be right back."

Hannah burst through the door of the body shop, calling for Ethan.

"What's all the fuss?" Ardy said, lumbering up to the front.

"I need to talk to Ethan. Is he in the garage?" she asked, brushing past Ardy.

"Hey, you can't go back there."

Hannah pulled open the door and stepped into the large, echoing space, the hissing of hydraulics and whining of drills drowning out her calls for Ethan. She paced through the line of cars, some with the hood up, others on lifts, peering into the faces of the mechanics as they stopped working to give her confused looks.

"What the heck do you think you're doin'?" Ethan asked, walking up from the back.

"I need you," she said.

Someone whistled at her from one of the cars.

Hannah ignored it. "I talked to Christie," she said.

Ethan's eyes widened in guarded interest.

"She said she'd talk to *you*. Has she?"

"Nope."

"I need you to paint a mural for me right now."

"I already told you—"

"I know what you said, and I'm not listening to any of it." She grabbed his arm and pulled him with her toward the door, to the hoots and hollers of Ethan's fellow mechanics.

"Hey, where y'all goin'?" Ardy asked as they crossed the waiting area, heading outside.

"I'm stealing him for a bit," Hannah said.

"Ethan, Christie won't like this!" Ardy called after them.

"She's fine!" Hannah said over her shoulder. "I'm getting her dance lessons!" She opened the passenger side of the truck. "Get in. You're mine for the day."

"Dance lessons?" Ethan asked when she'd gotten in the truck.

"Yep." Hannah pulled off and headed straight to the paint shop.

Chapter Twenty-Three

"It's been a long time," Ethan said, hesitant, as he stood in his Wright's Body Shop uniform and steel-tipped boots among the cans of paint. He was facing the blank wall at the back of The Memory Keeper, the old bravado Hannah used to see in his eyes replaced by uncertainty. What had happened to that swagger? He'd been hemming and hawing the entire time they'd shopped for paints, when the younger Ethan had breezed in and grabbed them with barely a single deliberation.

"God's gifts don't fade. If He gave it to you, He won't take it away." Hannah put her hands on his shoulders. "You can do this," she said, as Georgia looked on with Jerry in her arms.

Ethan's shoulders seemed tense, his lips set in a line as he concentrated. "What do you want on this wall?" he asked, clearly still not convinced.

"A vintage Franklin Main Street skyline would be amazing," she said.

They'd picked up a variety of colors at the paint shop. Against the bright white walls and the furniture they were going to refinish, the colors would be a really nice backdrop to showcase the flowers, making the whole room bright and inviting.

"I don't think I can do it."

Georgia looked over at Hannah for an explanation.

"Ethan," Hannah said, walking up next to him. "You can do this."

Ethan folded his arms and shook his head, staring at the empty wall. Finally, he faced Hannah. "I'm sorry. I'm not doin' this." He started stacking the cans of paint against the wall.

"Ethan, you're the best. I need the best for this."

"I'm not the best anymore," he said through gritted teeth. "I've left the guys at the garage shorthanded, and I've gotta get back. I'll walk if I have to."

"It's just the one painting," she said, trying to think of anything to help. She stood in front of him and looked into his eyes. "We've both changed, I know that," she said gently. "A lot of time has passed since we were partners in crime." She allowed a nostalgic smile. "But when I look at you, I see *you*, not only the guy in your dad's uniform. That's just a part of your life. But there's so much more to you than that one thing." She reached down and grabbed a paintbrush, holding it out to him. "I trust you. Now trust yourself, because you're absolutely fantastic."

His jaw clenched harder the more she talked, his whole body tensing up. "Hannah, I need you to respect the fact that, the same way you're not that girl I drove home from school with her boots propped up on the dashboard of my truck, I'm not that kid who drove you home. And while those parts of us are in our pasts, neither of us is the same, and we will never be those people again."

He strode over to the door. "You'll find something else to put on that wall." He opened the door and left.

"Why did he walk out?" Georgia asked, her words tender, clearly affected by the exchange he and Hannah had just had.

"I thought if he just got in here…" She gazed up at the blank wall. "Let's make a list of the other things we need done, and then we'll get started on those," she said. "I'll work on Ethan."

Hannah's phone suddenly went off in her pocket with a message from Liam asking, *What are you doing tonight?*

She texted back, *Georgia is here with me. She's staying at Gran's. We were planning to work at Gran's shop. Why?*

I was wondering if you'd like to go out to dinner with my mother, Noah, and me—my treat. You could bring Georgia with you. Would you all be free tonight?

"Well, that's a surprise," Hannah said.

"What is it?"

"Are we free to go to dinner with Liam?" Hannah asked, glad for the distraction after what had just transpired with Ethan.

Georgia had moved over to the back door and was letting Jerry out on a leash. "Of course," she said. "That's really kind of him."

"I'll text him that we can, then. It'll be nice to meet his mother and see Noah again." Her fingers were already moving on her phone screen.

"He'll meet us downtown at six," she said, reading his response when it came in, "so I suppose we should get home and get cleaned up. We'll pick up where we left off tomorrow."

They gathered up their things and turned off the lights. As Hannah shut the door, that blank wall glared at her. "We've still got a lot of work to do," she said, thinking about Ethan.

"It'll all work out," Georgia said.

"I hope you're right." Hannah locked the door behind them.

Mary McGuire was a tiny thing, shuffling across the street next to Liam in navy-blue flats coordinated with her tailored belted coat, while she held Noah's hand.

"So you're the casserole maker," she said when she'd reached Hannah at the door to the corner restaurant.

Noah wrapped his arms around Hannah's legs and gave her a squeeze.

"Hey, buddy," she said, the little boy instantly lightening her mood. "Yes, that's me," she answered Mary. "And this is Georgia."

"Lovely to meet you, Georgia," Mary said.

Liam held the door to let them all in, the lamplight and candles giving the whole place a warm, cozy glow against a backdrop of black-and-white photos of town residents through the years that peppered the walls. He gave his name to the hostess, who walked them over to their table.

Mary turned her focus to Hannah, fondness showing in her expression. "Hannah, it's lovely to finally meet you. Liam has told me so much about you."

"He has?" Hannah asked, interested.

Liam pulled out Hannah's chair and she took a seat. "Actually, Noah has," Liam said. "He was very excited to see you tonight."

"I want to sit here," Noah said, pointing to the chair between Hannah and Georgia.

Hannah scooted it away from the table to allow Noah to climb onto it.

The waitress put a child's paper menu with a pack of crayons in front of Noah and took their drink orders.

"Why don't we all share a bottle of wine?" Mary suggested. "I'm feeling festive. It's so lovely to be out with family and friends."

"Of course, Mom. What are you thinking—red or white?"

"What would you ladies prefer?"

Hannah and Georgia both shook their heads politely, sending the choice back over to Mary.

"I'm fine with either," Hannah told her. "What's your favorite?"

"We should have Mickey's red then, and our little guy will have milk," Mary said to the waitress, who hurried off to fill their orders.

"Mickey's?" Hannah asked, having not heard of that wine before.

Noah pushed his menu closer to Hannah and handed her a crayon. Then he wrote an X in the center of the tic-tac-toe board printed on it. Hannah marked her O.

"Mickey Jones has a very exclusive private winery down the road from our farm," Mary explained. "No one knows this, but he drops off only a couple of bottles here every day, and if you know to ask for it, they serve it, but for everyone else it's off-menu."

"I feel like James Bond," Georgia said with a sparkle in her eye, making Mary chuckle.

"So I've heard about Hannah and how she's here to visit her grandmother. Georgia, what brings you into town?" Mary asked.

The waitress returned from the bar nearby with a bottle, offering a taste for Mary before pouring them each a glass. Hannah took a sip of the deliciously fruity and aromatic wine.

"I'm here to find my parents," Georgia said.

Mary looked on, captivated. "Oh?"

"I was adopted, and the agency can't give me anything to go on, but I have a couple of photos."

"Oh wow," Mary said, leaning forward on her forearm and taking a sip of her wine with her other hand, enthralled.

"Yes, but no names, sadly. My dad dropped the photos off, apparently. He and my mother had signed a document statin' that I couldn't find out who my parents were, but a few years later, he came back to the agency and slipped the photos to the woman at the front desk, tellin' her to give 'em to me if I ever came looking. I suppose I was just hopin' he'd had a change of heart." She grabbed her handbag and rummaged around in it. "Would you like to see the photos?" She handed them over to Mary.

"And what if they haven't—what will you do?" Mary asked, looking down at the photos. She smiled at the one with the baby before handing them back to Georgia.

"I haven't thought that far," Georgia said. "But even if I don't find them, I'm glad I came because I got to meet you, Liam, Hannah, and her parents. Hannah's been so nice, letting me work in her grandmother's shop. We've had an absolute blast…"

"Oh yes," Mary said, addressing Hannah. "Liam tells me your grandmother owns the local florist's, is that right?"

"Yes."

"Are you still considering closing?" Liam asked, taking a sip from his wine.

"Well, Georgia and I have been brainstorming and we're completely redoing the whole place. I think it will really surprise Gran, and hopefully revitalize the business and bring in some new customers."

"It's gonna take a lot of customers to cover the spike in rent," Georgia added, "but it's worth a try."

Liam's attention seemed to sharpen at the mention of Hannah fixing up The Memory Keeper.

"How lovely," Mary said. "I'm not sure how I could help, but I always have a supply of fresh, seasonal fruit and vegetables… and I make a mean lemonade recipe."

"Actually, Gran always offered muffins and lemonade to her customers. I'd love to feature your farm's lemonade. That would really give it a local flair."

"Oh, that's a great idea," Georgia chimed in.

"I'd be delighted to help," Mary told them.

The waitress came to take their food orders and only then did Hannah notice the undecipherable look on Liam's face. What was it—uncertainty? Was he wondering if she'd stay in Franklin, or was something else on his mind specific to Gran's shop? He'd been acting differently ever since she'd mentioned it.

"You okay?" Hannah asked.

"Yes," he said, pushing a smile across his face. He picked up his menu. "Ladies first," he offered to the waitress so she could take their orders.

Chapter Twenty-Four

Just after the sun came up the next morning, while Georgia stayed back at The Memory Keeper to design the display window, Hannah went to see Gran. Since Georgia hadn't had any luck finding her birth parents, Hannah took the photos of Georgia's family with her to see if Gran knew anything about them, by chance.

"The woman I rode from the airport with—Georgia—she wanted me to show you these photos to see if you recognized the people in them." Hannah slipped them out of her wallet and handed them over to Gran.

"Could you get my glasses off the table, dear?" Gran asked, setting the photos on the white knit blanket that covered her legs. When Hannah handed them over, Gran took a closer look. "No," she said, inspecting them. "I'm sorry to say that I don't." She handed them back.

Disappointed for her friend, Hannah put them back into her wallet. "That's okay," she said. "I feel bad for Georgia. She really just wants to find her people."

Gran chuckled. "That's all any of us want." She smoothed the blanket. "How's the shop?" she asked.

Hannah moved the walker Gran had been using to get around the hospital out of the way, and sat down in a nearby chair. "I've got everything under control," she said, not wanting to tell her much to spoil the surprise, but at the same time wanting to set her mind at ease. "I've been working hard to get it into shape, and I've even gotten a local farmer to provide some fresh lemonade for your customers."

"Oh, Hannah, that's lovely," Gran said, sitting up straighter. "And how's Speckles?"

"I've made sure milk has been put out for her every day," Hannah said carefully, not wanting to tell her that she'd had to dump the milk at the end of the day because it had gone untouched.

"I knew you would come through for me," she said, leaning back with a satisfied crossing of her arms. "And how are *you*, my dear?"

"I don't know, Gran," Hannah answered honestly. "I don't know what I'm meant to be doing anymore."

"What do you mean?"

"I've worked really hard to get where I am in my job in New York, and I've been very successful… But there's a problem with one of the projects I'm working on and something occurred to me. I'd been avoiding the problem, not even wanting to think about it or try to figure it out—that's not like me. I should be leading, but instead I've been sidestepping."

"You're just giving yourself time to process what you really want," Gran said. She always had the kindest ways to spin things. "And you've been a bit frazzled in the last day or so. Give yourself a break."

"I've been pulled back into my old life, and all of a sudden, here I feel like I'm alive," she confessed. "I'm still that same woman from New York, but she feels comfortable here, too."

"We feel the most alive when we are doing the things God intended for us. Just because you're here doesn't mean you have to become the girl who grew up in this town. You've changed, Hannah. But that's not necessarily a bad thing."

"Are you saying I should be here and not in New York?" she asked.

"I'm saying you should give yourself permission to be where you thrive the most."

"I wish I knew for sure where that was."

"You'll figure it out. I have no doubt about that."

"Wait a minute!" she said, beginning to pace the room as an idea came to her. "The magazine feature photos should depict how we find our people..." She rushed over to Gran's bedside, kissing her. "You are amazing!" she said, giddy. "Thank you!"

Gran laughed. "I'm not sure what I've done, but you're welcome."

Hannah burst through the door of The Memory Keeper. She grabbed Georgia and spun her around, making Jerry bark and come tapping over to them, climbing Georgia's leg.

"I have the best idea," Hannah said. "I've had an awful time with this project at work, and I think I can fix everything, but I'll need your help! And then I'll be able to put all my focus on getting the shop ready for customers."

"What is it?" Georgia asked.

"I need your photography skills. Would you help me?"

"Of course," Georgia said. "What are we doing?"

"I have to call Liam. I want to ask him if you and I can come over and take photos of his family and Mary's farm. I can already see about ten to twenty shots in my head," she said. "The oak tree in the middle of the field, the front porch with its rocking chairs, all the hand-painted signs labeling each set of crops... There's so much out there."

"Call Liam to see if he'll do it," Georgia said, excited. "I'll keep painting."

Hannah dialed his number, pacing around eagerly. When he answered, she explained everything.

"He said yes! I'm going over right now to scout locations," she told Georgia. "Once I have an idea of what I want, you and I can go shoot it. Sound good?"

"Absolutely. Somehow you've managed to get me a job as a photographer for *Farmhouse Living*," she said with a squeal.

"If this works, you could be the *lead* photographer for *Farmhouse Living*."

Georgia stared at her wide-eyed for a second, before slapping an excited hand over her mouth.

If Hannah's hunch was correct, Georgia might have just helped save her career.

"Are y'all gonna be okay out there in the freezing cold?" Mary asked, folding her arms across her chest as she shivered while Hannah and Liam walked around the farmhouse.

"We'll be fine, Mom," he assured her. "We won't be out that long."

"All right," Mary said. "I'll put on a pot of coffee for when you two come in."

"Thanks," Hannah told her, while she opened the sketchpad she'd bought on the way over to a clean page.

"Let's have a look at the barn first," Liam suggested. He led the way down the long dirt path. The ground was soft under their feet. "I used to climb that tree when I was kid," he said, pointing to a maple tree at the edge of the path. Its branches stretched endlessly, the trunk so large that Hannah wouldn't be able to get her arms around it. A low-hanging branch gave her an idea.

"I wonder if we could do a generational photo on this tree with you and Noah. Would you be okay doing that?"

"And be in a national magazine?"

"Yes," she said, offering a cheesy please-say-yes grin. "You both have the perfect look for magazines."

"Are you flirting with me?" he teased, a smirk emerging at the corner of his lips.

Hannah laughed. "Call it what you want."

He eyed her playfully, raising his eyebrows. "You aren't saying no." He grabbed the branch of the tree, looking up to the top of it. "I'm going to tell everyone you said I look like a magazine model." He hit a pose, making her laugh again.

"Wait," she said, her drawing pencil poised above her sketch paper. "Stay just like that." She dragged her pencil across the paper, quickly outlining the tree and then placing him in position as he was. But then she added Noah, sitting on the branch, his legs dangling over it, Liam looking up fondly at his son. She turned the pad of paper around and showed Liam her idea.

He broke pose, astonishment on his face. "Wow," he said. "That's amazing. You're clearly great at what you do."

"I don't know," she said, shrugging it off.

He took her hand. "Come on. Let me show you the barn—I think it'll be right up your alley. I built it with my dad."

Liam led her to the brick-red structure. He tugged on one of the large doors, sliding it open. "My mom uses this for parties," he said as they stepped inside. He clicked on a light switch.

Hannah gasped, her mouth dropping open. "This. Is. Perfect!"

An enormous chandelier hung from the ceiling, sparkling like a rare jewel above them. Bales of hay were stacked against the walls and lining the cement floor, acting as chairs for the rustic whiskey-barrel tables. One of them held two glasses and a bottle of wine. She pointed to them questioningly.

"Local," he said, popping the cork and pouring them each a glass.

She took the offering and tipped it up against her lips. A rush of fruity nectar mixed with the bite of alcohol tickled her taste buds. "I'm supposed to be working," she teased.

"You are," he said, patting the top of the barrel. "Draw what you envision for this space. I want to see."

Hannah took another drink of her wine and then went to work, sketching her suggestions for Georgia's photos. Her pencil flying over the paper, the ideas were coming faster than she could draw them.

"I had no idea you were so creative," he said.

She turned her sketch around for him to view. In the drawing Liam sat on a block of hay in the center of the room under the chandelier, with Noah on his knee, teaching his son how to play guitar.

He studied it for a moment. "Alison was the teacher of the two of us. One time, she and I talked about how she'd wanted to teach Noah to eat with chopsticks when he got older… It seemed so silly a thing to consider at the time, but now I always think about who will teach him how. I've never used chopsticks… You know, when Alison died and I grieved for her, Noah was so young, and he didn't understand. Raising him is challenging and terrifying. Noah was fussy—he had tantrums, cried out with nightmares in the night, but he wouldn't allow me to comfort him."

"He was heartbroken too," she noted.

"I know. And I just froze. A friend recommended our nanny, and when she intervened, it provided the relief I needed to move through my grief, but then I didn't know where I belonged in his life. So I threw myself into work, building the business with Alison's brother."

A moment of hesitation flickered across his face, but it was gone before she could make out the reason for it.

"Because," he continued, "if the role I had was breadwinner, then I was going to be the very best provider for Noah that I could be. Alison grew up quite wealthy, and I felt like I had to prove myself, both for her memory and for Noah."

"You put a lot of pressure on yourself," she said.

He nodded. "I just want the people I care about to know they're loved."

Hannah put her hand on his arm. "I think Noah might have felt more loved by you at the tire swing and dancing in the kitchen than he has any other time."

"Yes," he agreed. "But I needed you to show me how to do it. You're so good with him—different from his nanny."

"How so?" she asked, interested to hear his answer.

"Elise is sort of like a schoolteacher. Your interactions are more natural. Like a mother would be."

The pang that surfaced whenever she allowed herself to think about motherhood washed over her.

"He really enjoys you," Liam told her. He took a drink from his glass and gazed at her, the vulnerability in his face undeniable. "I enjoy you too," he admitted.

A flutter spread through her like wildfire. Liam was so different from Miles. He listened to her, and he was open and honest. "You're pretty great yourself," she said.

As Hannah stood in the middle of that barn with Liam, New York just didn't feel like the right place for her. She was falling for Liam, but he and his adorable child would be heading back to Charleston in the coming days. Just when things were starting to feel right.

Chapter Twenty-Five

September 7, 1943

I could scream with happiness! I've quit my job at the metal company. I just walked right out. Minnie gave me a job with full wages at her floral shop! I'll be working five days a week with two whole days off! I told Warren all about it, and he said he's going to call my parents and ask if he can take me to dinner to celebrate! I couldn't be more excited. And this will give me more time to chat with him. I like our talks. We discuss art and music instead of the politics of war like my parents do. He reads me things I'd have never considered before, and I simply want to soak in every word he has to tell me.

Hannah closed Gran's journal and set it on the dresser in her room, as daybreak pushed its way through the bedroom window. Things certainly did happen for a reason—look at Gran now. Hannah's need to make The Memory Keeper a success felt stronger after reading Gran's words firsthand. Pop-pop and the shop were Gran's happily ever after, and Hannah couldn't bear to watch Gran spend her last years knowing things hadn't turned out like she'd hoped.

Her gaze fell upon the open closet door, noticing her old riding boots. She didn't know Gran had kept them. They were the shorties she used to love to ride in. The sides were still dirty from the last time she'd ridden, causing a memory to surface.

Eighteen-year-old Hannah put her dusty boot up on the fender of Ethan's Bronco, which they'd driven around in all summer after he'd cashed in his life's savings in lawn-cutting money for the hunk of tin he'd sworn he'd restore one day. Hannah fiddled with the hem of her jeans until they felt comfortable around the leather of her boot and then, for good measure, she stomped her foot on the gravel path leading to the old horse barn to shimmy the denim down into place.

The sun had slipped below the horizon, and the lightning bugs danced around them as they stood between the two wide cornfields on Ethan's grandparents' property out in the country. The small plot of land boasted a barn and a grazing area for Ethan's horses, Flash, Emma, and Nugget. Hannah secured her hair with the tie that had kept it out of her eyes earlier today while she'd been riding Flash, her favorite of the three, and jumped into Ethan's truck.

"Why would you ever want to leave here?" He stretched his hand out the open window, adjusting his side-view mirror to keep the reflection of the bright-orange sunset from blinding him as it peeked from between the rolling Tennessee hills sliding past them.

Thinking about it now, she wasn't so sure why anyone would want to leave…

"Whatcha thinking about, snugabug?" her father said from the doorway, before he came in and sat down next to Hannah on Gran's bed. He used to call her snugabug when she was little, the name catapulting her to simpler times.

"I don't know," she said on an exhale. "Life, I suppose."

"You've had a huge amount of change in a very short time," Chuck said with a doting pat on the leg. "You keep pushing forward, giving your all to the next thing, before you've tackled what's in front of you."

"I thought my job in New York was a culmination of everything I've ever wanted, and all I've worked for. But when I'm home, it seems so far away from who I want to be…" She grabbed a throw pillow and hugged it to her abdomen before lying back on the bed in defeat. "I thought I had my life all figured out."

"Wanna know a secret? None of us have our lives figured out. Life isn't stagnant; it doesn't stop until you get to the end. It's an ever-changing dynamic of experiences and desires. The key is to try to do the best you can for yourself in every moment, and listen to your inner voice when it tries to tell you something."

"But that's just it." Hannah sat back up. "I'm not sure what I want anymore. I think more and more that I want to be here, running Gran's shop, but I haven't figured out how the rest of it fits."

"Then keep going on the path you're on, and listen as you go."

"I've never gone through life without a solid plan. Is that wise?"

"Sometimes you have to tread water for a while, waiting for the next wave, so that when it comes, you'll be prepared to ride it in."

"I suppose you're right," she said.

"I'm always right," he said with a wink. "Come on in for breakfast. Georgia's already up, and your mother's made pancakes. The weather's gloriously warm today, so she's setting up on the table on Gran's back porch."

"Pancakes and sunshine both sound delicious." She stretched, eyeing the boots again and wondering how they'd look with her designer jeans. With a deep breath, she got up, ready to face the day.

*

"What is it?" Georgia asked from behind her sunglasses, when Hannah's old boots came to a stop in the middle of the sidewalk on Main Street. Jerry pulled on his leash before turning around to see what the problem was.

Hannah peered into the window at the local bakery to view the flier posted inside. They were on their way to The Memory Keeper to meet with the reporter who was doing the story on the shop and, to take advantage of the appearance of nice weather, Hannah had asked if they could walk into town this morning. "Dance lessons." She pointed to the yellow sheet of paper. Setting her bag full of the supplies they'd picked up onto the sidewalk, she ran inside, grabbing one of the fliers off the counter as well as another for the upcoming Spring Festival, and stuffed them into her bag when she came back out.

"You want to take dance lessons?"

"Nope, but I will."

"Did the barista slip somethin' *special* in your coffee this morning?" Georgia eyed her.

Hannah laughed. "No. Ethan's wife Christie wants to be a dancer. I was going to call around to see if I could find her dance lessons, but then this appeared. I'm gonna call for an introductory class."

"Sounds fun," Georgia said as they started walking again. "Oh, let's not forget to stop and pick up the baskets we ordered to replace the silver buckets." They'd decided the baskets would give the shop a more laid-back, comfortable feel.

"The home interiors shop is just down here," Hannah said. "So did you find out if Mary had a suggestion for who could make the ladder for us?"

"Yes!" Georgia said. She reached down and stroked Jerry's head. "She actually said she has an old ladder up in her barn that would be absolutely perfect. She's going to see if Liam can adapt it to work on the track."

Hannah paused to focus on Georgia. "Oh, that's wonderful!"

"Yes! So we need to get those baskets so we can unpack the flowers."

They passed the road where Ethan's parents lived, and Hannah couldn't help but peer over at the house, noticing Ethan's truck there. "Would you feel comfortable picking up the baskets for me?" She checked the time on her phone—they still had an hour before the reporter came. "I'm going to walk to Ethan's parents' house to see if I can try one more time to convince Ethan to do our skyline painting."

"Think you can?"

"I have no idea, but I won't know until I try."

"The heck you doin'?" Ethan said as he came out onto his parents' front porch.

"Persuading you to paint Gran's shop," Hannah said from the driver's seat of his old truck. She had the door open and her boots propped up on the dash next to the steering wheel as she sipped her coffee.

His gaze flickered to the dusty shorties and then up to her face. "Well, I ain't gonna do it." His lips were set in a defensive pout, but his affection for his best friend showed in his eyes.

"I'm not getting out of this driver's seat until you tell me yes."

"Looks like you'll be doin' a lot of drivin' then. I need to be at work in five minutes. Better put those old boots on the gas pedal."

She swung her legs down to the ground and twisted toward him. "If this is about me leaving all those years ago, you don't need to punish Gran for that. I'll take the full brunt of it."

Unsaid thoughts flashed across his face.

"It's my fault, Ethan. Not Gran's," she pressed.

"It's bigger than you leavin'," he said.

"What is it then?" She stood up to face him. "Tell me. I'm your best friend."

He shook his head, walking off, but then stopped and turned back. She walked over to him. "Tell me, please."

He tipped his head back as if the answer were above him. Then he looked her straight in the eyes. "Growin' up, you gave me hope that my life could be different, that I could be somethin' more than a small-town guy in my dad's shop—I loved the way you thought. I'd never met another person in this town who had that kind of fire for life. Your dream was New York but mine was even bigger than that. And yes, when you left, it took the wind out of my sails. My boat stopped, Hannah—dead in the water. But I still held on to that possibility. And when Christie got pregnant and I had to be able to support my family, my future was laid out in front of me. Paintin' reminds me of the life I'd hoped for but didn't get to live. I know I can still paint. I get that. But if I paint, I'm worried I'll resent the life I've got, and Christie and Wesley don't deserve that."

Without warning, Hannah pressed her hand to his chest as he looked on curiously. "I still feel that heart of yours beating," she said.

"I hope so," he said.

"If your heart's still beating, then you're definitely alive, and whatever life you want is out there for the taking. You've just gotta make it happen."

"Easy for you to say," he said, clearly frustrated. "This ain't the shiny land of opportunity like that big city you come from. You waltz in here with these grand ideas with no one to worry about but yourself. Sure, it's easy as pie for you to change your life. But what if I can't put food on the table for Wesley? That would kill me."

"What if you *can* provide for him?" she challenged. "You're choosing the safest route, which is commendable, Ethan. But you're also ignoring your God-given talent. You owe it to yourself *and* your family to explore that. You don't have to quit your job. Just do what you love as often as you can, and your path will be made clear."

That last sentence gave her pause. She sounded like Gran.

"You done?" Ethan asked, reclaiming her focus. "At this rate, I'ma throw you in the back and take you with me, so you can explain to my father why I'm late."

"It's your choice, Ethan, but you could agree to do this one painting and then decide if it's something you want to keep doing."

He didn't answer, so she upped the stakes. "I'll tell you what. If I can get Christie to do dance lessons, will you paint The Memory Keeper for me?"

"What?"

"I'm serious. I want to try to convince your wife to dance."

"Good luck," he said with an indignant chuckle.

"Deal?"

He blew air through his lips. "Deal, I guess."

Hannah threw her arms around him, and squealed, "I love you," making him laugh.

"Don't love me until I paint somethin' decent," he said. "And I need a firm yes from Christie before I even pick up a paintbrush. I ain't agreein' to your harebrained ideas unless she does too."

"Absolutely."

"Now, can I go to work?"

"Yes," she said with a giant grin.

"Want a ride to the flower shop?"

"I'd love that." She gave him one more quick squeeze, and then got in on the other side of the truck, putting her old boots on the dash like she had when she was a girl.

"Those look amazing!" Hannah said, as Georgia switched out the old silver buckets for the baskets they'd bought.

"I'm glad you like them," Georgia said, turning her head to the side and squinting one eye to examine the display's straightness.

"I'll check with Liam after work to see if he can do anything with that ladder," Hannah offered.

"I love coming into this shop with you," Georgia said, as she placed a container filled with water in the bottom of each basket. She grabbed a handful of red roses and placed them inside it. "Look how great that looks!" She stepped back and admired her work. "I feel like I have purpose here."

"I'd love to talk to Gran about giving you a job if you'd want it. But we have to become profitable first."

"You would? Oh, I'd love that."

"Then we'd better start making some money," Hannah teased, wiping a vase with a towel to get the dust off of it. "I think that on the heels of the article we're doing for the paper, the Spring Festival would be our best shot to pull in some serious business and get the word out." She retrieved the flier from her bag and held it out to Georgia.

"But that's in three days," Georgia said, peering down at the paper.

"I know…" Hannah chewed on her lip. "And I was also wondering if you'd like to run a display for the festival. We could put a table with some bouquets under our vendor's tent outside."

"You want me to run it?"

"Yeah. I figured you could make little bouquets of some sort for the festivalgoers, and I can be in the shop for anyone who comes in with bigger orders. I'd pay you... You interested?"

Georgia jumped up and down, clapping her hands. "That sounds amazing. Thank you for letting me do this."

"I'm glad you're excited." Hannah looked around the shop, remembering the grievance bouquets Minnie had thought of during the war. "I wish we could find something unique to offer at the festival..." She eyed the different flowers, trying to figure out what they could sell that would be exclusive to what they usually had in the shop. Then suddenly an idea came to her. "What if we did tiny take-away bouquets, and we offered an artful keepsake notecard with a photo of the bouquet with each one?"

"Flowers are forever..." Georgia said.

"No. *Memories* are forever."

"That's perfect."

"Okay," Hannah said, feeling the push to get the shop ready. "We've got three days." She dropped the dusting towel onto the counter. "I'll be back. I've got some business to take care of with Christie Wright."

Hannah set a bottle of water on the grocery checkout in front of Christie.

"Just this?" Christie asked, clearly more questions on her mind than that one.

"And this." Hannah flattened the dance lesson flier onto the conveyor belt.

"You buyin' a piece of paper?" she asked.

"Nope. I'm buying the lessons *on* that piece of paper."

"You learnin' a new skill?"

"You are."

"And when am I supposed to find time to do that?"

"Look." Hannah pointed to the time listed on the flier. "It's only once a week to start. I'll watch Wesley for you if you need me to do that."

A woman who'd stepped up behind Hannah, holding a loaf of bread and two bags of shredded cheese, cleared her throat.

"Say yes," Hannah said, handing Christie her credit card to pay for the water.

Christie swiped it, ripping off the receipt and handing it to Hannah with her card. "You're holdin' up my line," she said.

"Then say yes," she repeated.

The lady behind Hannah coughed and shuffled on her feet.

"The first class is the day after tomorrow. I'll pick you up," Hannah said, as she headed out the sliding doors. "I'll get us both registered."

Christie rolled her eyes, but she hadn't said no, which was a good sign.

"Whatcha doing, Hannah?" Noah asked, walking across their farm toward her as Hannah unlatched the tailgate of her father's truck and jumped up in the back.

After Hannah and Georgia had met with the reporter and finished up for the day at The Memory Keeper, Hannah had called Liam to arrange a time for her and Georgia to do the photo shoot, and to make sure the whole family was okay with being in the shots. While they chatted, she'd suggested they surprise Noah with a game of baseball. The parks office had hooked her up with everything—batting helmets, gloves, bats, and field equipment. She just had to return it by sundown. When Liam reached her, she lifted the bucket of baseballs over the side and handed it to him.

"Baseball," she said, tossing the bases onto the grass with a smack.

Liam set the bucket down onto the field, which had been cut short to give the ground a chance to rest before they planted crops for the next season. He reached in and grabbed a glove, sliding the well-worn leather over his hand and pinching it closed as if he were catching a ball.

Hannah handed him both a child's bat and an adult bat, grabbed a couple of batting helmets and hopped down. Then she put a few balls into the pockets of the new joggers she'd bought at the boutique in town. She grabbed the pitcher's mound and ran to the center of the field to set it up.

"You can pitch?" Liam called over to her. He looked as excited as his son.

"There's a reason my best friend growing up was a boy," she replied. She took a ball out of her pocket, reared back, and sent it sailing toward him in a straight shot.

Liam reached up and caught it in his glove, causing Noah to gasp.

"Can I catch one?" Noah asked.

"Sure!" Hannah called over to him. "Grab a glove."

Liam handed Noah the little league glove and showed him how to squeeze it to catch the ball.

"Do you want one in the air or a ground ball?" Hannah asked from the pitcher's mound.

"I'll try a ground ball," Noah replied.

"Okay! Let your dad show you how to catch it like an alligator. Show him, Liam."

She couldn't hear from way over there, but she knew exactly what Liam was saying because her father had taught her the same way. Her dad had explained that she had to get in front of the ball, put her glove on the ground, and keep it open like the mouth of an alligator, chomping on the ball the minute it hit her glove.

Noah was squatting down, his mitt ready. "Here it comes!" Hannah rolled it in a slow, straight line right to him and Noah scooped it up, jumping around and cheering, making Liam laugh.

"Y'all want to help me set up the bases?" Hannah asked.

"Yes!" Noah ran over to her with his glove still on his hand.

The three of them assembled the makeshift baseball field, and then Liam held a bat out for Noah. "Ready to hit a few baseballs?" he asked as Noah got into position. Liam stood behind Noah, bringing his arms around his son, placing his hands on Noah's to show him where to grip the bat. He explained where to put his feet and then he pointed at Hannah.

Hannah sent a slow pitch to Noah and he missed.

Liam swooped right in to coach his son, and Noah looked up at Liam, nodding, then cocked his bat up, ready to hit. Liam offered one more quick pointer before Hannah tossed another pitch.

Noah swung and smacked the ball. It rolled on the ground to second base.

"Wow!" Hannah said, running after it. "I think you might have some hitting skills! Most kids use a tee at your age."

Noah puffed his chest and, for the first time Hannah had witnessed, he turned to his father to share in the excitement rather than Hannah. Her heart sang with joy at the sight.

Chapter Twenty-Six

Hannah woke up in the morning still thinking about playing baseball yesterday. She couldn't remember the last time she'd spent a whole evening outside. She, Liam, and Noah had had so much fun, hitting balls until the sun had completely disappeared.

Wondering what time it was, she reached over to Gran's bedside table, grabbed her phone, and peered at the screen, sitting straight up in bed when she noticed the date. Today, she was supposed to be flying home from Barbados. She'd completely forgotten to schedule her return flight to New York. While that was fine, the fact that she had to work in a few days wasn't. She'd purposely taken more days' vacation than she'd needed for her trip to Barbados, to ensure she had enough rest and time to be prepared when she was back to the grind on her first day in the office, but she was going to need more. She'd figure it out in a bit. She wasn't going to start her day in a frenzy over work.

Hannah set her phone back on the table and picked up the journal. She couldn't wait to see Gran today. She decided to read a quick entry before getting up and ready.

December 23, 1943

I am utterly in love with Warren Townshend. Things have certainly changed for me this year. Warren is graduating from the University of Kentucky this spring, and he's found a job at a historical concert auditorium in Nashville. It's supposed to be pretty great, having sold out so many shows that it needed to move to a larger venue. The change in venue location opened up a position for Warren—they need someone to research the history of the place, create tours and curate memorabilia. He just got word today that he'd been given the job, and he came straight over to tell me. When I became sad about him leaving, he told me not to worry. He took me to the soda fountain, and we sat on the same two stools where we'd met. Warren ordered us both a soda and then he took my hand. Before I even knew what was happening, he'd reached into his pocket, opened a jewelry box with a gold band, and proposed! He'd already asked my father permission and everything! He's found a house in Nashville to rent, and he's even asked around to get the addresses of all the local florists, just for me! So much has changed that I don't even feel like the same person I was before I met Warren. I'm the luckiest woman alive.

Hannah understood what her grandmother had meant about feeling like a totally different person. Ever since she'd arrived, she hadn't had that driving interest in her work deadlines or in keeping up with what was going on in New York. She'd spent all her time enjoying other people. And her heart was full doing that.

Hannah and Georgia walked around the farm, trying to get the perfect scene that Hannah had sketched out earlier. Georgia pulled the camera away and cupped her hand over the lens to view the shot, when a smile spread across her face.

"What is it?" Hannah said.

Georgia focused the camera and took another shot of the porch, peering down at the screen again. "That's gorgeous," she said, turning the screen toward Hannah.

The shot was the whitewashed siding of the farmhouse with one window off center, but there was an unexpected addition that made it the warmest image of them all. Noah's face was in the window, looking out. It screamed personality and gave it the most amazing hometown feel.

"Oh, I love it!" Hannah said.

She waved at Noah, excitement showing on his face.

"This one has to be the focus image of the whole montage. It's just perfect… Let's go in and show it to Liam."

Hannah and Georgia had spent about an hour walking the grounds of the farm, and they'd gotten some really great shots out in the field, so they went in to see if Mary, Liam, and Noah were ready.

Mary answered the door. She was made-up, her face lightly dusted with powder and blush, her lips glossed. She had on a pair of jeans and a white button-down shirt with the sleeves rolled three-quarters up her arm.

"You look perfect for a casual farm spread. I love it," Hannah said. "Thank you so much for letting us do this."

"It's a pretty easy decision if I get to be in *Farmhouse Living*. I had no idea that you worked there, Hannah. I'm so thrilled—I have a subscription to that magazine." Then Mary hunched over with a shiver. "I'm heading inside. Y'all just come in. I'll put a pot of coffee on to warm you up." She walked off toward the kitchen.

"She's such a nice woman," Georgia said quietly from the front door of the farmhouse, as she peered through the lens of her camera.

Georgia snapped a shot, turning it toward Hannah. The photo was spectacular: a shadow of Mary striding down the hallway, flanked by the incoming sunbeams that fell in oranges and yellows onto a beautiful side table with a curling wooden sculpture.

"Stunning," Hannah said, running her hand over the table. Hannah wanted to take her time with this and make Mary proud of the feature. She pointed, directing a side shot of the porch. "What if we get one with the light coming in on the old steps like that?" she asked. "We could pair it with the one you just took."

"Oh, excellent idea." Georgia pointed her camera and snapped, tilting it up and down and capturing a few different angles. She squatted down and twisted the focusing ring, snapping another of the rustic barrel that sat next to the front door.

"Let's take a wider shot of the porch before we head in with Mary," Hannah suggested.

When they got to the kitchen, Mary swished toward them in a country-blue apron with yellow flowers, and handed them each a cup of coffee.

Noah came running in and gave Hannah a bear hug.

"Did you get all the photos you wanted outside?" Mary asked.

"Yes," Hannah replied. "Show her the one of Noah," she said to Georgia, before squatting down to Noah's level. "We got a picture of you in the window."

Noah giggled. "Can I see?"

Georgia showed the shot to Mary while Hannah lifted Noah up to see it.

"That's incredible," Mary said, putting her hand on her chest. "You are certainly talented," she told Georgia.

"What's this about a photo of Noah?" Liam asked, joining them in the kitchen. He was clean-shaven with his hair combed and styled just slightly. He had a well-fitting T-shirt on with a pair of rugged jeans. He leaned over Hannah to see the picture, giving her a jolt of happiness when she caught his scent of cedar and fresh cotton. "Wow," he said.

Mary bent down to address Noah. "You're going to be in a magazine," she said to her grandson.

Noah's eyes grew round. He pumped his little fists.

"Let's celebrate everyone being home," Mary said. "Coffee's ready, and I've got heavy cream, milk, and my secret spice."

"Secret spice?" Georgia asked as they followed her to the table.

Hannah took a seat and Noah climbed up next to her.

"I sell it at the farmer's market," Mary replied, handing her the jar with a label that said *Mary's Secret Spice for Coffee and Cakes*.

Georgia held it up and shook the container. "What's in it?"

"It's a secret," Mary replied with a grin, tapping the label. "But there's cinnamon, cloves, nutmeg, and cocoa powder in it, if that helps you to decide."

"That sounds amazing," Hannah said.

Mary poured them all a steaming cup and joined them at the table, the scent of spice dancing into the air around them.

"So do you run this whole farm all by yourself?" Hannah asked.

"I do. Ever since my husband Harvey passed away. My sister Sarah handles some things remotely for me—she lives in Georgia. But most of it falls upon my shoulders."

Hannah couldn't imagine managing an entire farm by herself.

"It's okay, though," Mary added. "I love it. I built this life with my husband and we raised Liam here... Every late night I spend doing the things Harvey used to do, I feel fulfilled and happy." She threw a teasing look over to Liam. "I keep trying to convince my son to take over when I retire, but he has this wild idea that buying buildings is his future."

"Mom," he said, clearly not wanting to air their differences.

"I just don't understand it," she said anyway with a sad smile. "If you worked less, focused on the farm, it would give you more time with Noah."

Liam didn't reply.

"I'm gonna go color," Noah said, climbing down from his chair. He ran off to another room, which was probably a good thing, given the turn in conversation.

"He needs his father," Mary continued. "I know you have your friends here and it's not really the best time to talk about it, but it needs to be said before you leave. One day, you'll be all he's got." Her eyes glistened with the truth of that statement.

"You're right, we don't need to talk about this now," he said.

"When should we, then?" Mary asked. "The only time you've stopped working lately is when Hannah comes over. And you're amazing with Noah when she's around. Noah tells me about the times you all are together. But you want to run away to some city where you have no roots whatsoever, and for what? To buy up useless buildings."

"I had a similar choice," Hannah intervened, wrapping her hands around her mug. "I could've stayed here in Tennessee and built a life around my family, but instead, I chose to do my own thing. I went off to college in New York and didn't come back until now. I built my life there."

Mary sipped her coffee, pensively listening. "And do you feel like you did the right thing?" she asked.

"At the time, I did. But now I'm not so sure that it was the best thing for me."

"Why not?" Liam asked.

"I've lost time with my loved ones, I didn't keep in touch with my friends… I worked too much."

"That's exactly what I keep telling him," Mary said. "You'll never bond with Noah if you're not at home. Here, you could be near me so I could help with him, and running the farm would give you time to spend with him. Remember when you and your father used to drive the tractor together? All those days you two worked side by side?"

"It's clear that I'm outnumbered here," Liam said, his lips set in a straight line.

"I didn't mean to imply that you aren't doing the right thing," Hannah said, although she did wonder, having witnessed his relationship with his son firsthand.

That sadness she'd seen glimpses of came rushing back over him, and he was closing up right in front of her. Hannah had come into his family's home and ganged up on him without even meaning to. His choices weren't up to her, and she needed to get him by himself so she could properly apologize.

"Can I talk to you for a second?" Hannah asked Liam, nodding toward the doorway.

Mary jumped in, clearly allowing Hannah and Liam time alone. "Georgia, I'd love it if you'd show me all the photos you've taken. Maybe I can get out the cookies I made and you, Noah, and I can all take a look at them."

"Sure," Georgia said, pulling out her camera.

Liam stood up from the table and Hannah followed his lead. He motioned for her to go down the hallway first. "Grab your coat," he said. "Let's take a walk."

The two of them stepped outside and then followed the narrow dirt path that led between the fields. The clouds had given way to a gloriously blue sky, the sun providing just enough warmth to keep the chill at bay.

"I didn't mean to throw you under the bus like that," Hannah said as they walked. "I was trying to explain that I did the same thing, but then my own insecurities about leaving surfaced and I spoke before I'd thought it through. I'm sorry."

"It's fine," he said, but she wondered if it actually was. "My mother is going to have her opinion, no matter what anyone else says. My job keeps me away from the farm, but I can't help it."

"Look, I'm a firm believer in doing what you love—I've been giving that idea a lot of thought, myself. So what do you love so much about your job?" she asked.

She considered what she loved about her career. Initially, it had been the creative outlet, but with her new position, she'd been doing less and less of the creative part, delegating more, and overseeing the process as a whole. It had been her push to get the execs to allow her to accompany the photographer on the shoot, and everything she did creatively these days was because she'd pressed her colleagues to allow her to do it. She'd taken the promotion without even once considering what she would love about it. It had all been about forward movement, her life beginning to take shape the same way Miles's had.

His silence caught her attention.

"I love the security that the income provides," he said finally. "And Alison was going to start the business with her brother, Jonathan. They had the whole thing ready to go when she got sick, so I took over to keep it running."

"That's commendable, and would've been necessary if she'd been able to come back to the job at some point. But it's not up to you to save her business and continue on indefinitely, if that's not what you want to do with your life, right?"

"Sometimes it isn't about doing what you *want* to do. But that aside, it's more about the financial security, anyway."

"That's it?" she asked.

"Financial security is a pretty big deal when I have Noah to think about," he replied.

"Well, I know, but if security is all you're looking for, couldn't you get that working at the farm?"

By the set of his jaw, she seemed to be frustrating him, and she wondered if, despite what he'd said, this had more to do with making Alison proud than job security. "I'm not suggesting you work at the farm. I'm just trying to figure out why your job is so important to you that you spend time away from your son and refuse to take on your birthright."

"You wouldn't understand," he said with an exhale.

"Try me."

Liam began walking. Hannah ran to get in front of him, stopping him.

"I'm asking because I don't understand, not because I *can't* understand," she said, stammering when he strode past her, clearly exasperated. She stumbled to try to get ahead of him again. "Because I think you're pretty awesome, and you've been fantastic with Noah. It makes no sense to me why Noah can't see that side of you every day."

Liam stopped, giving her his guarded attention.

Hannah reached out and took his hands. "Talk to me," she urged.

He hung his head, his gaze moving across the gravel path.

Hannah took a step closer, intertwining her fingers with his. "What is it?"

"I've failed him."

His statement was like a punch in the gut. She realized that while he put a ton of pressure on himself for everything else, he'd also put those same demands on himself as a father, and his fears were clouding reality.

"I don't think you have," she said. "I see him warming up to you. He just needs your permission to do it, and the way you give him that permission is by spending time with him."

To her surprise, he pulled her close to him and wrapped his arms around her. "You make it seem so effortless."

"You don't have to try so hard. Just be with him. Let me help you some more with Noah," she said.

He leaned back and looked down at her.

"The Spring Festival's coming up. Why don't we take him together?" She'd thought about working at the shop during the festival, but she could probably figure something else out. Perhaps her mother could fill in for her and help Georgia. "Let's give Noah another opportunity to see how much fun you are."

"Thank you for having faith in me."

"It's easy to have faith in you. You're a wonderful person."

He opened his mouth as if he were going to tell her something, but then it seemed he thought better of it. Instead, he leaned down and kissed her nose. "Shall we go back in with the others?"

As they walked back down the tire-tread-shaped dirt path, Liam didn't let go of her hand.

"Thank you for allowing me to take photos at the farm today," she said.

"It's no problem. I'm just glad I could help fix the issue at work." He stopped walking. "I should take you out for a drink in the city tonight to celebrate. Would you be up for it?"

"I'd love to."

As they reached the end of the path, she had no idea where it would take them from here.

After the photo shoot, Hannah went to see Gran. When she got to the end of Gran's floor, she met her nurse, Lanelle, at the door to her vacant hospital room. The emptiness was odd, causing Hannah to instantly worry.

"Where's Gran?" Hannah asked, her heart plummeting into her stomach at the thought that something might have gone wrong and Gran had been rushed somewhere. Since their last visit, she'd gotten caught up in registering herself and Christie for dance lessons, chatting with her mom over coffee, and doing her photo shoot when she could've been here. She'd never forgive herself if something had happened to Gran.

"Don't worry, sweet pea," Lanelle said with a smile that enveloped her entire face, making it impossible to have any concern. "Ms. Faye is walking around the unit."

"Wait, walking?" Hannah asked, as a plume of hope rose in her chest.

"Yep. She's been doing so well on her new meds that we have her on an exercise regimen. No walker at all."

"Really?" Hannah nearly shrieked. She couldn't help herself. She threw her arms around Lanelle, who gave her a big squeeze right back.

"She's doing great."

"How great? Like coming-home-soon great?"

Lanelle let out a laugh of happiness that ballooned from her contagiously. "We've got her on some new heart medication, and if she tolerates it, she can go home." She held up a finger. "On *one* condition, however. She won't be able to work. I know that's gonna make her crazy, but she just can't be on her feet like that. She'll have to take it easy and be sure to take her medication."

"She'll never agree," Hannah worried aloud.

"She has to."

If they could just make enough money to hire Georgia, they'd have enough help to do the work, and Gran could still pop by and enjoy the shop. Hannah didn't know if she'd be able to make it happen, but she'd do everything in her power to try.

Chapter Twenty-Seven

Hannah had done her hair and makeup, and put on the new sweater and boots she'd gotten at a boutique in town, along with her most stylish pair of jeans. She stared at herself in the full-length mirror, as she fiddled with her dangly earrings. When Liam had mentioned drinks, had he meant it to be a date? Or were they just running out to grab a beer at the local bar? She hoped it was a date.

Hannah headed down the hallway to check on Georgia before she left.

"Oh, you look like a million bucks!" Georgia was dressed up more than usual, with her hair pulled into a clip, fine tendrils falling delicately around her face. She'd powdered her nose and was wearing lip-gloss.

"You look nice too. Are you going somewhere?"

"While you and Liam were outside at the farm, Mary and I couldn't stop talking—she's so nice. She was headed into town to grab a few groceries, and since you and Liam are going out, she asked me to come over for dinner. She's picking me up in about ten minutes."

"That's wonderful," Hannah said.

"She's letting me bring Jerry too. I've got his leash, so he won't get lost in the fields chasing after rabbits."

Hannah laughed. "It sounds like you're going to have a nice night."

"Yes!" she said, and then she changed gears. "Hey, before you go, I wanted to ask you about the flower collection in the room I'm staying in."

"My shadow box?"

"Yeah. It's beautiful. I was thinking, wouldn't it be great if we did the whole shop in a vintage floral theme? We could have a whole wall of these shadow boxes opposite the basket wall. With a mural at the back and the old record player out where people could see it, it would be amazing. I could take photos of the arrangements and do up some artsy prints for the tables and display window. I can put a filter on them to make them look vintage…"

"That sounds amazing! It would go so well with the historic town mural I was trying to get Ethan to paint," Hannah said. "Gran used to give names to different arrangements. Wouldn't it be cool if we did the catalog up so each arrangement has a keepsake name?"

"I love your ideas," Georgia replied. "I've already called and gotten a turnaround time on the prints we need for the Spring Festival."

"Oh, that's so great!" There was a knock at the front door and Hannah rushed over to get it. "I can't wait to chat more about this. I'll catch you later." She opened the door and greeted Liam, stepping out into the night.

"Where are we?" Hannah asked, as she and Liam walked uphill on a steep path through a residential area of Nashville.

"You'll see," he said, shifting the backpack that dangled from his shoulder.

When he'd mentioned having drinks in the city, she'd put on her new boots, knowing that the flat heel would be best for walking the city blocks. She was glad for the comfort of them now. They'd parked the car on a side road and taken to the asphalt trail that paralleled the road. They rounded the corner to face another hill, this time flanked by a grassy bank.

"Last one," he said as they began the ascent. "I promise it's worth it."

They climbed the final leg of their journey.

"Close your eyes," Liam said, leading her by the hand. "Hold on to me."

Hannah took careful steps forward across the grass, her eyes squeezed shut, wondering what all this was about. She didn't mind though, with Liam so close behind her, his hands gently on her shoulders, his face near her ear.

"Ready? Open your eyes."

Hannah gasped at the view. "Where are we?" she asked again, breathless at the city skyline in front of her, orange and red streaking the sky like a violent protest to the sun's descent.

"We're seven hundred forty-four feet above sea level," he said from behind her. "It's one of the highest spots in Nashville." He stepped back, pulling out a large plaid blanket from his backpack. It shimmied in a wave as he shook it loose and set it on the ground. Then he took out a camping mug, handing it to her. "Have a seat." When she did so, he draped another blanket over her legs before retrieving a thermos and filling her mug, as well as one for himself.

She leaned over it and inhaled the sweet chocolaty scent. "Hot cocoa?"

He held up a finger to let her know he had something else. Then he rummaged around in the sack and set out a fold-up wooden tray, emptying bags of cheese and crackers, cookies, and rounds of bread, and arranging them into a platter.

"I have marshmallows too," he said.

"You've thought of everything."

"More than you know," he said, holding up a quarter. "Want to guess which hand?" He rubbed his palms together quickly and pulled them apart into two fists. "I've been practicing this," he said with a laugh.

Hannah had no idea which of his hands held the quarter, but she took a guess and tapped his right hand. He opened it. Empty.

"The other one's probably empty too, isn't it?" she asked.

"Nope."

He opened his left hand, but instead of the quarter, a round clear pendant had replaced it. Hannah plucked it from his hand and held it up. Inside the transparent circle was a tiny pressed flower.

"I saw it in town the other day, and it reminded me of your collection, so I bought it for you. It sort of looks like a butterfly, doesn't it?"

She peered down at it, thinking about what Gran had said about caterpillars and butterflies. The time she'd spent with Liam and Noah at the tire swing, playing baseball, reading Noah's bedtime story, and then dancing in the kitchen—she'd made more memories in the last few days than she had in years.

"It's so pretty. Thank you. I wish I could wear it right now."

"I thought of that too," he said, grabbing a box from his backpack and handing it to her.

Hannah opened it to find a delicate silver chain necklace.

Liam helped her get it out of the box. He unfastened it and she slid the pendant on. Then he got on his knees and scooted behind her as she lifted her hair so he could fasten it around her neck.

"Where did the quarter go?" she asked, lovingly adjusting the chain.

"I have no idea," he said with a laugh. "I tossed it somewhere in the grass."

Hannah laughed, fiddling with the pendant, getting acquainted with the feel of it around her neck.

"Thank you for thinking of me," she said.

"Ah, it happens a lot lately." He came back around beside her.

Hannah leaned over and kissed his cheek, lingering there, wanting to kiss his lips but unsure of whether to make the move. Slowly, he turned his head, his lips brushing hers, his breath intoxicating, the warmth of him as his hands found her arms making her lightheaded.

"The problem with kissing you," he whispered, "is that every time I do it, it gets harder to wait until the next time."

He pulled back, and she took in a steadying breath.

"And that's terrifying," he said.

"It shouldn't be terrifying to care for someone," she said.

He sat back, leaning on his hands, confusion written across his face. "I carry this constant weight of needing to make sure that I honor the memory of my wife. But I couldn't get you out of my head, and all I could think about was how soon is too soon? Have I proved to Alison how much her life meant to me yet? It makes moving forward very difficult."

"Remember when we talked about how the universe lines things up? Maybe that's why I got into the car with you at the airport. Perhaps it was a sign to say it's okay."

"I stood there in that shop the other day, staring at the pendant and wondering if I should buy it, and I kept thinking about what might have happened if I'd have mustered the courage to talk to you instead of your friend Morgan all those years ago."

She gazed into his emerald eyes.

Liam put one hand on her face and drew her in, pressing his lips to hers as his other hand moved behind her head, laying her down on the blanket. Under a deep-purple sky, the sun having dipped behind the city skyline, his mouth moved on hers urgently, the feel of it like heaven. Her fingers found his and she laced them together, their breath mixing as their lips moved perfectly together, the clean, spicy scent of him intoxicating, and Hannah knew she didn't ever want to be without this feeling. This was the start of something huge.

Chapter Twenty-Eight

Hannah sat outside in a rocking chair on Gran's porch with her cup of coffee, her laptop on her legs. The morning sunlight filtered past the budding trees in the back yard, giving them all a golden shine. It was shaping up to be a glorious day.

"Hey," Georgia said, coming outside and dropping down in the chair next to Hannah, holding her own cup of joe. Jerry sniffed his way around the porch.

"I just sent the gorgeous photos you took to my art department at work, so they can get them cropped and filtered for the magazine spread. And, uh…" Her heart thumped in her chest just saying it. She swallowed.

Georgia leaned toward her. "What?"

"I sent in my resignation."

Georgia's eyes grew to the size of quarters.

It was the strangest thing. She'd sent over the photos for the new feature, explaining the vision to Amanda and how the new images could replace certain previous ones. Then, as if on autopilot, she opened another email to her boss and told him she'd made the decision to explore other opportunities. She'd sat there stunned for a second, before she realized that her brain had just had to catch up with her heart.

"You what?" Georgia asked.

Hannah nodded in response to Georgia's question, fear and excitement like a whirlwind inside her, making her feel alive. "I gave them my two weeks, but when I said I needed to be here for Gran, my boss responded, telling me that I'd never taken a day off in the entire time I'd worked there until now, and I'd been on call seven days a week for years, so he was going to give me paid leave for the month. Then he wished me luck and happiness in my new life. My assistant director, Amanda, will take over immediately. I couldn't believe it."

"How do you feel?" Georgia asked.

"Nervous," she replied honestly. "But amazing. It's time to start a new chapter in my life."

Georgia crossed her legs underneath her in her chair. "You know, I've been thinking the same thing," she said. "I've been holding on to this need to find people like me, grasping at anything to pin down some reason why my father dropped off those photos. But at the end of the day, my parents signed the veto and didn't want me to find them. Maybe it's because, while they're decent people, and wanted me to see where I came from, they aren't actually *my* people. I look around at you and everyone I've met here in such a short time, and I feel more myself with y'all than I ever have. And I'm arranging flowers, taking photos, designing the shop—all the things I'm good at. It just feels right to stay here."

"I wish I could guarantee that you could work at The Memory Keeper," Hannah said honestly.

"Even if I can't, I know this is where I'm supposed to be. I'll figure it out."

"*We'll* figure it out," Hannah corrected her.

Georgia reached over and gave her a hug. And Hannah knew that this was where she belonged too.

*

"Oh my goodness!" Hannah said, when she came into the shop after stopping by the hospital to see Gran. Liam was on the brand-new rolling ladder he'd converted for them, adjusting the wheel on the old track. "That's gorgeous, Liam!"

"Surprise," he said. "I'm glad you like it." He pulled a pencil from behind his ear, marking something and then putting it back, then looked down at her with an affectionate grin. He pushed against the track and snapped a piece of the ladder in place.

"Any evidence of Speckles?" Hannah asked Georgia as she peered out the back door.

"It looked like some of the milk was gone, but I can't tell for sure," Georgia replied.

Hannah went over to the computer and turned it on, the screen coming to life. She opened the email and perused the incoming messages, stopping at the electronic bill for the rent. She opened it, her good cheer sliding away. "Look at this," she said to Georgia, pulling up the latest remittance on the shop computer. "The lease just went up again."

Liam peered down at her, quiet, interested.

"There's no way we'll have enough to cover the cost of the lease payment *and* turn a profit this month." Hannah felt deflated, like everything they'd worked for so far might be for nothing.

Liam climbed down the ladder, and set his tools and the pencil he'd been using on the counter.

"Why don't you try to call the leasing agent?" Georgia suggested.

Hannah peered at her screen under the Mercer Properties email signature, noting their phone number. "You know what? I think I will."

Liam went over to her but she held up a finger, stopping him. She dialed the number, waiting for someone to pick up.

Just as it started ringing, Liam's phone went off in his pocket, sending her eyes straight to him.

"I had the phone calls transferred to my phone while our receptionist is out," he said. "Mercer Properties is the company I own with Jonathan Mercer, Alison's brother."

Hannah stumbled back a step and hung up, his phone immediately ceasing to ring.

"What?" she asked, needing an explanation. He'd known this whole time that this was Gran's shop, and he hadn't said anything? Not during *any* of the countless times they'd been together. She'd told him they might even have to close, given the rent, yet he'd still sent the latest remittance. He'd even stayed in Gran's house! Why hadn't he offered to do anything?

She prayed there was some kind of explanation other than the fact that it was his company who'd been running Gran's shop into the ground. He was silent just long enough for Hannah to wonder if she'd made a colossal mistake trusting him.

"You?" she asked, hearing the hurt in her question.

"Yes," he confirmed again quietly.

She pulled back, trying to keep her utter disappointment at bay, squared her shoulders, and cut her eyes at him. "I have a complaint about the hike in rent," she said, her voice flat, feeling betrayed.

"I'm so sorry…" He stepped closer to her.

"You own the company—you said yourself—so you can fix this," she said.

After last night, she couldn't believe she was even having this conversation. Wouldn't he want to do whatever it took to make this right, given their growing feelings for one another? Or had he planned the whole time to go back to Charleston without a second thought?

"It's not that simple…"

"So you don't even care if we have to close?" she asked. Her heart felt like it was breaking, this moment adding to the anxiety she already felt from everything else she'd been through.

"That's not fair. The rent isn't any higher than the rest of Main Street," he replied. "I've already spoken to Jonathan about it, and it's just not feasible to bring it down."

She'd witnessed Liam choose work over family, and now she was seeing it firsthand. When it came to his profit, he chose money over people, and right or wrong, she couldn't deal with that right now.

"It's bigger than just this one shop," he said, but his excuse fell flat.

At the end of the day, while she adored the great parts of him, she didn't need this. "You know, I've been with someone before who put building his business ahead of us. I don't want to make that mistake again," she said, feeling the lump in her throat.

"Hannah…" He reached out for her arm, but she pulled back.

"Thank you for the ladder. I'd be happy to pay you for it."

He shook his head, clearly consumed with his thoughts. "That's not necessary," he said, looking up and finally making eye contact. "I'm trying here," he said.

But she wouldn't listen. Trying at what? Yes, he'd let Hannah in, breaking down his walls a bit, but she needed someone who could be there for her through everything. The shop was important to her.

"I'm stuck between a rock and a hard place here," he said. "I tried—"

She stopped him. She didn't want to hear any explanations. Even though she wanted to relent, she stood her ground and shook her head.

"I'll let myself out," he said, defeat in his eyes. He turned around, but she refused to acknowledge the gesture.

And despite the pinch in her chest, she let him go.

Hannah pulled up at Ethan and Christie's rancher on the edge of town. It was neatly kept with a spring wreath on the door that read "Welcome" in pink flowers. She could only see half of it, however, because Ethan was standing in front of it with his hands on his hips. He was wearing jeans that fell over the old pair of paint-splattered riding boots he used to wear when he did his murals.

"I s'pose if you and Christie are off dancin', that means I'd better get paintin'," he said.

"Did I mention how much I adore you?"

"Doesn't matter." He walked up to meet her.

"It hasn't gotten past me that you still have your painting boots," she said.

"Pure coincidence."

"You make me laugh." She shook her head in amusement and slugged him in the arm.

"You'd better watch all the flirtin'," he teased. "Christie's territorial. But that's why I love her. I knew she was the one the minute I met her. You know why?"

"Why's that?"

"'Cause I was chattin' up some random girl at the bar downtown, and Christie walked over to her and said, 'Excuse me, but that man's taken.' I thought she had me mistaken for someone else, but I didn't care—she was so pretty. Then she sat down beside me and bought a beer on *my* tab. I thought she'd lost her ever lovin' mind." Ethan laughed at the memory. "She pointed to the back of the bar and said, 'I've been waitin' over there all night for you to come ask me out, and it's takin' you too long, so I had to take matters into my own hands.' I haven't spent a day away from her since that minute."

"I wish I could've been at the wedding," Hannah said.

"I should've asked you to come. But I was too busy bein' mad at ya."

"You had every right to be mad at me. I was so preoccupied with trying to follow my dreams that I forgot about what really mattered for a while, but I remember now. I promise not to ever forget again."

Ethan nodded, emotion showing on his face. "Well," he said, "I guess I've got some paintin' to do…"

"Thank you. Gran's gonna love it."

Chapter Twenty-Nine

"You're talented, you know that?" Hannah said to Christie, as they walked out to her father's truck after their first dance class. They'd been taught the fundamentals for salsa dancing tonight, and Christie could match her steps to the rhythms like a champ. "You're a natural."

"I'm rusty," Christie said modestly. "And salsa wasn't the style I practiced as a kid. But I like it."

"It won't take you any time to get back up to speed." The two of them climbed into the truck. "I think you should try to teach Ethan."

Christie threw her head back in a loud laugh. "Can he dance?" she asked.

"Your guess is as good as mine," Hannah said, laughing. "One time I made him take me to a school dance because you couldn't get in without a date, and I wanted to hang out with my friends. He left me there and went out the back door of the gym to buy a pizza. I found him sneaking slices to his friends in the locker room. That's about as close to dancing as I've ever seen him."

"Sounds about right," Christie said, rolling her eyes, but her fondness for him was clear.

"Should we go see how he's doing at the shop?"

"Sure."

Hannah put the truck in gear and headed down the road to The Memory Keeper.

"Can I ask you somethin'?" Christie said. "Why are you doin' all this? Let's be honest. Even though I wasn't thrilled with the idea, Ethan would've probably painted the shop if you had kept on about it. You didn't need to pay for dance lessons. So why did you?"

"Because I should've been there. For your wedding, for Wesley's birth, for all of it. You and I should've been friends. You married my *best* friend, and that makes you like family. So now I'm trying to make up for that, I think. When you came into the shop and I realized you thought I was a threat, I couldn't believe it."

"Sorry I jumped to conclusions. I just always worry about whether Ethan is in this for love or duty."

"Before we left for dance class, he told me about the first time he met you," Hannah said as she made a turn toward the shop. "He told me he knew you were the one right away. Ethan doesn't say that about just anyone. I've been his friend through countless girlfriends and breakups, and never heard him say anything like that."

Christie's eyes glistened with emotion. "I always felt like I held him back."

"Not at all." They pulled up at the shop but continued their conversation. "And you can't hold him back, anyway. If either of you have something you want to do, you should try to make it happen together. There's no holding back, but rather lifting up."

"I like that," Christie said. "Thank you."

Hannah turned off the engine. "Let's go see what he's up to, shall we?"

The landscapers had come—the lawn was all spruced up, with flowers in the beds leading down the walk to The Memory Keeper—and the sign was being painted. Knowing Ethan was inside gave Hannah a feeling that things would somehow work out and the shop would be a success, even though appearances weren't the only issue. She opened the door, and she and Christie went inside.

"Oh my gosh, Ethan," Hannah said with a delighted gasp. "That's magnificent."

Christie's mouth hung open. "You did that?" she asked, pointing to the mural. "I had no idea…"

The back wall was alight with a vintage design in tans, oranges, and browns—subtle like an old photo, but full of life and character. The buildings of Main Street curved as if they were musical notes dancing along the wall. Crowds of people filled the doorways and windows. An old truck sat along the curb outside one of the shops. And the sun was setting, drawing long shadows along the road.

Hannah clapped her hands excitedly. "I *knew* you still had it in you!" She walked over to hug Ethan, but he stopped her.

"I'm full of paint," he warned. "You'll ruin your sweater."

"I don't care." She wrapped her arms around him and gave him a squeeze, the cold wet paint soaking through to her skin. Then she turned around. "Christie, I'm coming for you next." She held out her paint-spotted arms. "Thank you for dancing with me and being supportive of Ethan painting this for me."

"That's fine," Christie said, backing away. "Just don't touch me with all that mess on your shirt."

"Oh, come on. You know you want a big hug," Hannah teased.

"Yeah, she does," Ethan said, coming toward his wife.

Christie put her palms up in the air, waving them. "Ethan, if you dare… There's a couch with your name on it!" She started running around the shop as Ethan chased her, making her hoot with laughter.

He caught her and scooped her up, making her squeal, but she wrapped her arms around him and kissed him.

Hannah went over to the old record player and put on a 45-record with a dance beat that would work for their salsa moves. "Let's teach Ethan what we learned, Christie."

With a swipe of white paint on her cheek, Christie grabbed Ethan's hands and pulled him to the center of the room.

"What in the world are y'all doin'?" he asked as Christie moved him into position.

"Dancin'," his wife replied.

"I don't dance," he said, giving her a spin. "But I will for you." He leaned in and kissed her again.

Christie pulled back. "There's plenty of time for all that sweet talkin'," she said. "But right now, we're dancin'. Move your left foot like this," she said, showing him.

As Ethan and Christie danced to the music in the empty shop, the new mural behind them, Hannah caught a glimpse of the freshly painted sign: The Memory Keeper. So many memories were already being made.

"Don't kill me," Georgia said, as Hannah walked up to the front door when she got home. Georgia put Jerry down on the porch, letting him sniff around. He inspected the leg of one of Gran's rocking chairs.

Hannah bounded up the steps. "What's up?"

"I was talking to Mary, and she said that Noah is so excited about going with you to the Spring Festival tomorrow."

Hannah sat down on the porch swing, dismay washing over her as she remembered offering to go with Noah.

"I wasn't sure if you could stomach being with Liam after the rent thing…" Georgia gritted her teeth together in dramatic nervousness. "I'm heading out to see her after dinner, so if you really don't want to, I can think of something to say to cancel."

Liam had hurt her, and the thought of spending an awkward night with him that should have been a blast made her apprehensive, the loss of something wonderful settling on her shoulders. "No, it's fine," Hannah said. "If Noah wants me to go, I'd feel terrible not going." She didn't love the idea of spending an entire afternoon with Liam, but she could be adult about it.

Georgia scooped up Jerry before he headed down the steps into the yard. "Mary will be happy. She seemed just as excited."

"You and Mary have been chatting a lot," Hannah noted.

"Yes." Georgia shifted Jerry into her other arm to open the door, and they went inside. "She's the sweetest woman."

They went into the living room and sat down on the sofa. Jerry curled up in Georgia's lap as Chuck came in and joined them. Jerry perked up at his entrance, jumping down to greet him. Chuck picked up the dog and petted his little head. "Maura's at the grocery store, and I've been dying for some company," he said, plopping down in an overstuffed chair Gran had decorated with a yellow-and-navy-blue throw pillow.

"You know, I told Hannah that I've felt so comfortable around your family since I got here," Georgia replied. "My birth parents brought me into the world, but I have to admit that if I don't find them, while I haven't known you very long, you all feel pretty darn close to family to me. I've never felt like I was a part of something until now."

"So maybe you *did* find your family," Chuck said.

"I think I did," Georgia said.

"I think she did too," Hannah added. "And I'd love it if she could work at The Memory Keeper."

Chuck looked over at her. "Georgia told me about the genius idea for the mini bouquets and photos you're gonna take tonight for the festival. But she certainly doesn't want to work for free," he said, grinning in solidarity with Georgia. "I mean, a Chihuahua's gotta eat, right?" He stroked Jerry's head.

"You're right," Hannah said, feeling overly optimistic, despite the rent issues. "Georgia and I will work together at The Memory Keeper, and we're going to make it so successful that we'll be able to take her on permanently," she told him. "I quit my job to run the shop full time."

"Oh my gracious!" He set the dog down. "You're staying here in Franklin?"

"Yes." A warm wave of affection for her loved ones, for the shop, and the town she'd grown up in, washed over her. "I'll be able to take it over and Gran will enjoy it for the rest of her life."

Chuck's eyes filled with tears. "Oh, Hannah, that's the best thing I've heard. Gran will be over the moon." He gave her a big bear hug. "I love you, honey," he said.

"I love you too," she told him. Then she sat up. "It'll be sunset in about an hour. If we want to stage the bouquets for photos, we should probably get a move on."

Hannah and Georgia had taken some gorgeously artistic images at sunset. They'd photographed their little bouquets in front of horses lingering in meadows of wildflowers, old silos and red barns, rope swings hanging from trees, farmhouses tucked into the hillsides, with the purple peaks on the horizon forming a backdrop against the vibrantly striped sky. The printing company had done Hannah a favor and said that if she sent them the images tonight, they could have them all done by 9 a.m., just in time to set them up for display at 10 a.m.

Georgia was in her room with Jerry, and Hannah had finally taken the time to email Amanda and congratulate her on the promotion. Afterwards, she decided to take advantage of the mild temperatures March had brought in by sitting outside in one of the rockers on Gran's back porch, which was becoming one of her favorite places to unwind. She'd brought out the yellow blanket Gran used whenever she sat out there to cover her legs, and settled in with Gran's journal. What a wonderful life her grandmother had built for herself here.

The three-and-a-half-year gap in entries between the one she'd last read and the next one caught her eye.

June 5, 1947

Hello, Journal, my oldest confidant. I haven't written in years, choosing to spend my free time with Warren, building the amazing life we have in lieu of jotting down my thoughts. So much has happened since the proposal I told you about last. Warren and I moved to Nashville, and in moving here, I just know I've found who I was born to be. Warren has made quite a few friends in the music industry through his job here, and one of them let us get married in his lavish historical home, an old estate on 3,000 acres with marble fireplaces and crystal chandeliers in every room! I felt like a princess. We danced into the night, mingled with new friends, and drank French champagne, which I'd never had before. It was an absolute gas. What I've never told anyone until writing it down this minute is that I thought of Charles that night. Just once. I realized how different my life would've been if he had come home from the war and married me. The thought made me feel terribly guilty. Being a housewife back in Kentucky was absolutely what I'd wanted back then, and it would have been an honorable life, and even a happy one. However, it wouldn't have been the life I was meant for... I hadn't even been looking for this life; I'd say it found me. And I'm so glad it did.

Gran got her happy ending. Hannah flipped through the rest of the journal, the other pages empty. They may have been blank, but Hannah knew how much had come after that last documented moment.

She listened to the crickets singing in the nearby woods. Her life was feeling more like that happy ending with every day she stayed in her hometown, but she couldn't deny the hole in her path, the empty spot where Liam had been. She kept telling herself that maybe it was hitting her hard because they had such a connection to this place together, but in the back of her mind, she felt like it was something more. Hannah fidgeted with the pendant Liam had given her, remembering the way his arms had felt around her that night. Tomorrow was their last day together and then he'd be heading home with Noah, taking a piece of her with him. She'd miss Noah so much. She adored him. Perhaps she could go see the little boy when he visited Mary...

She closed her eyes and leaned her head back on the rocking chair, thinking.

Without warning, something thumped into her lap, startling her, her eyes flying open to find a purring black cat. It snuggled into the blanket as she sat there, stunned.

"Speckles?" she whispered.

The cat meowed.

"Oh my goodness," she said, stroking the cat as it purred. "You've been looking for Gran, haven't you?" Hannah asked, relieved. "Have you been getting your milk?"

The cat meowed again.

"Gran will be so happy to hear about you," she said. "She should be coming home soon, you know."

Hannah set the journal down on the table beside her and stroked the cat, rocking back and forth like Gran had done so many times when Hannah was growing up. As she looked out at the tree-lined yard, holding that sweet cat, she felt the serenity Gran must have felt sitting there. What a wonderful feeling it was.

Chapter Thirty

"How's my favorite person in the world?" Hannah asked, as she set down the oversized bouquet of fresh tulips on the counter of Gran's hospital room. She'd made the arrangement this morning to celebrate Gran's discharge, after she and Georgia had set up everything for the festival.

"I'm doing well," Gran said, pushing herself into a sitting position. She had on her pink cardigan set rather than the hospital gown, giving Hannah a fizzle of happiness. "I walked down to the cafeteria this morning unassisted."

"That's amazing!" Hannah pulled a chair over to the side of the bed. "I can't wait for you to come home."

"Nor can I. How's the shop?" she asked.

"It's… good."

Gran perked up. "What do you mean, 'good?'"

"Well, before we get into that, I thought I'd let you know that Speckles showed up at your house yesterday. She sat on my lap on the back porch."

Gran clasped her hands in delight. "Oh, I'm so excited to hear that."

"That cat has been giving me fits. It was the first time I've seen her since I've been home. I didn't want you to worry, so I hadn't told you."

"I would've worried," Gran said.

"I know."

"Have you told me everything when it comes to The Memory Keeper?" Gran asked. "Hannah, I know the shop looks like it could fall down at any moment. My worst fear was that I'd lose it before I was well enough to make it wonderful again. Even though I know my head's in the clouds."

"Maybe not entirely," Hannah said. "I've decided to stay and run it with you."

Gran threw her hand to her heart. "Oh, my dear! You have?" Without warning, she broke down into sobs.

Hannah grabbed a tissue, handing it to her and wrapping her in a loving embrace.

Gran sat back, the tears still falling. "You know," she said, sniffling, "The Memory Keeper is a tangible reminder of the life I've lived. And when it looked like the shop was closing, it was a shocking thought that everything I'd built during my time here was finished. I've waited for you to come home for years, praying for you to see that this is where you belong. I felt it in my bones."

Hannah could hardly keep her emotions in check. As always, Gran was right.

The sound of live music made its way through the laughter and conversations of the crowds as they gathered around lemonade stands and perused craft tents, the scent of funnel cakes, caramel corn, and barbecue in the air. A little girl ran by Hannah holding a silver balloon, her face painted in bright colors. She disappeared into the crowd, beside the street performer spinning a line of hula-hoops on top of his head. The Spring Festival was underway.

Hannah stopped at the juice tent and bought herself a raspberry Popsicle, nibbling on the end of it while she looked for Mary, Noah, and Liam. Darlene broke through the mobs of people, waving armfuls of carrier bags from various stalls.

"How are you?" she said when she reached Hannah.

"I'm doing well," Hannah replied. "Looks like you're having a good day."

"Yes, ma'am," she said, wriggling her arms excitedly. "I got a bouquet and print from the shop too! Your new employee Georgia is holding it for me until the end so it doesn't get crushed."

"That's wonderful," Hannah said, taking a lick of her Popsicle.

"I love what you've done with The Memory Keeper," she said. "Your gran should be proud of you."

"Thank you."

"It's definitely bringing in business. Georgia could barely keep her head above water."

"Really?" Hannah had considered the idea that the tent outside might increase business, but she hadn't thought it would do so by that much.

"Yes. You'd better go help her out. She was behind by about ten orders when I left her. They're coming in faster than she can keep up with them."

"Oh my goodness. Thank you for letting me know," she said, chucking her Popsicle into a nearby trash can, the excitement that their idea was working bubbling up. "I'll go right now. It was great to see you, Darlene."

"You too!"

Excited to see what Darlene had described, Hannah rushed across Main Street, and turned the corner headed to the shop, weaving through people while she texted Liam to let him know to meet her at The Memory Keeper. She stopped at the edge of the lawn and took in the sight in front of her.

Georgia was chatting animatedly with a group of customers as they stood under the tent outside, half a bouquet arranged on the table at the back of the tent. She was moving excitedly as she explained the concept of the prints, handed out mini bouquets, and took money. Others had their hands on the glass door of The Memory Keeper, peering inside, while more had settled at the tables and chairs which were now set up out front. Hannah put her fingers over her grinning lips, a thrill like she'd never felt before rushing through her. While she knew that every day wouldn't be a festival, they might have just done enough to get people interested.

"Need some help?" she asked Georgia, walking behind the table, dropping her handbag down and grabbing a vase.

"Yes," Georgia said with a giggle, obviously just as giddy at their success.

Hannah grabbed the half-filled vase from behind her and held it up. "Who's waiting for this arrangement?" she asked the crowd.

Two elderly women raised their hands.

"They've already paid," Georgia said, her focus on the order she was taking.

"Come on inside," Hannah told them, unlocking the door, and beckoning them in. She called to the crowd, "The showroom's now open! Feel free to look around. We've got complimentary, farm-fresh lemonade for all our guests." She set the bouquet on the antique counter and turned the record player on low, to give them the festive atmosphere she hadn't experienced since those days with Gran. Then she began filling glasses with lemonade from the bar fridge and setting them on a silver tray.

"It looks like you've ordered our arrangement called 'The Twin Irises,'" she said to the two women, holding up the bouquet to take a look at the flowers Georgia had started arranging.

"Yes, ma'am," one of the women told her, her gaze roaming the space. "It's just lovely in here."

"Thank you," Hannah said, pulling the rest of the flowers from the various baskets on the wall where the silver buckets had been to add to the arrangement. "Would you like a glass of lemonade?"

The two women each took a glass.

Hannah trimmed the ends of the flowers, threading them into the vase. "This is a beautiful bouquet," she said. "It's one of my favorites." She finished the last few flowers and handed the vase to the women.

The bells on the door jingled and Mary, Noah, and Liam walked in. Liam showed his surprise at the renovation, though he hung back at the entrance of the shop. Noah ran past the tables of displays and behind the counter, throwing his arms around Hannah. Without even thinking, she grabbed his hands and spun him around, dancing to the song on the record player the way Gran used to do with her.

Noah threw his head back with laughter and wriggled around. "Do that again!"

Hannah had gotten so wrapped up in the excitement of the shop's success that she only realized just then that this must be how Gran had felt every day. She gave Noah another twirl, making him giggle some more.

"I've walked past this shop before," Mary said, "so I know what you've done with it. It's simply stunning, Hannah."

"Thank you," Hannah said. "I couldn't have done it without Georgia." Hannah peered through the freshly designed display window at her new friend, who was just as busy as she'd been when Hannah had come inside.

Hannah's attention shifted to Liam. He was still near the door, his eyes on her. Their lost opportunity ate away at Hannah. Just looking at him, it felt like coming home, and she wanted to run over to him, to delight with him in the excitement of today, but his business decisions were hanging between them like a heavy fog. She wanted to move beyond it, but she just couldn't.

"Ready to go?" Noah asked, taking her hand.

"I'm not sure I can just yet," she replied, finishing the bouquet. She wanted more than anything to go off with Noah and play at the festival, but she couldn't leave Georgia to man this by herself. "It's busier than I expected. But I'm going to get someone to help us so I can join you very quickly, okay?" Hannah's mom would certainly come to relieve her if Hannah told her what was going on.

"Why don't I take Noah to play some of the games until you're ready?" Mary suggested. "He wanted to try to win the big sombrero on the ring toss."

Hannah smiled at the memory of his call on her birthday.

"Liam will stay here and work with you until your help comes."

"It's really fine," Hannah said as two more people came in, causing Liam to step closer to her. "I've got it. I'm going to text my mom to come in. Liam doesn't need to stay."

"No, I will," he said, walking toward the counter. "Once Hannah's mother gets here," he told Mary, "Hannah and I will meet you and take Noah around. Save the bungee bounce for us, buddy, okay? We'll all do it together."

"We will?" Hannah asked, happiness bubbling to the surface at the fact that Liam had initiated a bonding moment with his son.

"Yeah," he said, clearly more thoughts behind his answer than he'd verbalized. He came behind the counter, joining her, and peered down at the cash register. "Show me how to ring people up, and Georgia can send them inside to pay."

"Okay," Hannah said.

"I'll let Georgia know," Mary said. "Noah, let's give these two some time to get through the heaviest of the crowds. You and I can get an ice cream and find all the fun things to show them when they meet us."

"Okay," Noah said, running over to her.

Mary and Liam held the door for another group to enter the shop.

Hannah texted her mother and she texted back that she'd be right over.

"It does look amazing in here," Liam said to Hannah. "You've done an incredible job."

"Thank you."

His attention shifted to her necklace and then back up to her eyes.

An elderly man came in with a bouquet and print, interrupting the moment. He set them down on the table and pulled his wallet from his back pocket. "I'm getting this for my wife," he said with a smile. "We've been married for sixty-five years."

"That's incredible," Hannah said.

"Being with her is the easiest choice I've ever made. Want to know the secret?" the man asked.

"Yes." Hannah was all ears.

"It's about bringing out the best in one another and not letting the problems that plague this life eat away at it. When you find someone special, you hang on for dear life and weather the seas together."

"That's beautiful," she said back to the man with the bouquet. "I hope your wife loves the flowers."

"I'm sure she will." The man handed over his credit card and Hannah showed Liam how to ring him up on the register. She returned the man's card just as three others came in, lining up at the counter to pay. Business was positively booming.

The crowds at The Memory Keeper had reached a more reasonable level, and after Hannah's mother had arrived and gotten things under control inside, Liam and Hannah left to find Noah. A tense silence hung between them as they walked down the now quieter street together. It was jarring after working side by side in the buzzing shop. Hannah paced beside him awkwardly, not sure what to say, nothing feeling right.

At the end of the street, Liam suddenly stopped.

"When we were kids, I wanted to tell you how I felt about you, but I never did, and I learned from that," he said with intensity in his eyes. "I've also learned that the if-onlys get bigger the older we get, and I don't want you to go away not knowing what I have to tell you now."

She waited for what he had to say.

"I've been going back and forth with Jonathan to see what, if anything, we could do to lower the rent on The Memory Keeper. Jonathan won't budge, and I struggled to get him to even listen. The rent on Main Street and the surrounding area is high due to the demand. I can't lower it because it truly is a competitive rate."

Hannah nodded, unable to hide her disappointment.

"I knew you'd be upset, which is why I didn't want to tell you all this before."

"Thank you for trying," she said.

"Well, remember what I just said about the if-onlys?"

"Yeah."

"I told you they get bigger. If I didn't make it right, I'd regret it for the rest of my life. I thought moving on after Alison would be too difficult, but you helped me see that with the right person, it isn't as hard as I'd feared it would be. The last piece of my life with Alison that I needed to handle involved my brother-in-law. I told you before that he and Alison started the initial plan for Mercer Properties together—well, when I took over after she died, we suddenly found ourselves dealing with some pretty substantial real estate. Jonathan was counting on my inheritance to buy the building in Chicago—we'd planned on it—and I felt that if I pulled out, it wouldn't have been what Alison had wanted for her brother, so I pressed on. But after you and I spent time together, I lay in bed and all I could think about was this town, the farm… you."

Hannah hung on his every word, hoping that he could somehow make this all better because she wanted so badly to see where things went with the two of them.

"So last night, I offered to sell Jonathan my half of the business. It's a deal he can't refuse. After all, it was his and Alison's dream, not mine. But I asked for one provision."

"What was that?" she asked, breathless.

"That he let me buy 110 Ivy Lane."

She threw her hand to her gaping mouth. "What did he say?"

"He agreed to it."

She gasped. "You own The Memory Keeper?"

He shook his head. "No. *You* do."

"What?"

"I'm going to reimburse you for the renovations and your grand-mother's debt that you covered, and then you can make me an offer to purchase the property." He reached out and took hold of her waist, pulling her in. "And I'll accept all terms."

She looked up at him through her eyelashes. "All terms, you say?"

"Yes."

"Sooo, I can write in there that you and Noah have to stay in Franklin?"

He laughed. "Unusual for a sale of contract, but I suppose you can ask for whatever you want."

"That's what I want."

He pulled her in and leaned down toward her, his lips brushing hers. "Then we think alike." With the sounds of laughter and Skee-Ball slides, the bells from the carnival games as winners hit their marks in the distance, Liam pressed his lips to Hannah's and her path suddenly felt very clear.

The crowds had died down a touch as everyone had gotten a chance to spread out around town. Ethan and Christie caught her eye, waving from across the road. Ethan had his son on his shoulders, laughing at something Christie was saying, and Hannah couldn't have asked for a better view. The lights of the carnival games and the twang of country music swirled around her as she and Liam walked up to Noah and Mary. The little boy waved madly when he saw them, his mouth covered in sticky candy, a sombrero on his head, and a stuffed animal in his arms.

"Noah won a caramel apple in the cake walk," Mary said.

"And I played lots of games! Look what I won, Hannah!" he said, wiggling his head to show her the hat.

"That's awesome, Noah," Hannah said. "There's the bungee bounce." She pointed to an inflatable platform with kids strapped to bungee harnesses, soaring into the sky. "Are you ready to do that? The line looks short right now."

"Yes!" Noah sprang up and down.

"Let's go do it then," Liam said, taking his hand.

By the time they got over to the bungee bounce, the line had dissolved, the last child coming off the large inflatable. Liam paid the attendant. "Three, please."

"You're really jumping?" Hannah asked.

"Of course."

Noah's face lit up with a mixture of delight and astonishment. He kicked off his shoes excitedly and set his winnings down.

Liam took his shoes off and climbed onto the air-filled platform, reaching down and pulling Noah up with him. Then he helped Hannah up, their faces mere inches from each other, taking her back to the other times they'd been that close. She swallowed, righting herself and moving over to her bungee harness.

When they were all strapped in, the attendant gave them the go-ahead as the bungees were pulled taut, causing Hannah's knees to straighten. Mary waved at them from the edge of the platform. Noah pushed off first, his little body sailing into the air until the bungee caught him, bringing him back down. He kicked off again and flew through the air, giggling the entire time.

"Jump, Dad!" he said.

Noah called to his father as though it were the most natural thing in the world for him to do now. Liam pushed against the floor and soared to the heavens next to his son, both of them laughing together. Hannah couldn't imagine a more perfect sight. She began to bounce herself, the three of them bobbing up and down, the pure joy of that moment something she'd hold on to for a very long time.

Chapter Thirty-One

The morning sun cast its bright shine on the tin roof of Nell Winter's old barn, which she'd converted into a garden center for the locals. The deep-red structure with bright white trim sat in the center of a lush field, the large windows and doors all open, filled with pots of flowers in a rainbow of vibrant colors, bags of potting soil stacked by the main entrance.

Gran had called early that morning to say that she was coming home around noon, and Hannah wanted to be sure she arrived to an abundance of flowers. She'd fluffed the pillows on the porch, bought her a few new candles for inside, and she and Georgia were shopping for a pair of brightly colored perennials to fill the planters at Gran's house.

Georgia picked up a white basket with a raspberry-colored mophead hydrangea, and held it up for Hannah's approval.

"That's gorgeous," she said.

"Do you think your grandmother will be surprised by what we've done with The Memory Keeper?" Georgia asked.

"She'll probably cry tears of joy," Hannah said. "I can't wait to show her. But that's not the only thing I have to tell Gran." Hannah told Georgia about Liam selling her the store.

"Oh my God! He loves you," she teased.

Hannah shook her head with a grin, but this time, she believed Georgia. And Hannah felt exactly the same about Liam. "Let's get these," she said, pointing to the hydrangea. It was time to make some memories.

"Close your eyes." Hannah helped Gran walk slowly down the path to The Memory Keeper, lining her up to show her what they'd done.

Maura and Chuck were there, along with Georgia, Christie, Liam, and Ethan. They'd all come to see her reaction and celebrate with her.

"Open them," Hannah said.

Gran gasped when she saw the exterior, her eyes misting over. She peered up at the freshly painted sign in bright-yellow letters, her head swiveling to the new porch swing, all done up with color-coordinated yellow and teal pillows, the picture-window display Georgia had crafted with a stunning array of bouquets in all the newest shades for spring. Hannah took Gran's elbow and walked her carefully along the landscaped yard, lifting her arm to help her up the two steps and through the door of the shop.

When they went inside, Gran couldn't keep herself together; the tears rolled down her cheeks, just as Hannah had thought they would. Gingerly, she paced over to the pressed-flower boxes, running her fingers along the bottoms of the frames, peering in to get a closer look at the different petals. She made her way around to Ethan's mural.

"You did this, didn't you?" she asked Ethan, her trembling hand on her chest. "I can spot your work out of all the art in the world. You're so talented, Ethan."

"Thank you, Mrs. Townshend," he said, a smile of gratitude also directed at Hannah.

Gran turned and faced the ladder, her hands flying to her mouth to cover the surprise. More tears brimmed in her eyes. "Who did this?" she whispered, touching it lightly, following the grains.

"Liam McGuire," Hannah replied, introducing Liam. "The man who drove me home to see you."

Gran reached out and took his hand. "Thank you," she said.

She held on to the ladder, pushing it slightly back and forth, her eyes closed. "I can see Warren right now, moving this around to get flowers down for me." She opened her eyes and held out her arms to Hannah. "I couldn't have asked for a better surprise. My heart is full. And what a miracle it is that I've been given more time to spend in this beautiful shop. I am so blessed."

"Well, I didn't do it myself. Georgia helped," Hannah told her grandmother. "And the surprise isn't finished." She took her grandmother's hands and gave her a gentle spin, making her laugh. "You'll dance here for many years to come, but not because Georgia and I have made the shop prettier. Liam is selling me the building. Gran, we *own* the shop."

Gran stood speechless for a moment, and then she embraced Hannah and began to sob on her shoulder. She grabbed Liam, pulling him into the hug. "I can't believe it," she said, breathless.

"Look," Georgia said suddenly. Through the glass of the door, Speckles was lapping up the milk from the bowl they'd left out for her.

Gran let out a satisfied exhale.

"Ready to go home, relax in your own house, and have a big celebratory dinner?" Maura asked Gran.

"You all go. I'd like to stay here just a while longer."

"Liam and I will stay with her," Hannah offered.

When everyone had left, Hannah stood next to Gran.

"Life definitely has its surprises, doesn't it?" Gran said.

"It sure does." Hannah thought about how different she felt now from the way she had that morning she'd prepared to surprise Miles at the airport.

"*I've* got a surprise too," Liam said. "Ms. Townshend, I do hope you're all right with Georgia manning The Memory Keeper in Hannah's place for a week."

"Of course, dear, why?" Gran asked him.

"Well, the airline I was supposed to be traveling with called and offered me a voucher for my next trip. I can apply the cost of the missed flight to any future itinerary. So I got two tickets to Barbados... since Hannah never got to go on her birthday."

"You did?" Hannah nearly squealed.

Gran pressed her weathered fingers against her smiling lips.

"Yes, but you'll have to wait a bit. I scheduled the trip for May." He grinned at her. "No snowstorms."

Hannah thought of the many storms that had brought her to this moment. And she remembered Gran's advice: *To get to the treasure, sometimes we have to go through the stormy seas.* Hannah couldn't help but think she'd found her treasure. And she couldn't wait to spend the rest of her days discovering how rich her life could be.

Epilogue

"The tractor's all ready," Liam said, coming up behind Hannah in the kitchen of the farmhouse and wrapping his arms around her protruding belly, kissing her neck, and making her squirm with laughter.

When Liam had decided to run the farm, Mary retired, settling in a compact apartment downtown where she could lunch with her friends and pick up her own bottles of Mickey's wine for book club. She gave the farm to Liam, Noah, and Hannah. They'd had their wedding there, the tree-lined path to the farmhouse decked out in magnolia flower arrangements that Gran had helped her design at the shop, taking a horse-drawn carriage ride to the steps of the farmhouse and to say their vows with a tuxedo-clad Noah standing beside them.

"Did you have enough hay?" she asked, leaning into him, and tipping her head back against his chest. She'd been tired lately, their growing baby taking all her energy. But today was Noah's sixth birthday and they were giving hayrides through the farm to all the kids.

"Yep," Liam replied. "Ethan helped me load them. He hasn't been able to get Wesley off the tractor," he said with a grin, turning her around to face him.

"What's Noah up to?" she asked.

"Swinging on the tire swing outside with Mom and Georgia."

"I should've guessed," she said. Liam had hung the swing for Noah a few weeks ago, and the two of them spent every spare moment outside on it. They stayed out until the only light left was the blinking of lightning bugs at the edges of the fields.

"Hey, y'all," Ethan said, coming into the kitchen with Wesley. "I brought my new pony over so we could give the kids rides," he said.

"Oh, I'm so glad," Hannah said. "I know you were worried the horse wouldn't be ready yet."

"I just picked him up this week," Ethan said. "Used my first painting money to buy him. I named him Flash."

"Oh," Hannah said, "Flash was my favorite horse of yours to ride."

"I know," he said. "I remember. He was my favorite too. I wonder if Wesley and Noah will love to ride this one just as much."

"I hope so," she said.

"I made it," Gran's voice came from the hallway, before she hobbled in on a cane, carrying a gift for Noah. Maura and Chuck walked behind her to make sure she was steady. Gran sat down and ran her hand along the edge of the leather journal that sat on the kitchen table. "What's this?" she asked.

Hannah peered over at the new book she'd bought the other day. She'd liked it because it had a butterfly etched into the leather on the cover. "It's a journal I bought," she said. "I thought I'd write the first entry tonight."

Hannah wondered what the pages in that journal might hold for her own grandchildren one day. As she looked around at her family and the beautiful life she was living, she knew that her unborn baby boy would have so much love around him that she'd undoubtedly have volumes to write. But she wouldn't start just yet. It was time for birthday cake, hayrides, and making memories.

A Letter from Jenny

Hi there!

Thank you so much for reading *The Memory Keeper*. I really hope it filled you with warmth, had you snuggling up for hours on end with your hot cocoa, and got you thinking of making memories with your own family, and friends both old and new.

If you'd like to know when my next book is out, you can **sign up for my monthly newsletter and new release alerts here:**

https://www.itsjennyhale.com/email-signup

I won't share your information with anyone else, and I'll only email you a quick message once a month with my newsletter and then whenever new books come out. It's the best way to keep tabs on what's going on with my books, and you'll get tons of surprises along the way like giveaways, signed books, recipes, and more.

If you did enjoy *The Memory Keeper*, I'd be very grateful if you'd write a review online. Getting feedback from readers is amazing, and it also helps to persuade others to pick up one of my books for the first time. It's one of the biggest gifts you could give me.

If you enjoyed this story, and would like a few more happy endings, check out my other novels at www.itsjennyhale.com.

Until next time,
Jenny xo

7201437.Jenny_Hale

jennyhaleauthor

@jhaleauthor

jhaleauthor

www.itsjennyhale.com

Acknowledgments

I am forever indebted to Oliver Rhodes and his teams that I've worked with over the years, for shaping me into the author I am today and setting the bar for publishing. His example inspired every choice I've made along the way.

I owe a huge thank you to Ami McConnell for listening to my initial concepts for this book and Harpeth Road Press, offering suggestions, and cheering me on from the start. I wouldn't have made the leap to writing and publishing this book without knowing she was there.

To my amazing editors—Emily Ruston, who has overseen various works of mine from the early days to the present; Kelli Martin, without whom I could not have gotten the book into its best shape; Claire Gatzen, quite literally the most fabulous of all copyeditors; and my lovely proofreader, Lauren Finger—I am truly thankful. I couldn't have had a better team than these women to help me get this story into the best version of itself.

To Tia Field, one of my oldest friends, I am grateful to have her at the end of my string of texts about medical questions as I moved through the plot. In the midst of the busiest medical crisis in recent history, she was always there to give me an answer. She's a true friend and a great person.

And to my husband Justin, who had to live with me in quarantine (with no escape) while I wrote two books at the same time, started a publishing imprint, and taught two kids in online school, I am blessed to have his support. He handled the crazy like a champ and was always in my corner, cheering me on to follow my dreams as far as they'll take me.